The Scald Crow

The Scald Crow

Grace Daly

Creature Publishing
Charlottesville, VA

Copyright © 2025 by Grace Daly
All rights reserved.

ISBN 9781951971311
LCCN 2025935122

Cover design by Luísa Dias with scald-crow illustration by Jaya Nicely
Spine illustration by Rachel Kelli

CREATUREHORROR.COM
@creaturepublishing

This book is dedicated to:

Claudia

Dr. DeMeo

Dr. Luthringshausen

Lisa

Paige

Dr. Syed

Dr. Noone

Dr. Mahajan

Dr. Chou

Megan

Sue

Dr. Holm

And every other healthcare provider who believed me
and refused to give up on me.

Contents

"I'm so proud of you. I love you just the way you are."

—Your mom, probably

. . . That's the sort of thing good mothers say, right?
Don't ask me.
I wouldn't know.

Day 1

The bird is on her front porch. My front porch.

How is the bird still alive this many years later? How long do birds live? I suppose different types of birds live different lengths of time. I know some parrots live longer than their owners and have to be written into wills to be left to grandchildren. This isn't a parrot, though. Its feathers are ashy grey, apart from the head, wings, tail, and legs, which are a deep, scalded black. Black with a somewhat-blue sheen visible in the setting summer sun. The black also scorches from the large beak down its chin, choking out the lighter grey, overtaking it.

It also seems to be wearing jaunty feathered pantaloons, which detract from the otherwise ominous effect. I squint at it from the cracked asphalt driveway, through the windshield of my car. It cocks its head and returns my consideration with one globular eye.

It looks like a crow to me, but maybe I just think all black birds are crows. There are other types of black birds, aren't there?

Clearly, I don't know what I'm talking about. It does look like a crow, though. I grab my phone from the cup holder it was propped up in so I could see the directions and type "how long do crows live?" into the search bar. I know, I know. I could just type "crow lifespan," but I like to phrase it as a question. It's good to be polite.

According to the World Wide Web, there are lots of different types of crows, which live different lengths of time. Of course there are. I try again. "What types of crows live in Chicagoland?"

The internet helpfully provides me with an article about native Illinois wildlife, displaying a photo of the aptly named American Crow. That can't be right, though; the American Crow is solid black, not mostly grey with a scorched stain threatening to devour it. Besides, the lifespan of the American Crow is only seven or eight years, and this bird has been following me since I was six years old. Since I became unlovable.

The logical explanation is that the bird hasn't been following me for two decades, that I have just happened to see different black birds very frequently and I am a crazy person who imagines a bird is following them. In my defense, I do acknowledge that the bird wasn't following me when I lived in Wisconsin. Not that I never saw black birds in Wisconsin, of course. I'd seen my fair share of shiny purple-teal-black grackles bullying finches away from the feeders filled by the downstairs lady in my old apartment building.

But I didn't see this bird in Wisconsin. The one that follows me.

I hate this bird.

I scold myself, dropping my phone into my lap and taking off my sunglasses to rub my eyes. The bird isn't following me. I'm just stalling: looking up bird facts so I don't have to go into the house. I'm in a bad mood. I don't want to be here, and even though it's a comparatively low-symptom day, my constant and mysterious pain is still gnawing at the organs in my pelvic girdle. It's my body I hate, not the bird. The broken wreckage of a body that's forcing me to return to this house in the first place.

I also hate this house.

I grab my phone and sunglasses and keys and get out of the car, shoving them all into my tiny, womanly pockets. Taking a few steps toward the bird, I expel my anger with a threatening swipe of my arms. I toss in a few choice curse words, too, for good measure. I can't get close to it, but it still flies to a low branch on the nearby oak tree, mocking me with a rasping call.

Always the bigger person, I ignore its harsh words. I open the trunk of my car that's old enough to vote, grab a laundry basket filled with my sheets and quilt and a bedside lamp, and begin the process of moving into the childhood home I swore never to return to.

I guess I'm bad at keeping promises too. Add that to the list of things wrong with me.

Immediately upon opening the front door, I am whisked off to the Emerald Isle. The small hutch across from the front door displaying a crowd of fine porcelain dishes bearing hand-painted shamrocks is one reminder. The stuffed bear perched atop the hutch wearing a step-dancing dress and holding a small Irish flag is another.

Perhaps most reminiscent of Ireland is the large framed print of Jesus Christ, our lord and savior, looking reverently toward the heavens while his glowing heart, wrapped in thorns, beats inexplicably on the outside of his robed chest. Mammy loved that painting, and, as a teenager, I often stared at it while enduring lectures on how I was an ungrateful, lazy, and/or whorish daughter who did not appreciate the sacrifices Jesus or Mammy made for me.

Of course, the little chats about my shortcomings in front of Jesus were relatively mild. The true gauntlets were saved for Mammy's room, where she could trap me in the stiff wooden chair for hours at a time. I hope she's gotten rid of the chair; I don't want to have to face it. Odds are she kept it, though. After all, Jesus is still here, merciful as ever.

I shake my head to clear the memories away. It won't help me to dwell on them now; I have work to get done. Namely, carrying my stuff inside.

When I let go of the door, it slams shut with a screech and a bang. I jump in alarm and then laugh at myself. Of course. I forgot about this door. It has some old-fashioned spring mechanism on it so it never hangs ajar; there's a bit of a trick to getting it to close quietly. I'll remember next time.

Without the fresh breeze coming in from the door, there's a rancid undercurrent on the stale indoor air. I sniff curiously; it's something rotting, a sweet smell of decay. If it were a stronger scent, it'd be turning my stomach, but even as is, it makes me feel vaguely queasy. I can't afford to be any sicker than I already am. Whatever it is, I'll have to deal with it as soon as possible.

But first, I drop my basket and take the picture of Jesus down. The spot it hung in is a slightly darker color than the rest of the wall around it. I put the painting in the corner near the door to the garage. It'll be the first thing to go to the charity shop.

Sorry, Mammy. Sorry, Jesus. It's my house now.

I'll leave the shamrock dishes and the bear, though, at least in the short term. I sort of like the reminders of Ireland. We used to go all the time to visit family; my parents emigrated to Chicago in the '80s for Da's work. I had good summers in the midlands with my cousins when I was little, playing with the barn cat's kittens and drinking thick milk straight from the cow. But that was before I ruined everything and we stopped going. It's been so long since I was there, Ireland feels like the scenery of a favorite book fondly remembered. I often forget it's a real place, where real people live. I'd like to go back someday if I ever have the money, which I won't.

I make a few more trips between the car and the entryway, carrying in the suitcase I packed with my necessary items and a few boxes filled with marginally valuable things that I probably ought not leave outside overnight (laptop, external drive, jewelry, the like). My lower abdomen starts hurting more, the pain going from a dull drone to sharp stabs of punctuation. I look out the window: It's getting dark, and I still have to figure out how to get rid of whatever that smell is. The rest of the boxes can wait until tomorrow.

I sniff at the air as if I were a bloodhound, feeling my revulsion grow as I zero in on the noxious scent. I open the door to the garage, take a few experimental sniffs, and find the smell is fainter there. It's the same story when I walk down the hallway toward the bathroom and bedrooms. I step through the entryway to return to the kitchen and hit the jackpot: The smell is noticeably worse in here. My stomach flops in earnest.

The fridge is almost certainly full of only spoiled food since no one's been here for well over a month, and of course it would be too much to expect the police who performed the wellness checks and discovered Mammy's disappearance to have cleaned it out. They were only ensuring Mammy's wellness, not mine. I expect the source is some moldy cheese or a rotten roast, though I'm surprised the scent is able to escape the airtight seal of the refrigerator door.

When I pull the door open with a sharp tug, the smell doesn't get worse, new layers of mold and sour just get added, shaping it into an elegantly nauseating miasma. So, I was right about the fridge's seal being secure enough to imprison the revulsion within. Being right is shite sometimes. I shut the door and lean against it, breathing through my mouth for a minute until I can work up the courage to continue my search.

Once my emotional fortitude has been shored up, I sniff again around me. Yep, still disgusting. It gets worse as I approach the sink, so I check the trash can in the cabinet underneath but sadly find the trash bag empty aside from a few forgotten wrappers. I look at the sink, take a deep whiff, and regret my choice instantly, reeling my head back.

It's definitely coming from the sink.

At least I live in the Midwest and, therefore, sink-based problems have sink-based solutions. I turn on the tap, which sputters for a moment before remembering how to do its job, and, once the water is flowing consistently, flip the switch above the sink that operates the garbage disposal. I wait for the beautiful, reassuring growl of the grinding mechanism crushing whatever is rotting to a pulp, but am instead greeted by the screeching whine of something clogging the works.

Feck.

I flip off the disposal. The noise dies down, and I turn off the tap. The water drains more slowly than it ought to but does go down the drain, so it isn't completely stopped. That's good. But I'm not overly enamored with what the next step is going to have to be.

Under the sink, I find a pair of rubber cleaning gloves and a roll of empty trash bags. I prop a bag open on the counter-top next to the sink and pull the gloves on, then stare with trepidation at the opening of the drain. Garbage disposals are useful and convenient and ecologically friendly, but they are also deeply terrifying, which is why I assume they aren't as popular in the rest of the world as they are here. The rest of the world seems to have a better sense of self-preservation. In Ireland, they won't even have electrical outlets in the bathroom, to ensure you don't accidentally plop your running hair dryer in the bath. But us Midwesterners are made of sterner stuff. We don't let the fear of things like ice storms, moose, or having our hands crushed into a pulp whenever we drop something down the drain deter us.

I shoot a withering glance at the switch above the sink, warning it with my mind not to even consider turning itself on, then bravely reach into the disposal. I use my left hand, since that's my least favorite one. Between the stench and the anxiety, my stomach jolts sharply, which of course causes my pelvic pain to up the ante. I clench my jaw against the misery and grab around for the soggy, squishy, putrid mass of whatever it is in the drain and pull it out.

Immediately I drop it into the sink. It lands on the stainless steel with a gruesome, sodden smack. It's some horribly mangled mass of meat, meat colored with the sickly purple grey of rot. There are little bones in it, most of them snapped in multiple places and some completely pulverized.

See, this is why I don't feck around with garbage disposals. This is just some chicken or something, but the disposal would do the exact same thing to my hand.

Though, actually, it doesn't look much like chicken, not if I take a closer look at it. (Not that I want to take a closer look at it. I really don't.) Chicken meat is a different color, like a light tan, and this is dark. I imagine in its unrotten state, it was the deep red of a hunk of beef, or maybe venison.

Jesus, Mary, and Joseph, what did Mammy do? Decide to chuck a raw T-bone in the garbage disposal for a laugh before driving her car into the river and running off to Vegas, or wherever she ended up?

Actually, I have no idea what cut of meat this would be, with all the little bones. I'm not a butcher. Regardless, there's only one thing to be done with it now: I pick up the hunk and slop it into the garbage bag.

I make another brave foray into the depths of the garbage disposal and get another, albeit smaller, hunk. Meat clings around a small bit of bone shaped like a capital letter I. I try to think about what sort of bone this could be: maybe a bit of a deer's tail? But why would Mammy keep a deer tail, or even have one? And why would she put it in the garbage disposal? Come to think of it, there's no fur here. Did she skin it before tossing it in? What was she trying to accomplish? But before I can continue with my line of questioning, I shake my head and scold myself. I know better than to question Mammy.

After two more plunges into the drain, it seems like I've grabbed the bulk of the mess. All I'm getting at this stage are pieces of bone, which I pull out and put into the garbage bag without ceremony. At one point, a particularly sharp shard pokes me through the glove.

"Ouch," I mutter for no one's benefit but my own, and look at the shard closely. This bone has a weird look to it: It's cloudy translucent and more flexible than the others, and thin and broad. More like a flake than a shard, really. I'm bizarrely reminded of a toenail, and immediately force the image out of my mind. My imagination is getting away from me. I'm sure this is just some weird rotten bit of gristle or something.

The disposal is as clear as I'm going to get it, so I tie off the garbage bag and, double-checking inanely to make sure my hand isn't still inside, turn on the tap and flip the switch on. There are a few moments of foreboding grinding as the disposal works through whatever bits of gore and marrow I wasn't able to fish out, but then the sound turns smooth.

Thank heaven for small mercies.

After I take the stinking garbage bag to the curb, I decide it's time for dinner. The pain makes me wish I could stop moving and maybe never move again, but I can't afford takeout this week. I consider quietly starving to death, right here on the kitchen tile. But no, starving to death is probably even more painful than my mystery illness. I'm not one for melodrama anyways. It'll have to be a quick trip to the grocery store for a microwavable burrito.

The damn bird is still sitting on the tree branch watching me when I leave but is absent when I return. For a moment, I'm suspicious (what is it up to?), before I remember the bird isn't up to anything, because it's a bird. I go into the house with my paltry groceries and am again greeted by Irish knickknacks and Jesus's holy visage.

Frowning at Jesus, I take off my shoes and put my grocery bag on top of one of the boxes I haven't bothered to clear out of the entryway yet. Didn't I take him off the wall? I meant to. I was going to bring him to the charity shop.

I must've thought about taking him down but not actually done it. That would be just like me. I have a horrible memory; I was always losing stuff and forgetting things Mammy told me to do and misremembering the way things happened when I was a kid. I thought it was getting better now that I'm an adult, but here I am, imagining Jesus went and hung himself back up so he could be admired.

This time, I do take him down. I put him firmly on the floor by the door to the garage. For good measure, I go out to the garage, locate a hammer on top of the big chest freezer, and come back to pull the nail out of the wall. I nod to myself, satisfied. I put the hammer and nail down on the bottom shelf of the hutch, next to a delicate teapot with a basket-weave pattern and obligatory intricate hand-painted shamrocks.

Jesus makes plaintive eyes at me from his spot on the ground. I turn the picture around so he faces the wall.

It's only eight thirty, but I'm tired. Being in pain is tiring.

I feel like I spend 70 percent of my daily resources just trying to ignore the pain. It doesn't work, of course. The heavy, festering ball of agony in me drowns out my internal monologue. To add insult to injury, it gets louder throughout the day. A whimper of pain in the morning is a piercing, keening cry by the time I finally microwave a burrito or put a frozen pizza in the oven for dinner in defeat, wishing I had the energy to make something healthy. I don't have the energy. I never do. I take my unevenly heated burrito into my childhood bedroom so I can go to sleep as soon as it's finished. I won't brush my teeth tonight. I'm too tired.

My childhood bedroom is actually completely different than it was when I was a kid. Mammy turned it into a guest bedroom six months before I left for college; I interpreted it as a punishment for deciding to go all the way to the University of Illinois at Urbana-Champaign, a three hours' drive south, instead of enrolling in the local community college like she wanted. I slept in the basement while workmen redid the floors and painted the walls from pink to grey and replaced my cute twin bed and its floral-painted headboard with a sensible queen. I don't even think she ever had a guest stay the night, other than me visiting when I was on break from UIUC. I might be wrong, though. I've been no contact ever since I graduated. I didn't even tell her when I moved to Wisconsin. She could've grown two extra heads and I wouldn't have heard about it.

In between bites of burrito, I strip the sheets and comforter off the guest bed and replace them with my own. I couldn't afford a moving truck to bring my mattress or furniture here, but I don't mind too much. My mattress wasn't the best, and my particle-board furniture probably wouldn't have even survived the trip. Still, I want to make this place feel like mine as quickly as possible. Sleeping in Mammy's sheets would make me feel tethered to her, even if this isn't the room she actually slept in.

I still haven't gone into her room. I'll leave that for later.

I finish my burrito and change from my daytime pajamas (leggings, T-shirt, bralette: the uniform of the chronically ill woman) to my nighttime pajamas. I lie on the bed for a good fifteen minutes practicing the belly breathing that the pelvic floor physical therapist recommended, but it doesn't help the pain and doesn't help me fall asleep. If anything, the mindfulness it encourages only makes me more aware of my suffering, makes me more anxious. There are too many odd creaks of floorboards in this empty house, and the wind keeps blowing through branches and across the gutters in ways I'm struggling to ignore.

Grabbing my phone, I decide to give Emma a good-night call. She'll want to know how it's going. She's sweet like that. She would've called me already, but she's forgetful; the sort of person who's probably got ADHD but makes it work for themselves. Sometimes, she frustrates me, like when she's late just about every time we hang out, but mostly I love it about her. Mostly I love everything about her.

As I lie in the dark room, the phone rings and rings and rings in my ear until I get her voicemail.

"Hey Em," I whisper, as if she's the one in bed instead of me, "just calling to tell you about the house. It's going okay, but not great. But not bad. Nothing bad. I just feel sorta down. But I'm sure you're busy. No need to call back anytime soon."

As I'm about to say goodbye and hang up, the phone starts ringing. I scowl at the lit-up screen (who thinks this is an appropriate time to call someone?) before I see it's Emma. The scowl turns into a smile.

"Emma! I just called you," I effuse when I answer.

"Brigid! Hi!"

I smile larger when I hear my name pronounced correctly. Emma's the only one, other than Mammy, who gets it right.

"Are you busy?" I ask her. I can hear cars whooshing past and people chatting in the background of her call.

"Yeah, no, not at all! Well, I'm on the way to my pottery class, so I only have a few minutes, but I want to hear about the house. Tell me everything!"

I laugh a little. Her late-night pottery class. She signed up for it a few months ago because, and I quote, "lesbians love pottery." It worked; she started dating Jess from Pottery Class almost immediately after. But then it turned out that Jess from Pottery Class hated Emma's cats and also Jess from Pottery Class was a total bitch, so Jess from Pottery Class was left by the wayside. But I guess lesbians do love pottery (or at least Emma does), because she's still taking the class.

"It's kinda rough. But not too bad. Yeah, no, like, it's okay," I tell her. "Weird, you know? Being here. I keep expecting Mammy to pop up around every corner."

"Your mom's gone, Brigid," Emma says gently. It's been her refrain for the last few weeks, ever since it became clear that living in Mammy's house was the best option I had. "It's just a house, you know? A free house!"

"A free filthy house. It's full of her junk. Besides, she's not dead. Well, officially she's dead, but they never found the body. Just her car in the Fox River," I argue lamely, hoping to lose.

"She's been gone for over a month. She would've shown up by now if she was going to."

"Yeah, no, I don't know, what if this is a trick of her's somehow?" I respond with my half of our circular disagreement. "Mammy's clever, maybe she's just trying to find me. Trying to get me back under her thumb."

"Well, I don't think anyone's ridiculous enough to do that, but you know her better than me." Emma sighs, disappointed pottery night is being delayed by my obstinance, disappointed we have to have the same conversation again and again. "When's your next appointment with Carol? Could you chat about it with her?"

"Tomorrow." Carol's my therapist, and Emma's right, she's the one who gets paid to have these ridiculous talks with me. I feel bad for getting into this with Emma. I expect too much emotional support from her. "You're right, I'm sorry. This is a Carol talk. I shouldn't bug you with it."

"No, I don't mean that, Brigid. I love chatting with you. It's just that I'm a nanny, you know? Not a therapist."

"Yeah, no, but you're such a good nanny," I tease, trying to lighten the mood to assuage my guilt. "I feel so safe, so well cared for . . ."

She laughs and my heart sings. "Shut up."

I don't make a sound.

She laughs harder. "Yeah, no, don't shut up, but you know. Shut up."

"Shut up but don't shut up. Got it." I'm beaming a ten-thousand-watt smile into the dark room, all wisps of sadness gone.

"Good, don't forget it," she orders. I won't.

"Anyways, how is pottery class? Any sweet young things there for you to corrupt?" I ask her, trying to prove that I'm interested in her life, that I'm a supportive friend.

"There's the one cute girl, the blonde I told you about? But she might not like Black women. Or maybe she's not gay. Every time I catch her eye, she looks away so fast. But it doesn't matter, Jess is gonna twat swat me anyway if I try to pick anyone up."

"Ugh, Jess is the worst," I groan conspiratorially.

"Well, I did break her heart into a million pieces and now I don't even have the kindness to leave her to her pottery in peace," Emma answers fairly. For someone so self-assured, she's a bit too fair, too empathetic, sometimes.

"Just because someone got dumped for being the worst doesn't make them not the worst."

"Oh shit, here she comes now." Emma's voice drops. "Look, I oughta go, class is starting in a minute and I gotta go inside. We'll talk soon, yeah? Bye!"

"Bye," I reply, but she's already hung up.

I hug the phone to my chest for a moment before opening up Instagram. For a second, I review my own page, but it's a ghost town: I never think to take pictures, and I never wanted to risk posting something that would give away my location to Mammy, so I average about three posts a year. I only joined because Emma told me to. Honestly, it's more than avoiding Mammy; I don't really want people looking at me at all.

Over on Emma's Instagram page, I flip through the mountain of selfies and Outfits of the Day, even though I've seen them all a hundred times. I admire her micro braids, her pointed chin contrasting with her bounteous curves, her painted lips that are fuller on the bottom than the top. She always wears bold lipstick, and it looks amazing with her deep skin tone. I wish I looked more like her. I wish she posted more pictures.

In a blinding flash of self-awareness, I realize what I'm doing. I'm such a fecking pervert, memorizing her closet, obsessively cataloging every inch of her skin. Jesus. Why am I like this? Why can't I just be a normal person?

No more stalking. I plug my phone in and put it on the nightstand, face down. I don't even know what I get out of looking at her pictures, just that I like to. It's safe, like rewatching a favorite movie.

I am determined to sleep tonight. The pain is worse when I sleep poorly, and I need to have a low-symptom day tomorrow if I'm going to finish carrying my stuff inside. I ignore the ominous creaks coming from the other rooms of the house and renew my focus on my breathing (in two, three, four; hold two, three, four; out two, three, four; in two, three, four, etc.). It must work because one moment I'm breathing, and the next I'm having the dream.

I used to have the dream all the time when I was a child, but I didn't have it once when I lived in Wisconsin. What's strange about the dream is it doesn't feel like a dream. It lacks that sense of detachment; it's missing the gossamer threads of unreality and possibility dreams normally possess. It just feels like being awake.

In the dream, I lie in bed. When I was little, it was the floral-painted twin bed I liked so much. Once my room became a guest room, it was the guest bed. Now, it's the guest bed, but with the sheets and quilt I put on it today. No matter how old I am, no matter what else is happening in my life, it starts with me in whatever bed I fell asleep in.

The room is dark, and I feel like I was just awakened by an unidentified sound, but I can't hear anything at all. The door to the hallway is open, but the hallway is dark, too, so I can barely make it out. Standing at the foot of the bed, between me and the hallway door, is a willowy, womanly, ominous shape. It is, of course, the delicate form of my beautiful mammy.

As I rub at my own tired face, her pale visage swims into view. It is luminous and unmarked. (I got my freckles from Da; Mammy's skin is perfect as heavy cream.) Her high cheekbones and tight jawline cast shadows, even in the darkness. When she recognizes me recognizing her, her thin lips roll back upon themselves into a snarl before pulling to the sides in a wicked grin. Her eyes open wide but are dead looking; they are shallow, dull, devoid of any delight or sorrow.

"Mammy?" I might ask in a quavering voice laced with dread. Or I might remain silent. Or I might whimper. The dream happens the same regardless of what I choose.

She begins to speak in a voice similar to her own, but dark and with a bite, like she's letting the air from the absolute dregs of her lungs ferment in her chest before allowing it to escape. "I am not your mother," she says.

Her rictus grin grows minutely wider.

"Mammy!" I yell in terror. (I always yell at this point, my heart's frantic pounding forcing me to scream something, anything, but always, always it's for my mammy I scream.)

"I am not your mother," she repeats louder, her grave voice booming in my blood-rushed ears.

I lower my cries to a whimper and listen closely, knowing what she says next is important.

Still with a voice like death, she speaks softly now, almost tenderly, explaining a delicate fact to a sensitive child. "I killed your mother and put her in the closet. And now, I'm coming for you."

I squeeze my eyes shut tight and tense every muscle in my body, waiting for her horrible jaws to part and for her white teeth to lovingly rip out my throat. Usually, I wonder how long it will take me to die, whether I will still be alive when she drags me to the closet and locks me away to rot alongside my real mammy's corpse. Will I still be able to smell when she uses mothballs and scented candles to cover the putrid stench of my corpse emanating from behind the church dresses and wool coats?

But the jaws never approach. Death never comes. When I force my fear-twitching eyes to open, Mammy is gone and the hallway door is shut.

I think that's actually when I wake up, when I open my eyes, because I always stay awake the rest of the night, staring at the door, praying Mammy doesn't return. Or, when I was younger, before I realized I was unlovable, praying she would return but as the mammy who loved me, the one who would comfort me, the one I missed so much.

She never comes back, neither wicked nor gentle. Whenever I see her next, when I'm awake, she will be the same unpredictable and incalculable Mammy I love despite my own better judgment.

It's been nearly four years since I had the dream. I thought it was over, thought I had outgrown it. I guess I was wrong.

Like the bird, like me, it's back.

Day 2

In the morning, legging-clad and Cheerios-filled (alright, you got me: technically they are Oaty-O's, Cheerios's generic cousin, because I'm not made of money), I finish the last of my cup of coffee and rinse the cup out in the sink, upturning it onto the nearby drying rack without properly scrubbing it. There's no point to washing it, really, since it'll be me drinking the same store-brand, self-brewed coffee tomorrow and the next day and the next and the next until the end of time, in an endless procession of lonely, mediocre cups of joe. Besides, the sink is so filthy after last night's little garbage disposal adventure, I don't think washing the cup would get it any cleaner. The whole house is filthy, to be honest. My bedroom is dusty; the bathroom is layered with soap scum; and the sour, bodacious scent of spoilt cheese and rotting veg is still spilling out of the fridge whenever I dare to open the door. Luckily, I haven't had to do that very many times this morning; since I forgot to get unspoiled milk from the grocery store last night, I ate the Cheerios (Oaty-O's) dry.

I'm feeling overly grateful for my subpar coffee. I didn't end up sleeping well last night after all, thanks to the dream, so my pain is even worse than usual, and my energy levels are critically low. I need to rev up the old meat suit chemically. And I still harbor emotional scars from the months after my most recent surgery when I wasn't allowed to drink coffee.

Not that anybody else ever needs to worry about that. Most people are allowed to have coffee after surgery, no problem. The gynecologist who performed my second surgery didn't even mention it as a possibility beforehand. Of course, she wasn't planning on misdiagnosing me with interstitial cystitis if and when the surgery didn't turn up what she thought it would, but misdiagnose me she did.

It was probably an honest mistake, but I would like to point out how convenient it is that the wrong diagnosis she came up with allowed her to wash her hands of me. She handed over a few pamphlets about diet changes, wished me luck, and, like magic, I was no longer her problem.

After a few months, I gave up on the diet. I missed coffee and citrus and not checking ingredient labels, and by that time, I had figured out for myself that it wasn't helping.

I also eventually figured out that if you're out of work on disability, most companies will only hold your job and pay their part of your health insurance for a year, even if they told you they'd wait however long it took for you to get better. At least the disability insurance I had still pays 50 percent of my salary. I'm a lot luckier than most disabled people in that way. But 50 percent of my salary is 50 percent less money than I had been previously living on. My savings account wasn't massive to start with, and the health insurance I desperately need isn't cheap; COBRA is expensive and only lasts eighteen months after you officially lose your job. I'm not sure what I'll do when that timer runs out. I've applied for Social Security Disability, and if I get that, I suppose I could sign up for Medicare, but it takes years of appeals to get approved. All of this to say: After I became disabled, I couldn't afford my apartment in Madison anymore. It was only a matter of time until I became homeless.

And then Mammy (the mammy I've been hiding from ever since I graduated from college and realized she wasn't any good for me, the mammy I never told when I followed Emma to Wisconsin) was gone. The police declared her dead when her car was found in a deep spot in the Fox River right off the Route 14 bridge. Somehow, they found my phone number and called me. I was next of kin and she didn't have a will. What did I want to do with her house?

A house. A free house. I looked around the apartment I had already begun selling my few belongings to afford, and admitted defeat. Somehow, even when she was absent, Mammy always won.

So here I am, moving in, drinking coffee. I peek into the entryway, see the porcelain in its hutch and Jesus on his wall, and realize I brought in even fewer boxes last night than I thought. Groaning, I place a hand across my tender abdomen. I'm not sure how I'll manage today. Probably more weed edibles. At least they're legal in Illinois. And probably more coffee, thank God.

Wait, Jesus? On his wall? I took him down. I remember. (Don't I?)

I shove a few boxes from the entryway into the kitchen with my foot to make room as I approach the picture. As I pass the window set into the front door, I glance out and see that the bird is on the porch again. I look away, not wanting to give it the satisfaction of seeing how angry it makes me, and turn my attention to the offending wall. Jesus hangs there, gazing beatifically upward toward our Father who art in heaven, hallowed be thy name.

I took him down. I remember. I went out to the garage to get a hammer to remove the nail from the wall and everything. A loop in my small intestine kinks rudely, anxiously, either from fear or from irritable bowel syndrome. It is surprisingly difficult to tell the difference between the two.

Someone must have broken into the house. Is anything missing? I haven't noticed if anything is gone. The box with my laptop is still here in the entryway; my cell phone is still in my pocket. I look at the front door: It's still locked. There are no footprints on the floor. The only thing of note is that damn bird watching me through the window.

My bowel kinks again, more assertively and urgently this time. Irritable bowel syndrome it is. Though let's be clear, I do still feel afraid. In fact, the two aren't mutually exclusive. *"Intense emotion can set off IBS episodes. You should avoid stressors as much as possible,"* doctors have told me, as if I'm not already trying to avoid stressors. My entire life is comprised of the avoidance of stressors.

I waddle like a penguin as quickly as I can to the bathroom, keeping my butthole clenched until I reach the toilet. You might think that upon reaching the toilet and voiding my bowels I would feel immediate relief, but actually my traitor of a body likes to make it painful to defecate. It's crafty like that.

At least the knife twist of agony in my gut is enough to push all thoughts of Jesus's holy visage from my mind. I focus on surfing the pain and consider that maybe I shouldn't be drinking coffee after all. Coffee, like high levels of stress, unfamiliar foods, and Mercury being in retrograde, can also trigger IBS episodes.

Several minutes (or hours, time loses all meaning when you have diarrhea) later, I return to the entryway and the dilemma at hand. Now that I'm over the shock, it seems less likely that there is anything nefarious about Jesus Christ. He's just cheap pigment on a cheap canvas in an even cheaper frame. There's been a lot of marijuana in my system recently to help me deal with the pain. I wasn't high last night, but there's a chance it could still be affecting my memory. Like I said, I have a bad memory anyways; I must've gotten that from Da along with my ugly freckles. I've also got an overactive imagination. Mammy loved to remind me of all of these facts.

I look at the hutch to see if the hammer is where I recall leaving it. Sure enough, there's no hammer and no nail. I head into the garage to peek in the toolbox on top of the chest freezer, and there the hammer sits, right where I "remember" finding it last night. Well, that settles it. I imagined myself taking Jesus down twice. I scratch at my forearm, too hard, a bad habit I have when I'm frustrated or anxious. I get the hammer, I really do this time, and go back to the entryway. I remove Jesus and pull out the nail, putting the nail and hammer on the bottom shelf of the hutch for real, and hold Jesus's face barely an inch from the tip of my nose.

"What are your secrets, Jesus?" I ask, suspicious of his motives. He's not talking. I toss him into the garage and hear his frame crack when it hits the concrete floor. I do feel a mild pang of guilt about that. He did die for my sins, after all. And now a charity shop won't be able to get as much for him.

I unlock the front door and shoo the bird away from the porch, but instead of leaving me in peace, it elects to stay on a nearby branch just out of reach and scrutinize me while I carry in my boxes. I get just about all of them stacked into the entryway before the pain in my abdomen gets severe enough to make it difficult to bend over. I pop four ibuprofens, unearth my laptop from the small tower of boxes, and limp to my bedroom to fire it up. It's just about time for therapy with Carol.

I connect to the Wi-Fi (I will always find room in my budget for Wi-Fi; it's right up there with indoor plumbing as far as I'm concerned) and log on to the telehealth service I use to talk to Carol. I always see her via telehealth; I've never actually met her, not in person. She lives in Kenosha, near the Wisconsin-Illinois border, so she's licensed in both states, which made her convenient in regards to the move but inconvenient to drive to, even for a normal person. And I'm not a normal person. Sitting immobile for long periods of time, like in a car, always seems to set off my mysterious pain. Besides, what would I do if I was out and my IBS flared up? Or I got hit with another one of the unpredictable immobilizing-agony stabs? No, it's best if I go as few places as possible. Therefore: telehealth.

I sit on the guest bed that I struggle to think of as mine and notice the window above the headboard is letting an awful lot of bright light shine directly onto the screen. I adjust the brightness on my laptop, and it works well enough, though I don't look wonderful lit up from behind like this. But it's fine. It's not like I need to be beautiful for Carol. She prefers I show up in my "authentic, natural state" anyways. Carol is big on honesty.

While I wait for her to join the video, I look around the room, making sure to maintain the neutral smile on my face. If she joins and I have my resting distraught face on, she starts the call worried about me. I don't like to make Carol worry.

My childhood bedroom, repurposed as a guest room, is studiously bland and covered in a coating of dust. The walls are a color that makes me feel no emotion, and the floor is unscored and untextured. The furniture is minimal and barely nice enough to not appear utilitarian, and the rug has an inoffensive pattern of interlocking circles. Even the knickknacks are dull: pointless glass orbs and unused scented candles. The only object with any real personality, aside from the crumpled pile of old sheets and comforter I left on the floor last night, is an abstract painting hanging above the dresser, next to the door to the hallway and opposite the bed.

It's large, overtaking the space on the wall that it has been allotted. The background is a grey that seems to have motion, shifting subtly from paler to darker tones. Atop the grey, lash thin strips of black, straight lines apart from a few broken in two, that overlap thickly in some places and thinly in others, giving the impression of tree branches or prairie grass or the fingers you peek through when you're too scared to look properly. And in the foreground, looms a shape. It seems to have a motive, seems to be swooping in toward the viewer, to land on them and claw at their throat and stick its horrible beak inside their mouth and peck at their uvula until the blood pours out of their mouth like thick house paint, covering the plain wooden floor and understated rug in an indelible stain.

But the shape isn't a bird shape at all. It's an abstract painting, it's just a shape. I don't know why I think it's a bird. I've got birds on the mind, I suppose.

Carol joins the call. I force my lips into a smile. If she caught the grimace the ominous not-bird conjured up, she doesn't mention it. Instead, she perfects the expression on her own face: one of delight and her signature enthusiasm.

"How's the new homeowner doing this week?" she chirps, reminding me we are trying to frame this move in a positive light.

"I'm doing alright," I answer on reflex.

"Are you? You're settling in?" Her face rearranges itself to be open and attentive. She's all ears to the point I'm surprised she still has eyes and lips: It seems like all her facial features ought to be ears instead.

I sigh. Carol is big on honesty, and I was just dishonest. "No, sorry, I'm not alright. It's not going great. I don't know why I said that."

"You have nothing to apologize for. You gave a normal response to the question."

"No, yeah, but with a therapist you're supposed to not do stuff like that."

"Stuff like what?"

I groan. Therapy is always hard for me, even when the questions are innocuous. "Give lazy answers. Thoughtless answers."

"I don't think you're lazy or thoughtless," Carol compliments. "I think you're polite and considerate, and don't want to burden others with your problems."

I break eye contact with the computer screen and begin scratching at my forearm. This little dance is Carol and I's thing. She compliments me, and it's so challenging for me to accept that I find myself wishing she would criticize me instead.

I force myself to answer, "Thank you."

"You're welcome. So, you're settling in?" she repeats.

"Not really," I admit. "I had the dream again last night."

"The dream?"

"Yeah, the one with my mother. Where she's in my room, and she tells me she killed my real mother?"

"Ah, of course, I remember. I know that dream scared you a lot when you were a kid. Were you frightened, as an adult? In the dream?"

"Oh yeah, terrified." I nod emphatically. "If anything, I feel more scared as an adult. Both in the dream and after I wake up from it."

"Why is that?"

I vocalize thoughtfully for a few moments, then hedge a guess, "I think . . . when I was a kid and I had the dream, it was scary, but it also sort of enabled this fantasy I had where it was true. Like, it'd be good if Mammy really wasn't my mother, and the mammy I remembered from before she stopped liking me was my real mammy, and all I had to do was defeat the not-Mammy and I would be free."

"You wanted to be free of your mother?"

"Well, I think what I really wanted was to know it wasn't my fault Mammy stopped loving me. If she had been killed by the not-Mammy, then it was sad, but I hadn't done anything wrong, you know? But now that I'm an adult, and I know for a fact there isn't some evil mammy, that she really is my mother, it means that I . . . well, it just makes it a scary dream. There's no more hope in it. I can't defeat her. She just . . . is."

"It's never a child's fault that they were harmed by those who were meant to take care of them." She delivers this line with great authority, then softens her tone to continue. "And I'm sure your mother always loved you, even if it was in a way that ultimately hurt you."

Carol's eyes are rich and comforting, a sharp contrast to my memories of Mammy's icy gaze. I wish Carol, or somebody like her, was my mother. Carol's real kids have all the luck.

"That's nice of you to say," I acknowledge, but she hears the disagreement in my voice and looks slightly downcast. I press on, because she'd rather me disappoint her than lie to her; she's made that clear to me before. "I just don't know. I was a bad kid. I think it's my fault Da left to start a new family and she had so much on her plate. I was a disappointment."

Something in my chest cracks a little, and my normally emotionless exterior falters, the way it often does when I talk to Carol. I sniff, tearful, pitiful. "I still am. Look at me, I can't make it by myself. Living in her house. I'm still relying on her, even when she's gone."

"Oh, honey." Carol's empathy is palpable. "Is it okay if I call you 'honey'? That's my nurture coming out, but I don't want to infantilize you."

"Yeah, no, I don't mind. It's nice. You're nice to me."

"You deserve to have people be nice to you. You are worthy of kindness and respect. You're a great young woman, and I feel honored to know you."

There she goes with the compliments again. I have to look away and scratch my forearm. "I don't . . ." I begin to protest, but remember Carol hates it when I refuse her compliments. I'm supposed to accept them. I'm supposed to practice liking myself. "I mean, yes. Thank you."

"Honey, we all need help from time to time. I don't think needing a little extra support because of your health issues means you aren't independent. You're very strong."

"I don't feel very strong," I admit, a few more tears spilling out of my eyes. I wipe at them messily with the back of my hand but only succeed in smearing them around. "My pain is bad today. I haven't even gotten all my boxes inside yet, and there weren't that many of them. And cleaning up the house, it's so dirty, and going through all of Mammy's stuff . . . I don't know how I'll manage. I already feel so tired."

Carol nods. "That sounds very tiring."

"It is! So tiring. Overwhelming."

Suddenly Carol's face switches from one of laser-focused empathy to one of diffuse confusion. She looks at something above my head and behind me. "I'm sorry, I don't mean to interrupt. It's just . . . Is there something outside the window?"

"Is there? It's just the backyard. I haven't even been out there yet," I respond as I move the computer off my lap and onto the bedspread so I can turn and look out the window.

"It was something sort of big? And dark colored? Again, sorry for interrupting, but if there's someone looking in your windows, I want you to know about it." Carol's voice is tinnier now that the computer is farther from my ears. My tears are gone; I'm focused on the issue at hand.

If someone's sneaking around my yard, then maybe I was right. Somebody did break into the house last night. I don't know if that makes me feel better or worse.

When I finally turn to see, it isn't a person at all. It's that same bird. The inky bastard is listening in on my therapy appointment. It's spying on me.

"Hey!" I shout and rap five times on the glass, *bang bangbang bangbang*, expecting it to fly away. "Get out of here!"

Instead of taking off, the bird looks offended, as if it has every right to eavesdrop on me. Petulant, it pecks at the glass in the exact pattern I just knocked. *Tap taptap taptap.*

"Are you mocking me?" I ask the bird. "Don't you have bird things to be doing? Eating worms or pooping on children or whatever?"

Carol's tinny voice comes out of the laptop. "What's going on? Who are you talking to?"

"This isn't over," I hiss at the bird before pulling the curtains firmly shut. The room gets significantly darker.

"Sorry, Carol. Let me get the lights." I have to get out of bed to hit the light switch by the door, giving me a moment to compose myself even as I wince through the pain spike my standing causes. By the time I'm back in therapy mode, with the laptop camera directed at my face, I am a composed adult instead of an immature child with a vendetta against a bird.

"Was someone outside?"

"No. Well, yes. Not really. It's just this bird."

"I heard you talking," Carol says, clearly wanting an explanation.

"I . . . Okay, Carol?"

"Yes?"

"I'm gonna level with you. There is no way for me to explain this that won't sound crazy."

"I don't think you're crazy," she tells me reassuringly.

"Okay, well, there's a bird that follows me. Or, well, it used to follow me. When I was a kid, and at college. It stopped following me when I moved to Madison, and I guess I thought I'd just imagined it, or maybe it had died. Either way, it was gone. But now that I'm back, it's back too. Ever since I got to the house, I keep seeing it. On the porch, in the yard, it's always there."

"You've only been at the house since yesterday, right?"

"Yeah, but still. It's really hanging around. Way more than normal. And it looks just like the bird I saw everywhere when I was a kid," I explain.

"Is it definitely the same bird? Or could it just be a similar bird, or maybe the baby of the bird you remember?"

"I-I don't know," I admit. "It looks different from any other bird I've ever seen, and I've never seen it with another bird. It's always by itself. But you're right. That would make more sense. It's probably multiple birds."

"Maybe there's a nest somewhere on the house? If it is only one or two birds, that would explain why they're always there," Carol offers. "You could try looking around outside, and call animal control if you find one somewhere it shouldn't be."

"Yeah, no, that would make sense." I sigh, crumpling up the plans for bird murder I had been plotting and tossing them in the trash can of my mind.

"Would it be helpful if we came up with a list of things that need to be done for the house, and then we prioritized them? I think it's possible you'd feel less overwhelmed if you could break it into manageable chunks. We can put searching for the bird nest on that list."

"Yeah, that's a good idea," I agree with a sigh. I'm not entirely convinced the bird isn't stalking me, but I think a reasonable person would be convinced and go along with Carol's plan, so that's what I do. We spend the rest of the hour coming up with a list of tasks and putting them in order. Cleaning the kitchen and the bathroom both end up outranking evicting the bird.

Also higher on the list than bird expulsion, is getting a third opinion on my pelvic pain. I don't want to, but Carol reminds me one of the conditions of my disability insurance payout is that I continue to seek treatment. She also reminds me the doctors in Chicagoland might have different experience and backgrounds than the doctors in Wisconsin. I agree to schedule something, even if it's only to make her happy.

Carol and I decide I should write the list out on a piece of paper and put it on the fridge, so I can see it every day and check things off. I'll be able to celebrate what I've accomplished and see what's next.

"Do you think this list will help you feel less overwhelmed?" Carol asks when our time is almost up.

"Yeah, I think so." Surprisingly, it's the truth. I do feel more in control of the situation. This is why I always ought to listen to Carol; she knows what I need. "I feel a little better about it already."

"That's great, honey! There's something else I wanted to ask you, and please tell me no if you don't think it'll be good for you, okay? You don't need to worry about hurting my feelings."

"Okay," I lie. Carol is always telling me not to worry about her feelings. I find it an impossible instruction to follow.

"I think for the next few weeks, until all the move-in stuff is completed, it might be helpful for you to have two sessions a week instead of just our regular one. Not that you can't handle it on your own, of course not, but a big move and going through their mother's things would be stressful for anybody. What do you think?"

Relief floods over me. I don't know why I didn't have this idea myself. The pressure-release valve of talking to Carol is wonderful, and I could definitely use more of it right now. "That would be great. Really, Carol, I'd like that a lot."

"Oh good, I'm so glad. Let's see. Today's Monday. I do have an opening Fridays at four o'clock if that works for you?" she offers.

"Friday at four o'clock is great," I confirm without bothering to check my schedule. I have nothing else going on in my life.

"Great! You'll be my last client of the week. What a great start to the weekend for me!"

From anyone else a statement like that would sound hokey, but from Carol it's another abundantly sincere compliment. I wrinkle my nose and scratch at my arm again. "You can't mean that."

"Oh, I do. Talking to you is a delight. I look forward to speaking to you on Friday." She waves goodbye to the camera.

"Talk to you Friday," I confirm, waving back at the screen and then exiting out of the telehealth platform.

Before I head to the kitchen to prepare myself some form of microwavable dinner, I pull back the curtains. The sun is setting outside; it's pink and lovely as dusk falls. At first, I don't see anything out of the ordinary in the backyard. But as I continue to sweep my eyes across the lawn, I notice the bird perched on the back of a deck chair, staring at the bedroom window. At me.

After eating an apple and a bake-at-home personal potpie (a luxury I don't normally allow myself, but they were on special, three for nine dollars, and I deserve a reward for doing well in therapy today), I curl back up in bed.

I try giving Emma a call, but I just get her voicemail. That's not unusual. She might still be at work; sometimes when she's nannying, she has to work late.

Or maybe she's hanging out with someone cooler than me, someone with bigger tits and nicer skin and progressive, actionable ideas about how to fix society. I imagine what the blonde from her pottery class might look like and conjure up an image of a real-life Sailor Moon with a waist so snatched it can hardly be said to exist at all. And the blonde likes pottery, we already know that, so she and Emma have that in common. Maybe the blonde will like Emma's cats too.

I pout, alone in my bed, for the benefit of no one but myself. I love Emma's cats. Does Emma know that? She has to. One of them always ends up on my lap whenever I'm at her place, and I am a champion when it comes to dangling bits of string.

Maybe I should get a cat so I'm not so alone. I bet Emma would like it if I got myself a cat, and maybe the cat would kill the bird. It's an elegant solution. Or it would be, if I wasn't such an incapable mess. I have no idea how to take care of one, not really. Mammy always hated cats; she was afraid of them and wouldn't let me near them. Dangling string near Emma's doesn't count as experience. And what about on my bad pain days, when I can hardly do anything? I can't trust myself to be able to take care of one, not when I can't even take care of myself. I pout harder at the unfairness of it all.

My heating pad is already turned up to eleven and I lay it across my pelvis. It doesn't really make the pain any better, but the sensation of my skin being slightly burnt is a good distraction. I pop a weed gummy in my mouth, letting the coating dissolve on my tongue so it'll hit faster, and use my laptop to start rewatching *Downton Abbey*. Ah, Mr. Carson, I think to myself, don't worry so much. It'll all work out in the end. And if it doesn't, there's always drugs to dull your sensations.

After two episodes, I am more tired than I am intrigued by the fictional rich British family's non-problems. The first two episodes aren't my favorite, anyways; they don't have Tom Branson, the Irish chauffeur, in them. He's my favorite character. He's not bad looking, and I'm quite loyal to Erin's Isle.

My thoughts turn into half-awake dreams as I start to drift off. I think that I might end up keeping all the Belleek porcelain with its basket-weave patterns and hand-painted shamrocks. Emma would like them, I think. I can clearly see Emma coming in through the entryway, telling me she's decided to nanny out here in the suburbs of Chicago so she can live near me. I put the kettle on the stovetop while she tells me about the rich white family that hired her because she's Black, specifically so their kids would respect other races, without realizing the irony that they've hired a Black woman to do work they consider below them. I laugh and interpret her words kindly. "You're not like that," I choose to hear her say. "You're different from those kinds of white people. I like you." My heart swells pleasantly. I serve her old-fashioned candy we bought together at the shop in the fancy downtown area, and pour her tea from the delicate shamrock teapot into a delicate shamrock teacup. It looks precious in her plump, excitable hands.

The hallway door opens, even though the kitchen where I'm pouring tea for Emma opens directly to the hallway and there's no door, and I'm sitting up in the guest bed, rubbing the sleep out of my eyes. A figure enters the room, tall, taller than me, the same height as my towering mammy, and it's Mammy again. The mammy of the dream.

Same dead eyes. Same grave voice. Same way of talking down to me, explaining things I already know and should understand by now.

She is not my mother. She killed my mother and put her in the closet, and now she's coming for me.

I cry in fear, my emotions heightened and marijuana-fuzzy around the edges. The pain in my pelvis skewers through my uterus while my muscles tighten automatically in defense. I pull the quilt over my head so I can't see not-Mammy and curl into the fetal position, cradling the pain that lives at my center. The tears run sideways across the bridge of my nose and my temple, pooling in my right ear. It's muffled, like drowning, when the hall door closes behind not-Mammy as she leaves.

Day 3

I stumble from the bathroom to the kitchen, rubbing my raw, overtired eyes. I put the kettle on the stovetop to heat water to make coffee and prep the French press I bought at a thrift shop a few years ago. I can't afford a coffee machine, and there's not one here because Mammy only ever drank Barry's Tea, like a good Irish woman ought to. It's alright, though; the French press might take more effort, but if I pretend I'm choosing to use it, it makes me feel fancy.

My gaze slides to the prioritized list of tasks Carol and I came up with yesterday, now dutifully stuck to the fridge. As grateful as I was for it then, today it seems to mock me with its ponderous length. I'll try to follow it, though, because I promised Carol I would. I take it down and sit at the small eat-in kitchen table to review it and plan my day.

Jesus, Mary, and Joseph, it is long. Probably nineteen or twenty tasks. My eyes jump over it, from the high-up items like "set up doctor appointment" and "clean rotten food out of fridge" to later tasks such as "go through books in the office" and "clean living room." I haven't even stepped foot into the living room or office yet. Or basement, or backyard, or Mammy's room. And I've barely been in the garage; I just went in for the hammer to get Jesus off the wall, but I saw enough to see it's full of junk.

It's not a large house, just a single-story ranch built early during the Cold War, like most of the homes in this neighborhood, but I fear I'll never get through it all. I start to feel the pain rise with my panic, the wave of overwhelm threatening to crash over my sleep-deprived body, and I take a deep breath. This is exactly what the list is meant to prevent. Just focus on the first item for now. Don't look at anything else.

"Set up doctor appointment." I can do that. I've set up a thousand doctor's appointments. I'll just have to pick a doctor first.

I go on my health insurance company's website and use their provider finder tool, filtering for gynecologists that are in-network and not men. Is it sexist of me? Probably. But a man has never seen my vagina before (at least not to my knowledge; I suppose it's possible there were men in the operating rooms during my surgeries, but I don't think those count, at least I hope they don't), and I don't want the first time it happens to be in a doctor's office.

The kettle boils and I pour the hot water over the ground coffee, stirring it the way the lady in the YouTube video I watched when I first bought the French press recommended. I rinse off the spoon and return to my search.

The list of doctors has appeared on my cell phone. I scroll through, reviewing their specialties, looking for someone who lists chronic pain instead of fertility. Right now, I have bigger fish to fry than having a baby, and it always seems like the baby-focused doctors don't care about my suffering as long as I could still be a functioning vessel for a fetus. Though, if I'm honest, my faith in the ability of any doctor, even one that hates babies, to offer me relief could not be lower. Most likely, they will review my existing records and tell me my pain is all in my head.

The first one I come across that I like the look of is Dr. Silvia Hämmerle. I click to her office's website and see she doesn't do obstetrics at all. As an added bonus, she has a nice little quote about prioritizing women's quality of life right under her picture. She wears thick-rimmed glasses and a somewhat sassy smile. I smile back at her picture and at her name, which I have no idea how to correctly pronounce. I might cave under my own impossible-to-pronounce first name and just let people say it as if it were *Bridget*, but here's Dr. Hämmerle, shoving that umlaut down everyone's throats, forcing them to swallow it along with her medical degree and expert advice. Yes, I think I'll like her very much.

Out of respect, I look up the correct pronunciation. *Heh-mer-lay*. I repeat in my mind.

I continue to scroll through her website as I absentmindedly open the fridge to get the half-and-half. I only see the man inside the fridge staring up at me out of the corner of my eye before he tumbles out and crashes to the floor. I shriek but mercifully don't drop my phone (I can't afford to replace it if I crack the screen), and realize after a moment that it wasn't a real man. It's just a framed print. A framed print of Jesus Christ.

"Jesus Christ!" I exclaim in frustration, not dwelling on my ironic choice of words as I crouch to look at the painting closer.

It is lying face down on the floor, frame slightly dinged but still intact. I broke the frame when I tossed it into the garage, didn't I? Is this a fresh Jesus?

Before I touch the picture, I quickly pop my head through the door to the garage. There is no Jesus sitting on the concrete in there. I return to the picture and gingerly pick it up, as if it might snap at me, as if it were alive. On closer inspection, there is a damaged spot on the frame where it looks like it was hastily glued back together. That answers that question. It's the same picture of Jesus as always.

I put Jesus on the kitchen table and finally get the half-and-half from the fridge, holding my nose against the smell, to make myself my cup of coffee. I also fetch another bowl of dry Oaty-O's. I really need to buy some milk that isn't spoiled. This, along with the stench, is why "clean rotten food out of fridge" is second on the list, right after setting up the doctor's appointment.

I crunch noisily and sip my coffee as I study Jesus. What are the most logical explanations?

Option one: Home invader. Someone is breaking into the house when I'm sleeping or distracted, and displaying Jesus to maximum effect. They aren't stealing anything, or leaving any footprints, or doing much else. Just spooking me with a picture of Jesus.

Option two: It's a miracle! Intent on renewing my faith and/ or turning me away from my sinful ways, Jesus has chosen to reveal himself to me by putting himself in the refrigerator. God works in mysterious ways, after all.

Option three: A ghost of some kind? A ghost that is very keen on Jesus, and is also capable of supergluing a picture frame back together? (A Catholic ghost? The ghost of Mammy?)

Option four: I am losing it, and my guilt over being a bad daughter and/or person is manifesting by making me subconsciously put Jesus in odd places to freak myself out.

Option five: I am very tired and am sleepwalking, or maybe I just put Jesus in the fridge on accident when I thought I was putting something else in there.

I suppose there is also an option four and a half, where I am both tired and losing my mind. Or maybe option two and a half, which would be a miracle caused by a Catholic ghost. Occam's razor would suggest options four through five, and, as Carol would remind me, this is a very stressful week for me. My stress levels are off the charts. It would make sense if I'm doing things I wouldn't normally do.

There is nothing nefarious about Jesus. Jesus is a nice guy.

I consider taking Jesus to the charity shop today, just so he's out of the house and I can stop using him to torment myself, but then I remember my to-do list. I promised Carol I'd follow it. I ought to stick to the list and make an appointment with Dr. Hämmerle. I can make the charity shop trip later, when I actually have a carload of stuff to donate. It won't take long. My 2003 Honda Civic is a small car.

I crunch the last of my cereal and wash away the Oaty dust coating my mouth with another sip of inferior coffee, then dial Dr. Hämmerle's office number. I press three to talk to a receptionist. I wait a few minutes while vaguely sexual saxophone hold music plays.

The saxophonist is rudely cut off mid-phrase. "Hi, this is Jenny with WomanWellness, St. Charles office. How can I help you?"

"Hi, Jenny." I put on a winning smile in case she can hear it through the phone. "I'd like to schedule an appointment with Dr. Hämmerle."

Jenny is to the point. "You've seen her before?"

"No, I'm a new patient. I just moved here."

"Oh, sorry, I just assumed since you said her name right. Okay, well, normally the wait for Dr. Hämmerle is about two months, but if you could make it next Friday in the morning at eleven, I could make that work. She just had a cancellation."

I feel a swell of pride at having gotten the name right. I wonder if Dr. Hämmerle will look up my name before she meets me. Probably not; that's a lot to expect, and doctors are busy people. "That works great," I say. "Could we make it a telehealth visit?"

"Mmm, we don't usually allow that, sorry."

Jenny is not sorry.

"Please, Jenny? I don't need an exam, really, I'm just looking for her to look over my records and establish care. I can email you everything she'd need." I beg a little, even though I assume she won't give in. I have a theory that medical doctors all have a mild allergy to webcams.

"Fine," Jenny grumbles, weary of me.

"Thank you so much, Jenny, you're a gem." I fist pump in celebration. That has never worked before.

"Okay, and what's the appointment for? To establish care?"

"That, and also, like I said, to review some records I'll send over. I'm a bit of a complicated case," I admit. "So, I have this constant pain, it can get really severe, like a stabbing pelvic pain. And I mean very painful, so bad that sometimes I can't stand. I also have some bowel issues and I bleed an awful lot when I menstruate, but I've had two laparoscopies done and—"

"Yeah, okay, I'm just putting down 'pelvic pain,'" Jenny interrupts, her well of mercy having officially run dry. "What insurance do you have?"

Jenny spends the rest of the phone call asking for every scrap of protected personal information imaginable, and ends it with a reminder that I'll need to fill out the forms she will be emailing me and send them back to her along with my medical records before the appointment. I agree to the terms and conditions, hang up, and set an alarm on my phone to ring two hours before the appointment, just in case I forget about it between now and next Friday.

And with that, I have succeeded. Children cheer, trumpets sound, angels sing. One item is checked off my list. Truly, like my namesake, I am a goddess among women.

Next on the list is cleaning out the fridge. I glance at the kitchen table, where Jesus still rests. Excellent. At least I know he won't be in the fridge. I open the door and, after forgetting to plug my nose and without the distraction of Surprise Jesus, am incredibly aware of the putrid stench that spills forth. If Mammy had to run off, she could've at least thrown away the perishables first.

I sigh and chide myself as I put the spoiled items from the door's shelves into a sturdy black trash bag. I oughtn't think cruel things about Mammy. She might not have been nice to me, but I'm sure she always tried her best. I ought to be worried about her, or in mourning. The police think she's dead, after all. For a brief moment, I imagine her corpse tossing about in the Fox River, bloated and tumbling down the rugged rocks of Blackhawk Waterfall, where she used to take me when I was small, before I made myself unlovable. I shake the image out of my brain and sniff at a carton of milk I know has gone off. The punch of sourness smacking my nose punishes me sufficiently enough to bring me back to the task at hand.

Once the door's shelves are clear, I turn my attention to the main fridge compartment. Its shelves are crowded with all manner of moldering fruit and desiccated veg and nearly empty condiment jars and cheeses slowly turning inventive shades of green. My stomach turns, and I remind myself I don't have to follow Mammy's rules about not wasting food; I don't have to eat things that are moldy anymore just because she'd tell me to. I repeat Carol's words in my head. *I am worthy of good food. I am worthy of good care.* I begin pulling out items one by one and putting them in the trash bag where they belong.

Until I come across something that isn't rotten at all. A hunk of meat sitting on a plate in a small puddle of juices, hidden behind a couple of nearly barren pickle jars. I shove the pickles aside and pull the meat to the front of the shelf. It definitely looks like beef; the deep red color is familiar enough.

It's not a cut I recognize, not a strip steak or T-bone, though I'm no expert butcher by any means. By the look of it, the person who cut this up wasn't a butcher either. The edges have been roughly sawed apart with small hunks hanging off haphazardly, and the bulk of the muscle is misshapen and somewhat mangled. As it turns out, my initial impression that it was just an amorphous hunk of meat was pretty accurate. I poke at it experimentally with a finger and immediately wish I had been wearing gloves. I don't know where it came from, I don't know what diseases it could carry, and I really can't afford to be any sicker than I already am. It's cold, cold, cold, though, like it was taken out of the freezer a few hours ago and left in the refrigerator to defrost, like it ought to be made into a nice roast with some potatoes and parsnips and sage for this evening's dinner.

I go wash my hands in the sink, still worrying about mysterious meat diseases in a bid to distract myself from worrying about how it got into the fridge behind the abandoned pickles. I must be more tired than I thought. Or I got more high last night than I realized.

That must be it. I got too high and I decided to take some meat that Mammy left in the freezer and put it in the fridge to defrost, and then I fixed Jesus's frame, too, because I felt bad about breaking it, and then I put him in the fridge for a laugh. Things are funnier when you're high. That's what happened, I decide.

Still, I won't eat the mystery meat. I might be strapped for cash, but I'm not broke enough for that. Not yet, anyways. I tip it into the trash bag and put the plate in the sink to be washed later. Unsettled by the meat, I make the impulse decision to raise the bar of freshness food needs to meet to stay in this fridge, and toss away everything I didn't buy myself. I scrounge up a bucket from under the sink and make a 50/50 water and vinegar solution to wipe down the shelves. Once they're wiped down and dry, I put a bowl of baking soda in to deal with the last lingering bits of stench.

I do the same for the small freezer that's attached, but oddly, I find no more mystery meat inside. I suppose it could've come from the chest freezer in the garage, but I'm not cleaning that out today. That's further down on my to-do list. The mystery will have to wait.

No, in this little freezer all I find are the frozen pizzas and potpies I bought, a slightly freezer burnt loaf of bread, a tub of half-eaten ice cream that's seen better days, and a few bags of frozen veggies. I actually smile at the bread. It's brown bread, the proper Irish kind Mammy would special order proper Irish flour for. She always refused to eat American bread, saying it tasted too sweet, like cake. I do like the Irish bread best; there's nothing better with a bowl of soup than a knob of brown bread. I take the loaf out of the freezer to defrost, placing it in an empty bread box sitting on the counter.

After I take the trash bags to the curb and wave my hands aggressively and ineffectually at the bird who continues to stand sentry on the front porch, I return to the kitchen to finish cleaning. I scrub and wipe at every surface I can, pushing through the increasing pain with the help of ibuprofen until I reach the point that I'm spending more time curled up on the floor than cleaning. I made good progress; the only things that still need to happen to the kitchen before it's truly mine are giving the sink a good scouring and deciding what should go to the charity shop with Jesus.

I lie on the floor in accomplished agony while my consolation burrito revolves in the microwave. After I eat it, I take a shower (sitting on the floor of the tub while the water rains down since it hurts too much to stand) and retreat to my bedroom for more *Downton Abbey*.

I try calling Emma before I go to sleep, but she must be hanging out with her cool friends or otherwise be too busy for me because she doesn't pick up, which is disappointing. Mammy visits in my dreams again, which is also disappointing. Well, more harrowing than disappointing, I suppose. Even though I know what she'll say, even though I know what she'll do, even though I've had this dream hundreds of times, the terror of her looming over me squeezes the breath out of my lungs.

This time, when I wake from the dream, I briefly consider looking in her closet, to remind myself there're no corpses in there and it really is simply a nightmare, but recoil from the idea like a live electrical wire. I tell myself that it's because Mammy's room is low on the list, one of the very last things, and I promised Carol I would follow the list.

I'm lying, of course. I won't do it because I'm scared of what I might find.

Day 4

I wake up late in the morning, snuggled under my quilt as the sun shines through the window above the headboard and onto my bed. I am cozy, and relieved I was finally able to sleep. I've never been able to fall asleep after the Mammy nightmare before, but then again, I can't remember having it three nights in a row before either. I suppose my exhaustion finally trumped my terror. It's good to know something can. I look at my phone (a bad habit, but it's always the first thing I do in the morning) and grin stupidly. Emma has texted me: She's sorry she missed my calls, she's been busy, would I be free to Facetime tomorrow night? *I'm free*, I answer, *can't wait!* For a fleeting moment, I have a sense everything will be alright, and that I am capable of handling anything that's thrown at me.

The feeling evaporates when I open my bedroom door and the smell socks me in the sinuses. It shares similarities with the miasma that emanated from the garbage disposal, but it's worse. A hundred times worse. My eyes water and I blink away instinctual tears, wondering how I didn't immediately notice the odor when I woke up. Too busy enjoying the sunshine, I guess. And maybe I'm not giving enough credit to the quality of my bedroom door.

Jesus, Mary, and Joseph, it is an oppressive stench, heavy and rough in my lungs. The initial impression is the acid tang of soured milk and yogurt, which then steps aside to allow the round, forceful scent of rotten eggs mingled with spoiling veg to take center stage for my olfactory receptors. At the edges of it all, a coppery and treacle-sweet hint of rotting blood and meat dance in and out of awareness. I try to breathe through narrowly open lips to avoid smelling it, but end up tasting it in the back of my throat instead. My esophagus closes reflexively against the threat.

I reel back into the bedroom and throw open the window to try to keep the smell from getting into my bed and my clothes. Once I'm brave enough to return to the hallway, I shut the door since it seemed to work well enough at keeping the odor at bay before. And with that, my search for the source of the stench begins.

One thing can be said for small Cold War–era ranch houses: They don't take long to search. I walk along the short hallway, poking my head into the office and bathroom and finding nothing amiss, opening the windows in those rooms as well to help clear the air, before reaching the kitchen. Of course the problem is in the kitchen. I should've guessed; I thought the smell was familiar.

It is the reek of the putrid ruins that had been in the fridge, with the added benefit of time, Midwestern summertime heat, and malevolence. The thick industrial black trash bags I carried to the curb yesterday lie slashed open on the kitchen floor, and the moldering food I had put inside of them has been spread across the tile, edge to edge, corner to corner.

I'll give whoever did this to me a compliment: The dispersion of this rotten food took a real sense of purpose and a dose of creativity. The contents weren't just dumped out, no, they were kicked and smeared and pushed to cover as much of the floor as possible. No single ceramic square is unmarred. Closed containers, like the half gallon of milk or the bag of rotten potatoes, have been stomped open, and if a material was capable of being ground into the grout, it has been. The pièce de resistance, the stroke of brilliance, is the ragged cut of mystery meat. A long length of twine has been tied around the center of it and attached to the light fixture in the center of the room so the raw slab hangs in midair, dripping its juices onto the mess below, majestically displaying the sickly grey-brown hue of beef that is beginning to spoil.

"Oh, Christ—" I start to exclaim, but when I take in a proper breath to speak, I taste the smell more fully and my body rejects the intrusion. My abdominal muscles clench into a fist and I reel into the bathroom, heaving the acid and bile out of my empty stomach and into the sink, adding the smell of saliva and thin vomit to the bouquet filling the house.

I rinse out the sink basin and go rest my forehead on the wall next to the open window, trying to breathe only the fresh outdoor air. The bird flies past, looking at me as it does. I narrow my eyes at it, unable to shout expletives through my shallow breath. I probably shouldn't be screaming swear words out the window anyways. There're a lot of kids in this neighborhood.

As the mostly clean air fills my lungs, my brain starts to order the jumble of thoughts I'm having into some semblance of sense. Obviously, there is something nefarious going on here, something beyond my forgetfulness and absent-mindedness. I'm not absent-minded enough to accidentally tie meat to the ceiling. That is some next-level shit.

I think back to my list of possible explanations. I suppose I could be dealing with a ghost or poltergeist, but I'm hesitant to believe in such things. First, I've never encountered a spirit before, so I have no real reason to believe they exist. Second, even if they did exist, why would there be one in Mammy's house? I lived here for my entire childhood without experiencing even a whiff of paranormal activity, and nobody ever died here as far as I know. Sure, when Da left us, it felt as if he had died because he disappeared so thoroughly, but he didn't actually die. Mammy told everyone he cheated on her and ran off with the mistress. I assume he's off somewhere else, living with a second wife and a second daughter who's less of a mess. No, it wouldn't make any sense for it to be a ghost.

This doesn't bring to mind any miracles I've ever heard of either. To my knowledge, which is extensive courtesy of my devout Catholic upbringing, miracles are generally positive or, at worst, benignly macabre. The Holy Trinity's shtick is more about burning bushes, curing leprosy, turning water into wine, painting lambs' blood over doorways, and bringing the dead to life. Watching a dead man walk wouldn't leave me feeling so unsettled, so desperate to crawl out of my own skin. Even when Catholicism is dark, it doesn't have such an undercurrent of revulsion. The Bible isn't a work of extreme or gross-out horror.

Honestly, the only possibility that's holding any water for me is a home invader. Someone with a sick mind, more focused on tormenting than stealing. Though, actually, I don't know for sure he hasn't taken anything, do I? Maybe, whoever he is, he's sneaking around and taking just a few things here and there, so I don't notice right away. I check my pocket automatically for my phone, though I know he didn't take it because I was using it just this morning. My laptop was still on my nightstand too. I'll have to search the rest of the house.

I take a deep breath of fresh outdoor air from the window before I begin my quick sweep through all the other rooms (except for Mammy's, I'll just leave the door to Mammy's room shut for now, wouldn't want to let the smell in and upset her). I open any still-shut windows as I examine the house. I don't find anything to be missing until I finally return to the kitchen, holding my breath and pinching my nose shut. I'm certain that yesterday I left Jesus's picture on the kitchen table, but it's nowhere to be seen.

Alright, so. A home invader who's surprisingly fond of Jesus. (Briefly I think that Mammy loved Jesus, she was a dedicated Catholic, and she would have keys to the house, and they never did find her body, but her car was in the river, and she's been gone for ages; she ran off and started a new life or drove into the water and drowned, and her body was swept away in the current; she can't be back, she can't be). He must've missed the commandment about not stealing, or perhaps felt it didn't apply to pictures of our Lord and Savior. Fair play to the home invader, though: I don't recall a specific commandment about not breaking and entering, or about not spreading rotten food all over the floor. If he's right about stealing pictures of Jesus being acceptable, he might still have a shot at heaven.

I call the police, because that's what you do when someone has broken into your house (or your mammy's house). I start to dial 911 but stop to consider this isn't a real emergency. I ought to leave the emergency line to the people who have real problems. I search for the local police department's non-emergency line and call that instead.

For a late Wednesday morning, I am on hold for a surprisingly long time. As I listen to the unfamiliar, crackling classical melody, I realize I can't actually get out the front door without stepping into the mess of the kitchen. To add insult to injury, all my shoes are in the entryway, as are my keys. I'd have to brave it barefoot, which I refuse to do. Instead, I exit out the side door, the one in the living room that's a bit stuck from underuse. I leave it unlocked as I head to the front porch to wait for the operator to answer and the police to arrive.

Of course, the bird is on the front porch, and as soon as it sees me walking up, holding my phone to my ear, it begins its mocking call. In a smooth motion, ignoring the twinge of pain in my pelvis, I bend and grab up a small rock and pitch it at the bird with my free hand. I miss because I'm terrible at sports. The stone ends up a good three inches to the right of where it ought to be and clatters harmlessly against the brick next to the front door, but the bird still takes off to return to its slightly farther post on the nearby oak tree. I consider fetching the rock and trying again, but the operator answers before I can give it a go.

"Hello, St. Charles Police Department, Greg Jeffries speaking. How can I help you?" the man on the other end of the line asks.

"Hi, I recently moved to the area, and I'm having some trouble. I think someone broke into my house?" I say it like a question, laughing nervously as though home invasion were funny, while I make my way to sit on the front steps. I'm still in my pajamas, with bare feet and no bra and messy hair and morning breath. Here, away from the smell, I realize I'm incredibly thirsty.

"Are you in danger, ma'am?"

"I don't . . . I don't think so. I think he's gone. They're gone. I don't know the gender of the person."

"Have you been away from the home?" He's asking only pertinent questions, but I'm still a little annoyed with Greg Jeffries. I want him to tell me how scary that sounds, offer some sort of comfort, give me the verbal equivalent of a cuppa. I guess that isn't his job, though. I'm being needy.

"No, but like I said, I only moved in a few days ago. But the break-in must've happened overnight, while I was asleep. At least, I assume it did. Everything was fine when I went to bed."

"I'll send an officer over immediately," he tells me with a voice that remains stubbornly all business. "Can you give me the address?"

"Of course, thank you," I say and tell him the street address. I ask, "Do you know how long it'll be?"

"Not long," he assures me. "Ten minutes. Maybe fifteen."

"Okay, thank you."

He reminds me to call 911 if I have a true emergency and hangs up.

Still tasting the morning breath on my teeth, I decide I can get a fair bit done in ten minutes and build up the courage to face the stench again. Once at the side door, I take a deep breath of clean air and plunge inside to change into daytime pajamas, gargle some mouthwash, and drink water straight from the bathroom tap as quickly as I can. I'm back outside and at the front steps in significantly fewer than ten minutes and feeling significantly less vulnerable, though I still don't have any shoes on.

When the cop arrives, it's actually two cops who casually amble their car past the park with a giant rocket ship–shaped playground and down the quiet residential street. I stand up and wave to them from the porch. They pull into the driveway, parking behind my little shitbox of a car. They're both white men, of course, which doesn't surprise me (this town is Wonder Bread white). I am also Wonder Bread white, and cops usually help young white women like me, but it still has me feeling vaguely upset and on edge. I don't know why, maybe it's just Emma rubbing off on me; I know she would be nervous with two white cops around. Maybe it's because it's another reminder Emma would never want to live here in this town, with me.

Regardless of how I feel about them, they are the cops I have. One of them is young, maybe my age, maybe even younger, with too much hair gel standing his hair into crunchy points and a neck that cricks like a crane's. The older cop, the one who seems in charge, reminds me of every nondescript middle-aged man I've ever seen at a Buffalo Wild Wings. I wonder if Long Neck will grow to resemble BWW in time, if all suburban cops gain certain morphological characteristics until they are an indistinguishable and interchangeable source of ever-present danger, like a gaggle of Canada geese skulking in a grocery store parking lot. Canada geese with guns. I wish they didn't have guns. Guns, like many other things, make me nervous.

Unfortunately, the cops don't seem to make the bird nervous. It hops down to a lower branch only a few feet away from the spot where I shake their hands on the driveway, clearly eavesdropping.

"Hello, miss. I'm Officer Purcey, and this is Officer Nelson. We're here because someone called about a possible break-in," the older one says in a cop-voice, with authority and practiced concern. Long Necked Nelson's Adam's apple bobs as he nods in agreement and pulls out a small notebook.

"Yes, thank you for coming so quickly." I try to make my handshake firm and trustworthy. "That was me."

"And could you tell us your name, miss?" Officer Nelson asks.

"Yes, Brigid Connelly," I say, pronouncing it correctly. When both officers look slightly baffled, I spell it out. "That's spelled *B-R-I-G-I-D*, Brigid, and then *C-O*-double *N-E*-double *L-Y*."

"Thank you, Brigid," Officer Purcey says, saying it like *Bridget*. I stop myself from sighing. Technically, he's not wrong; some people named Brigid pronounce it the anglicized way, but Mammy and Da always used the old Irish pronunciation. I've learned it's best to let it go. I don't want to argue about how to say my own name, and it shouldn't matter so much to me anyways. "So, what happened here?"

"Well, I'm not . . . sure exactly. I woke up late, I slept in a bit today, and I immediately noticed there was this horrible smell. I just moved in a few days ago and when I arrived, there was all this rotten food in the fridge, so I cleaned it out yesterday and threw it all away. But then, this morning, in the kitchen, the trash bags were back inside and it just smelled awful, and all the rotting food is all over the floor." I'm stumbling, telling the story poorly, but I don't know how to save it. "And there's rotten meat hanging from the ceiling too."

The older cop's face looks confused and perhaps a bit concerned, while the younger cop's pen steadily slows as I speak. I make myself stop talking so he can catch up, but the pen stops instead. He has given up on following the narrative.

"Okay, let's back up a little here." Officer Purcey takes the reins of my story away from me. "You said you just moved in?"

"Yes, on Sunday afternoon."

"Are you the daughter of the woman who lived here and passed away a few months back?"

"Yes." How does he know that? I rack my memories for Officer Purcey's face or name or voice, but draw a blank. "I'm sorry, I don't recognize your name. Were you one of the people looking for my mother?"

"Not much happens around here, miss, so we all worked on that case in one way or another," he answers with a shrug.

I don't know how much I like the entire St. Charles Police Department dipping their fingers into my backstory, but I suppose it's too late to stop it now. I push my frustration away. "Yes, I'm her daughter. Do you think she was the one who broke in?"

"Well, no, not if she's dead." He makes an awkward little laugh, as if I were a child who asked a stranger about a mole on their face.

"But you never recovered her body, right?" I clarify. "She was declared dead, but all the police found was her car."

"If she did survive, I don't see why she'd break into her own house, not when she could just make herself known." Officer Purcey speaks slowly, peering at me curiously, perhaps because I don't seem more torn up about my mother's death. Perhaps because he thinks I'm crazy for thinking she might still be alive. "Just an odd coincidence is all."

I frown. I don't know exactly what he's implying, or if he's implying anything at all, but I'd rather focus on the issue at hand. "Sure. Do you want to see what I'm talking about inside? Or do you need me to tell you more first?"

"No, no, we'll take a look," he says, and takes the lead, ambling toward the front door with his younger partner following behind.

"Uhm, I'm sorry, Officer, but the front door is locked. I couldn't get through the kitchen, not with all the trash, and my shoes and keys were by that door." I point down at my bare feet as a way of explanation. "I came out the side door. We'll have to get back in that way."

"Lead the way," he allows, gesturing a hand for me to walk in front.

Standing in the archway that connects the living room and the kitchen, I see the mess from a whole new angle. Again, I'm impressed by the attention to detail, or rather, I would be if I wasn't so frustrated. A package of rotten strawberries was not only opened and dumped onto the floor, but each individual strawberry was burst underfoot. Brilliant. Inspired. A stroke of evil genius.

By now, I've built up my defenses to the smell and am breathing shallowly through my mouth to avoid the worst of it. Officers Purcey and Nelson are not so accustomed and their eyes water as they pull their shirts up to cover their noses, as if that will help. Officer Purcey's body lurches and his stomach makes a foreboding gurgling sound, but unlike me, he succeeds in not vomiting. Their gazes land on the centerpiece, the ragged meat hanging ominously from the ceiling, still dripping and looking minutely more vile and rotten-brown than before.

They glance at one another for a beat.

"Alright, I think we've seen enough." Officer Purcey takes control of the situation. "I'm going . . . I'm going out the front door, so I can unlock it. Officer Nelson, will you walk Miss Connelly back around the side and meet me in the driveway?"

"Yeah," Office Nelson chokes out, and nearly bolts to the side door. I follow him at a more measured pace and hear the front door screech and slam loudly behind Officer Purcey as he leaves. Clearly, he doesn't know the trick to those old doors.

The three of us reconvene near the front porch. Like magic, the cops are now taking the situation seriously.

"So, when you woke up this morning, the kitchen was like that? What time would you say that was at?" Officer Purcey asks, nudging Officer Nelson. The younger cop scrambles to get his notebook and pen out of his pocket and resumes taking notes.

"About ten a.m., maybe a little after. When I opened my bedroom door the smell hit me and I followed it to the kitchen. I threw up in the bathroom and, once I got my wits about me, came outside and called the police station. I went back inside, got dressed as fast I could, and then met you two out here." I catch some movement out of my eye and see the bird is still here, hopping a little closer to us along its branch. "That's it."

"I see. And is anything missing?"

"There's this old, cheap print of Jesus I had sitting on the kitchen table that's gone," I tell them. I weigh the pros and cons of telling them about my forgetfulness and the way that made it seem like it was moving around on its own (was that my forgetfulness? I'm not so sure now), but ultimately decide not to complicate my story. "That's all, though. Nothing valuable is missing. Not that I've noticed."

"Hmm," Officer Purcey intonates skeptically. "Do you mind if we look around a bit?"

"Of course not," I tell him, and move aside to stand in the grass and lean against the brick exterior of the house, out of their way.

They poke about the exterior of the house for several long minutes, looking for footprints and signs of forced entry that aren't there. Eventually, Officer Purcey experimentally opens the front door a few times and lets it go, letting it squeal and slam shut loudly, the way it always does if you don't know the trick. "You said you didn't hear anything last night?"

"No," I tell him. "Nothing out of the ordinary."

"Are you a deep sleeper?"

"Not particularly." I shrug. "I think I'm a normal sleeper?"

"Hmm," he intonates again, and resumes his aimless search.

Officer Nelson is over by my Honda and calls for Officer Purcey. The older man places his hands over his eyebrows as he peers through the glass of the driver's side window.

"You said a picture of Jesus was missing?" He calls over to me. "Yes?"

"This is your car." He says the question like a statement.

"Yes . . ." I answer, not enjoying the leading questions, but not able to discern where he's leading me.

"Can you come here?"

"Sure." I make my way over, walking quickly over the hot pavement and shifting my bare feet casually when I arrive to make sure they don't burn.

"Can you look into the window, tell me what you see?"

I lean over, pressing the edges of my palms and pinkies against the glass, the same way he had done a moment before, and file the mild increase in my pelvic pain away as a problem to be dealt with later. Through the car window, my gaze is met by the noble visage of Jesus sitting on the driver's seat.

I sigh in defeat. "It's the picture of Jesus."

"That's the one you said was missing?" Officer Purcey clarifies.

"Yes," I admit, looking down at my feet, embarrassed and thwarted.

"Alright, so, just to make sure we're clear," he explains with a bored look on his face, "what you're saying happened is yesterday you cleaned out the fridge in your late mother's house, which you just moved into, and then today when you woke up, that trash was all over the floor and some of it was hung from the ceiling in some sort of bizarre mess. The only thing that was missing was a picture of Jesus, which we just found in your car. Nobody else has keys to the house, and you didn't hear anything, and you didn't see anything. Does that sound about right?"

"Yes," I mumble, not making eye contact. The bird makes three sharp mocking barks from its branch, joining in on the anti-Brigid brigade.

"Well, we'll file a report, but I don't see what else we can reasonably do." Officer Purcey's bored voice is in full effect. "Do your best to not lose any more pictures, yeah?"

"But what if he comes back?" I blurt out. I can't help it; I'm scared to face this all alone.

"If someone is actively inside the home, please feel free to call nine-one-one to report the emergency." It's clear from his tone that no follow-up questions are permitted. I cross my arms and furrow my brow as they get into their car and drive away.

I suppose I'll have to clean up the mess myself, all over again. At least the front door is open now and I can get my shoes. I get them, as well as more trash bags and rubber gloves, and clean the kitchen again. It's a repeat of yesterday, but worse, of course. There're more bits to clean up, like all those smashed strawberries, and I have to take a scrub brush to the grout. When I cut the meat down from the ceiling, it smacks wetly against the side of my face and I nearly vomit again. The shower I take later, once again lying on the floor of the tub due to pain as the water hits me, is desperately needed. I want the stench off of me.

The biggest change to my cleaning routine is, this time, I load all the stinking trash bags into my car with the windows rolled down. I drive them about half a mile away to a local elementary school and, after checking to make sure no one is looking, toss them in the school's dumpster. Whoever made the mess, whether it was a poltergeist or a home invader or me sleepwalking, will have to drag the heavy bags all the way back to the house if they want to do anything more with them.

When I get back to Mammy's house, I leave Jesus in the car; he's going to the charity shop any day now anyways.

After a paltry dinner, I return to my bed, and I'm so tired I don't even bother watching a show. I don't even call Emma. I'll get to talk to her tomorrow. That'll have to be good enough.

Day 5

Bad. Bad pain. Sharp sharp sharp if I, when I, no stop do not move sharp SHARP *sharp* when I move. *Sharpsharpsharp* no, lie still. Breathe in two-thee-four hold two-ouch-ouch out two-threefour it doesn't help, the breathing doesn't help *sharp*.

Try. Try try try the physical therapist said to try, so in two-thee-four hold two-three okay out two-three-four in two-three-four hold-hold out three-four I can. I can manage. I have managed before.

Stay. Still. *Still*. In my abdomen. But my hands, move hands, on the nightstand next to the bed there are the weed edibles and vape pen, and I can grab them as long as the pain holds off for just a sec-*sharpsharpsharp* just ride the wave of pain, it can't last forever it can't—and go. Grab them *nownownow* while you have the chance.

Drag on the vape pen twothreefour and hold it in your lungs and *coughcough* sharp sharp SHARP stabs with each cough but drag again anyways, then a third long drag. I need the pain to *stopstopstopstopstopstopstop.*

Sweet skunky sugar-coated edible gummy rescue, let the sugar dissolve on my tongue. Please hit fast please please fast, please.

Ride the pain. Ride the pain. Ride. Pain. Pain pain pain pain. Think distracting things, think about Emma and her pretty face, you'll talk to her tonight, think about getting a cat, maybe you ought to get a cat, but Mammy hates cats doesn't she? But Mammy is gone you can get a cat. But is Mammy gone is she really gone she was here again in your sleep last night but by her own mouth she is not my mother she is not my mother she is not my mother she is not and then—

Taptaptap on the window screen (the window is still open, got to air out the stench, ohgod ohjesusmaryandjoseph remember the stench) and it's the goddamn bird again. I try to get up to get rid of the bird, get out go away, but when I move, sharp SHARP *sharp*, so the damn bird stays. I think maybe I ought to get the cat after all. A cat would help with the bird.

What sort of cat would I like? I don't really know much about cats, aside from knowing they'd murder the shit out of that bird. Careful not to move my midsection, I grab my phone from the nightstand and unplug the charger. I search for animal rescues near me, and what do you know, there's one only a few miles away. It's even got a charity shop attached. They use the proceeds from the shop to take care of the animals up for adoption. That sounds like the perfect place for Jesus, doesn't it? Two birds with one stone or, more accurately, one cat.

I start to scroll through all the cats on the rescue's website and don't they all look so sweet? This one is sort of dopey looking, with eyes that are a little wide set, and this old one is white and black in ruffled formal wear, and this one's showing off a fuzzyfuzzyfuzzy belly I imagine burying my face in, and I giggle to myself, realizing I love every cat because I'm high. Head-spinning high, and I feel so much better because of it. It's not that the pain is gone, but I can take the pain and put it in a box and put that box in a cobwebby unused portion of my brain. I look at cat pictures for a long time. I can't say for certain how long, because time has ceased to have meaning.

Eventually, my treacherous bowel makes itself known by increasing my pain. I frown and try to weigh the options with my muddled mind. On the one hand, if I don't have a bowel movement, the pain will continue and I will become constipated and it will be worse later. On the other, if I do have a bowel movement now, it will hurt terribly while it happens, a horrible ripping, tearing, slicing, rending pain through my colon and pelvis and rectum. But then it will be over. I sigh in self-pity.

I hate chronic illness math.

Ultimately, I lurch myself to the toilet to suffer more greatly but for a shorter period of time. I'm not one for procrastination, and the pelvic floor physical therapists always told me it was important not to hold my bowel movements or it would make my pelvic floor symptoms even worse. When the worst of the agony is over and the toilet is flushed, I sit on the floor of the bathroom, leaning against the outside of the combination bathtub and shower, and brush my teeth. Standing is hard, after all. When that's done, I fill my water bottle, which I conveniently thought to bring with me to the bathroom, in the sink, and amble down the hall back to the bedroom.

As I stumble, the pain flares and I lean against the wall to find the emotional fortitude to press on. I push the fingers of my free hand deep into the flesh low on my pelvis to distract my nerve endings from the agony. I'm reminded of portraits of Napoleon Bonaparte, how he pressed on his stomach because he had an ulcer or something. People copied him to appear firm and stately for decades afterward, an unspooling procession of rich men pretending to have ulcers, not knowing that that was what they were doing. I wonder, if I was useful enough, important enough, would people pose for selfies with their fingers roughly palpating a spot only a few inches above their genitals? I doubt it. It doesn't have the same visual appeal. Ulcers are cooler than mysterious gynecological problems and irritable bowel syndrome.

I wish I could do something more for the pain, something other than getting high and burning my skin and digging my fingers as deep into my abdomen as I can force them. But I know the pain isn't real, that I'm imagining it. There's no physical cause, so there's nothing to be done. The second surgery proved that.

The second surgery had to happen because the first surgery didn't go so well. I just went to a garden-variety gynecologist the first time around, because I was clueless and thought all gynecologists were the same. She thought the symptoms I was complaining about were all signs of endometriosis, which made sense. I have constant pelvic pain that worsens around my period (check), I have extreme bloating in my lower abdomen (check), I have bowel upset (check), and I bleed uncontrollably, soaking through tampons and pads and pajama pants to leave little droplet trails of blood wherever I roam at least once a month (check check check). Bing bang boom: You've got endometriosis, baby.

The treatment options were birth control pills or surgery. Since I'm a virgin, and I doubted God would be coming down from heaven to impregnate me with his second son anytime soon, I chose surgery. I wanted the issue dealt with. As the gurney wheeled me into the operating room and the world slurred away from me courtesy of the anesthesiologist, I beamed like a bride on the morning of her wedding. This was the day my life would begin; I was sure of it. My pain would go away; my vagina would expel regular amounts of blood; I wouldn't alternate between having a lacrosse ball of constipated feces in my colon and shitting my pants, and the world would be my oyster.

Of course, as I previously explained, I'm not smart, so my predictions were woefully inaccurate. I woke up with the same pain as always, plus surgery pain. I did get a consolation prize: For a week afterward, I got to take hydrocodone. This was funny to me; the surgery pains the hydrocodone was meant to treat were much milder than the pain I had been living with for years. But after the opioids were gone, I was back to the drawing board, confused as to why burning away the small amount of endometrial scar tissue the doctor had found hadn't worked. She thought maybe the pain was caused by anxiety, which, of course, only served to make me more anxious.

Scared that I was imagining everything, scared of losing my job, scared of living the rest of my life in agony, I hired Carol to help me scrub my brain folds. I picked her because she's the child of immigrants like me, though her parents were from South Korea instead of Ireland, so I don't know how much we actually have in common. And I will continue not to know because like all good therapists, Carol doesn't tell me much about herself. I only know what I do because it's in her bio on her website.

Anyways, Carol recommended I join some support groups. I hate going places, so I joined support groups online, and proceeded to make a bunch of whiny posts I'm ashamed of in which I complained about how the endometriosis surgery didn't help me. It wasn't long before other endometriosis-havers piped up with helpful questions and comments.

Was the gynecologist an endometriosis expert? (No. Is that a thing?) Did the gynecologist ablate the adhesions or excise them?

(She burned them off, so, ablation, I guess.) Well, that's why you're still having problems! You have to find the secret Facebook group of forbidden endometriosis knowledge, beg the elders for access to the sacred tome listing the names of endometriosis specialists, and then have the adhesions excised, not ablated, because otherwise they immediately grow back. Everyone knows that, silly!

Following the internet strangers' advice, I ate the fruit of the tree of knowledge and made an appointment with a gynecologist who specialized in endometriosis excision. It was a three-month wait to even get to see her, much less get a surgery. With every passing week, my pain was getting worse, and I'd started getting migraines from the stress of it all. By this point, I was leaving work early almost every day. Gently, ever so gently, Carol asked if I'd considered going on disability. Not permanently, of course not, just until I felt better after this next surgery. I got a little mad at her (sorry, Carol) because that's morally wrong, isn't it? Going on disability is for people who are actually disabled, people with real disabilities, not for melodramatic pieces of shit like me who can't handle a little period pain.

But then I had a bad day, a day where the pain lanced like a javelin through my bowel and into my ovary when I stood up from the toilet. The agony was intense; the room spun and I fainted onto my bathroom floor. After I came to, the pain's grip was so all-encompassing, I couldn't stand or crawl or even speak for a couple hours.

As I lay there on my shower mat, crying until I was too dehydrated to scrounge up a fresh batch of tears, I realized maybe I actually was disabled. When I got back to work a few days later, my manager told me the same thing. He's a nice guy; he'd printed out information about the company's disability insurance policy and everything for me. For six weeks I could get paid my full salary, and after that I could get 50 percent of it until I was feeling better. He promised to hold my job for me until I got the second surgery. To be honest, I cried a little during that meeting. I didn't deserve so much kindness.

With the blessing of multiple authority figures, I temporarily left my job doing software quality assurance testing (only temporarily, of course). When the appointment day arrived and I finally met the endometriosis expert, I was impressed. She had no-nonsense shoes, no-nonsense hair, a no-nonsense face, and seemed exhilarated by the idea of slicing me open. Excision works, she promised. I'd feel better in no time.

Still, I was feeling less optimistic the second time around on the gurney. What if she found nothing? What if I was imagining everything?

She found nothing. I'd jinxed it.

She had the gall to remark on how perfect my reproductive organs looked, how I was the picture of health. At the follow-up appointment, she handed me a stack of high-definition photos taken from the inside of my abdomen to flip through, pointing at the unmarred slippery surfaces of the treacherous meat inside of me.

I was angry, livid (or maybe just terrified). I sat across from her, on the inferior side of a large oak desk, and demanded she tell me what the source of my pain was. But she had already dismissed me. She was an endometriosis expert, and I didn't have endometriosis. It was probably interstitial cystitis. She shrugged. My bladder must be enflamed. She recommended pelvic floor physical therapy, handed me a pamphlet about diet changes for bladder health and the stack of pictures of my meats, and ushered me out of the room.

The diet changes sucked so badly I preferred the pelvic floor physical therapy, even though that involved having a chipper woman palpate the interior of my vagina with clinical fingers. I did breathing exercises and ate bland foods, cutting out coffee and orange juice and alcohol and spices and hot peppers and tomatoes and pickles and soy sauce and chocolate and pizza and everything else I ever liked. Can you guess what happened next?

My pain got worse at the same reliable rate it had maintained for over a decade.

And worse and worse and worse and worse. And I'll never escape it. I'll never escape, never; it's part of me and I can't get away from it and I just, I have to, have to—

I have to stop thinking about it. I can't dwell on it or I'll become too depressed, and then I can't make myself accomplish anything. I need a distraction. I push myself off the wall I've been ruminating against.

Returning to my bedroom, I notice a book on the dresser, right under the horrible abstract/bird painting, that somehow hadn't gotten my attention before. I don't know how I could've missed it; it's right in front of me. For a moment, I think of the home invader breaking into the house and smearing trash all over the kitchen floor, but I instantly dismiss them as a culprit. What sort of thief leaves things? No, I banish the possibility before I even wholly consider it.

Besides, I recognize this book from my childhood: It's a collection of Irish folktales and legends Da used to read to me when I was small, before my big mistake, before he left. Irish myths make for odd children's stories; they loop and whirl and dance about one another with loose-weave threads of ill-defined magic and foreboding consequences difficult for an unfinished brain to parse morals out of. Still, though, I loved them. I loved the sound of Da's brogue telling me the sometimes funny, sometimes scary, often mournful tales in the matter-of-fact way Irish stories are always told. And every time Brigid popped up, he'd nudge my side to remind me I was named for a goddess.

I take the book back into bed with me and turn on my heating pad, poring over the heroes and villains of my youth. On this page, it is the story of the children of Lir, the four of them beautiful beyond compare, turned into swans by a jealous aunt turned stepmother and cursed to live a lonesome life of sorrow. Later on, there is the Morrígan, the goddess of terror and war, sometimes depicted as a trio of sisters, sometimes as one fearsome shape-shifting pillar of a woman, appearing as a scald-crow, striking fear into her enemies and chaos into the battlefield, washing the blood-stained clothing of those fated to die. On another page, you see Cú Chulainn, who grew up to be the most famous of all the warriors of the Red Branch. In his youth, through no fault of his own, he was forced to kill a great hound belonging to a blacksmith when the dog attacked him. Sorry for the death of the beast and being an honorable boy, he served as a hound to the blacksmith in repayment, and this was how he got his name.

Wait. Recognition hits me, a few moments delayed thanks to my weed edible. I turn back to the page about the Morrígan, the terror goddess, and her shape-shifting. There is an illustration of her favorite form: the scald-crow.

The crow in the drawing has an ashen body with an inky black stain covering its head and wings, and a clever, knowing eye. It looks very much like my least favorite bird. Slowly I turn my head to look out the window behind me. Sure enough, the bird sits on the other side of the window screen quietly, seemingly reading over my shoulder. I turn my head back.

I pull out my phone and search the phrase "scald-crow." It directs me immediately to the Wikipedia article for the "hooded crow," which is apparently what they're called in modern times. They're not endangered; in fact, they're quite common all across Europe and even into parts of the Middle East. Their native range does include Ireland, but not Chicagoland. Not North America at all.

So, this bird must have escaped from some zoo or aviary and decided to live near my house for whatever reason. It seems like they must be smart birds: Wikipedia says they know how to hide food to return to it later, and if they see another crow hiding food, they'll steal it when the first crow is gone. One could probably learn how to survive here. Even the lifespan is possible, if unlikely: Wikipedia says the longest-living known hooded crow was over sixteen years old. That's only a stone's throw from the twenty years I've been seeing this one.

But why would I have ever seen it at college? Was I imagining it then? Have I seen two escaped hooded crows? That seems unlikely.

I turn my head again to frown at the crow. I stare deeply into its eye, trying to determine if it seems more otherworldly than a bird ought to.

"Are you a goddess?" I whisper to it.

It caws in response.

I slam the folktale book shut and rub my eyes. The bird is not a goddess. That is an insane thought. I am just very, very tired and very, very high. I forbid myself from considering that the crow is a deity and lie down, trying to think sleepy thoughts.

This is how my high-symptom days generally go: me sailing the seas of agony in an anxious daze, floating on a raft constructed primarily of grit and marijuana, desperate to fall into the pull of sleep because if I am asleep, I am not aware of my own misery. It is a small mercy that marijuana and pain both make me tired, and

I successfully doze in and out for an hour or so.

By the time the pain begins to fade, so does the high. Everything is still gossamer around the edges, but my thoughts are more orderly and my ability to see a goal through has returned. I realize it's nearly time for the video chat with Emma I agreed to yesterday morning, and that I haven't eaten anything all day because the pain was making me nauseous. The only thing in my stomach is sips of bathroom faucet water. I'm ravenous.

In the cabinet in the kitchen, I come across some fancy soup. I know it's fancy because it has been packaged in a jar and the brand name is some lady's name; the soup I buy is always canned and generic brand. This one's label proudly proclaims it to be organic, non-GMO, and made only with ingredients you can pronounce. I check the expiration date and it's good for another several months. Thank you, Mammy, for leaving at least a little edible food in the house. I pour it into a small saucepan to heat on the stove.

I drum my fingers on the counter and wish wistfully for something hearty to go with the soup. With a start and with delight, I remember the proper brown bread I took out of the freezer on Tuesday, when I cleaned the fridge out. It must be completely thawed by now, if maybe a little freezer burnt or stale, but I'm sure dunking it in the soup would cover all manner of sins.

I slide the serrated knife from the block, untangle the bread from the tea towel I wrapped it in when I put it in the bread box, and thwack it down onto a wooden cutting board. I admire the look of it, thinking if I can find room in my budget, maybe I'll order a stockpile of the good flour for myself. I give it a sniff, treasuring a rare, happy childhood memory of good bread and hearty stew. I enjoy the way the knife slides through the crust and into the body. Not too stale after all. I smile.

The knife catches on something hard in the bread, and I

frown. Normally, things get stale from the outside in; it shouldn't be stale in the center. I saw a little harder to get through the rough spot but can't make any headway against it. The knife can cut to the left of the spot and to the right, but the thing itself is hard as stone.

Is there somehow a pebble in the bread? Maybe importing Irish flour isn't a good idea in the end.

I put down the knife and stick my fingers into the half-cut slice, feeling the squidgy-fresh center, and begin to pull the loaf apart. It crumbles into coarse chunks of dark bread in my hand and onto the cutting board, spilling onto the counter, but I tell myself it isn't a waste. I'll just pour those bits into the soup. I like when the bread is sopping with umami deliciousness anyways.

Once I've pulled enough bread away, the pebble is revealed, sticking out from what ought to be a clean-cut edge. It's an odd-looking stone, nearly white but with a yellow tinge about it, smooth on the sides but rough on top, with shallow fissures occurring in a regular, symmetrical pattern. I grab it with my fingertips and work it out of the loaf, and then drop it into the sink as though it burned me.

The back end, the end that was buried in the loaf, has roots coming out. Four roots. Like a molar. A tooth.

It pings around the bottom of the stainless-steel sink, rolling its way to the drain. My hand jerks frantically toward it and away, toward and away, as I wrestle between the impulse to keep it from tumbling down the pipe where it will either disappear forever or cause a blockage, and the desire to never touch it again. Responsibility wins. I cover the hole, allowing the tooth to come to a stop against the edge of my palm. I squeeze my eyes shut for a moment to calm myself and then peek at it with only my right eye, as if that will make it less alarming. It doesn't move. I wish I still thought it was a pebble.

Cautiously I move my hand away and look at the tooth resting there in the basin. It's clean, no blood or gore on it, though a few crumbs of bread are stubbornly holding on to one of the roots. It seems less threatening now that I'm over the shock. Could it be an animal tooth that somehow made its way into the grain? It seems human-sized, but I'm not a dentist or a veterinarian, so I don't know what I'm talking about. It could easily be some sort of animal tooth. Maybe a huge dog, or a small goat. How well are Irish food imports regulated anyways? Are the standards relaxed for imported products? Are animal teeth something flour is even checked for?

I hear an angry hiss and turn to the stovetop, swearing out loud when I realize the soup has boiled over. I ought've watched it, ought've put it on a lower heat, ought've used a larger pot. Stupid. I turn off the stove and watch my molten dinner calm itself, then return to the task at hand.

Carefully I rip through the rest of the loaf, plucking out tooth-sized pieces of bread from it as if I were plucking a chicken, creating a pile of breadcrumbs on the cutting board. I don't find anything else in the loaf; the bread is just bread, but the tooth remains in the sink, undeniably real against the stainless-steel backdrop. I have no intention of eating tooth-bread, no matter how wasteful that may be. (Mammy would make me eat it, Mammy didn't believe in waste, Mammy wanted me to not think so highly of myself all the time, but I don't want to eat it, Mammy, I want different things than you, Mammy.) I consider taking the crumbs outside to toss in the yard for wildlife, but I don't want to encourage the bird to keep hanging around, goddess or not. In a perfect world, in fact, the bird would starve to death. I pick up the cutting board and tilt all the bread remains into the trash can.

I pick up the tooth with a paper towel (it's an animal tooth, a large dog or a small goat, but I'd still rather not touch it, not more than I have to, which is entirely reasonable) and deposit it into a clear plastic baggie. I put it in the top drawer, the long shallow one that contains the cheese grater and potato peeler and can opener, just in case I need it later. Then, I eat my soup too quickly, scalding my tongue and forgetting to enjoy the lack of genetically modified organisms. I'm on high alert: nervous about the tooth, scared of my pain returning, excited to talk to Emma. I try to focus on the last one. The only good thing I've got.

I've ten minutes to spare before my (virtual) hangout with Emma, and I kick off this in-between time by grabbing a small mirror off the dresser and assessing my appearance. It is, in a word, dire. My high-symptom day, smothered as it was by a pillow comprised mainly of marijuana, has left my skin patchy and dull, while my eyes shine swollen and red. My short brown curls have gone rogue, exploring the space around my head in irregular patterns, and I ought to do a load of laundry because even I can smell the misery sweat that has dried into the fibers of my clothes. Mercifully, technology has not yet reached the level where Emma will be able to smell me through the screen. Everything else needs to be addressed, though.

I pull a precious cleansing wipe from its packet and scrub down my face (I save these only for emergencies, as they're an expensive luxury item I can't afford to waste), then slap on a film of moisturizer. A smidge of hair clay lets me shape my curls into something vaguely resembling a style, and eye drops take care of some of the redness in my sclera. I change my clothes, even my bralette and underwear, in case there's a stain somewhere I haven't noticed. It helps me to feel a bit fresher, too, though I know how I feel never matters.

With only a minute to spare, I power up my laptop and smear on some tinted lip balm as I check my reflection again. Much better now. I closely resemble a regular person.

Of course, Emma is late to join, and I kick myself for rushing. After so many years of friendship, I know better than to be on time for anything with Emma, but I'm always punctual anyways. The thought of her waiting, with her painted lips dripping into a lonesome pout on one side of an empty Zoom call, breaks my heart too much to risk it.

But she joins eventually. You can always count on Emma eventually. I smile too big when her image blips onto the screen. She's done this great thing with her hair: Her long micro braids are in these two spherical buns on either side of her head. With her being so short and plush, the hairstyle could look childish, but it doesn't; it looks flirtatious. Maybe it's the bold lipstick she's wearing, like she's always wearing. Today it's a rich berry color, bordering on purple.

"Brigid, hi! Ohmygod, I miss you so much, girl!"

My thousand-watt smile shines brighter. My name, said right, sounds so nice from her mouth. "I miss you, too, Emma, you have no idea."

"Sorry I haven't called you back, this week has been *cah-ray-zee*. The twins had this piano recital on Tuesday night that I totally forgot about until Monday morning, so I had to get their stupid little matching outfits rush dry-cleaned and figure out getting them there because—get this—their parents both had to work late on Tuesday and so they just 'caught the end' of their own daughters' performances and like, god, I just can't imagine the therapy these girls are gonna need in, like, seven years."

"Jesus, the parents sound like nightmares."

"Yeah, no, they are, of course they are, but they pay me well, and I'm doing my best for the girls, and what more can you do, you know?" Emma shrugs a nonchalant shoulder, totally confident in her boundaries.

"You're a better person than I am," I tell her. "I don't think I could handle your job. Like, watching parents be so shitty and still just trying to take care of the kids the best you can? And like, how do you know if you're helping the kids at all? How do you know you're not messing them up worse? I couldn't handle it. I don't know if I could take care of any kids, ever."

"Aw, nah, you'd be great at it, you're way more patient than I am. More giving. And that's all kids really need, you know? To be cared about and respected and stuff like that. The whole 'kids' thing is just rough for you, with your mom and everything. That's not your fault."

"It's kinda my fault. I should be over it by now." I shrug, but in a defeated way. Not nonchalant, like Emma.

She rolls her eyes but pairs it with a soft quirk of her lips so it comes across as gentle and loving. "You were abused as a kid and now you don't like to see kids be abused. I don't think that says anything bad about you."

I laugh a little at her exaggeration. "It wasn't so bad as all that. And I don't know if being late to a piano recital constitutes child abuse."

"It's child disrespect." Emma shrugs again but doesn't let the conversation drop. "And I thought you said Carol said you should call what happened to you child abuse?"

I scowl. I swear the two of them are in a league together. I would think they were texting about me behind my back if I didn't know it'd be illegal for Carol to do that. "No, yeah, that's what she says. I don't know. Mammy never hit me or anything, she just . . . wasn't nice all the time."

"Wasn't nice all the time?" Emma repeats incredulously, her eyes bugging wide. "Brigid, you told me she burned your homecoming dress in the backyard when she thought you were dating some guy behind her back."

"Yeah, well, it was really low-cut. I probably shouldn't have bought it in the first place," I mumble.

Emma carries on as if my argument has no merit. "And when you were little, she'd lock you in your bedroom all day without food if you argued with her, right?"

"I was a pretty difficult kid."

"Brigid, I don't believe that. You're not a difficult adult. If anything, you're too agreeable. You'll go along with anything, even if it hurts you. Hell, the only thing you're ever difficult about is this."

I apologize as a reflex, "I'm sorry."

Emma sighs, a weary sigh, and I curse myself. She'll avoid talking to me if I keep this whining up. I couldn't handle that. I need to be more agreeable.

"I really am sorry," I repeat, trying again, hoping she doesn't leave.

"No, don't apologize." Emma shakes her head. "That's sort of the point, you not apologizing all the time. Look, I don't mean to bully you about this. You'll come around on your own someday. I hope you will, anyway. It's just you're special to me, and your mom, even if she's dead, she pisses me off so bad. You're obviously terrified of her, it's clear she was awful to you, and I just wish you could see it wasn't your fault."

I hear a flutter behind me and turn my head to see that the bird is on the window ledge again, disgruntled looking, with feathers askew. I try to ignore it, focusing instead on getting Emma to stay on the call.

"You're probably right." I agree to end the topic and jump ship to a new one as deftly as I can. "How is your week, other than the piano recital?"

Emma frowns a little. She sees what I'm doing but goes along with it in the end. "Well . . . I did have a date last night."

"No!" I gasp, trying to disguise my distressed alarm as excitement.

"Yes!"

"Who?"

"The cute blonde from pottery!" She effervesces. "Her name's Kelly. I was able to get a seat next to her during class and Jess was stuck on the other side of the room and we got to talking and I'm gonna be honest, I brought my A game, I was flirting so good, and I got her number. And so we were texting like all day Monday and Tuesday, just like stupid jokes and stuff but still it was so much fun, and then we went and got a drink last night at the German place, you know, where that one bartender has weird facial hair and wears those leather pants?"

"Lederhosen," I say, buying myself time before I have to act happy about this news.

"Yeah, those," Emma confirms. "Anyway, we had a great time, and I looked so amazing, if I do say so myself. I got a manicure and everything." Emma waves her fingertips in front of the camera lens and, sure enough, Emma's usually bare, short fingernails are currently a berry color, an almost exact match with her lipstick.

"So, she is gay?" I clarify.

"Well, okay, so strictly speaking, she hasn't ever actually dated a woman before," Emma admits. "But she says she wants to try it!"

"I thought you didn't like to be the first woman someone dat-

76

ed? Something about not wanting to be someone's experiment?" I try to keep the scowl off my face. Emma's persistent distrust of bi-curious women is one of the reasons I let her keep thinking I'm straight. There are other, more important, reasons, of course. But still, it rankles me.

Though maybe she's right not to give me a chance. Hell, maybe I am straight. It's not like I know what I am.

"She's sooooooo cute, though, Brigid." Emma sighs, but this time, it's a sigh of longing tinged with hope instead of disappointment. "You know who she looks like? Like the blonde Ann in *Gentleman Jack*. She's got this amazing hair, it's so long and so bright. She keeps it up in a bun during pottery class, you know, because of the wheel, but at the bar she had it down and ohmygod, I could just about drown myself in it."

Self-consciously I touch my short, dull curls, entirely unsuited to drowning oneself in. They're a good reminder: Emma would never want me, anyways. I should be happy with what bits of herself she's willing to share with me. "She sounds great, Em." I force myself to smile. "I'm really happy for you."

"You don't like her." Emma, always the empath, can see through my shoddy façade.

"I just don't want you to get hurt," I lie as earnestly as I know how. "I mean, Jess seemed great at first, too, but we saw how that ended. Maybe pottery class girls are cursed."

Emma mock-gasps. "How dare you? The pottery class girls are . . . are . . . sacred! And I'm one of them, you know."

I laugh. "Of course, my mistake. I forgot about the holy communal bond of pottery-based sisterhood."

"Damn straight." Emma nods once, closing the argument, and pets one of her cats who's in the process of walking past her camera. "Anyway, tell me about the house! Is it going okay?"

"It's not going . . . great," I admit, not certain exactly how to describe everything without sounding like I'm losing my grip on reality. I go with the easiest explanation, "I got broken into the other night."

"I'm sorry, what?" Emma screeches. "Wait, that's so scary! Did they steal anything? Why are you still there? Did you change the locks? Get an alarm system?"

"No, I can't really afford any of that." I scratch at my forearm, too ashamed to admit I didn't even think of those solutions. Maybe I should replace the locks. I probably could dip into my savings for that. I don't know why I didn't consider it. Too overwhelmed, I guess. "The police didn't seem to think it was a big deal. Nothing got stolen."

"So, what happened?"

"I'd spent all day cleaning the kitchen, like emptying all the rotten food out of the fridge and wiping down the countertops and everything. Overnight, somebody came in somehow without waking me up and brought back in all the trash bags I'd thrown away and poured all the garbage all over the floor. It was disgusting, the smell was so bad, you can't even imagine. And it took me forever to get it cleaned up again."

I don't mention the meat hanging from the ceiling. I don't know how to explain it without making it sound vaguely serial killeresque, and I don't want Emma to worry about me. I couldn't handle the embarrassment if she didn't think I was capable of living on my own.

"So, it's, like, a vandal then? Do you think someone's mad at you for taking your mom's house? Maybe one of her friends or something?"

"I guess. Maybe." I hadn't considered that either. Emma's so smart; she always has different, better answers for things than I do.

She could be right, I suppose. But did Mammy even have friends? "I don't know who it would be, though. She mostly kept to herself, as far as I know."

"Maybe somebody from her job? She worked nearby, right?"

"Yeah, she was the manager for this nice boutique." I nod slowly, turning the thought around in my mind for closer examination. "They liked her there."

"Well, I mean, I hope you don't mind me saying this, but of course they did. She might've been a bitch, but your mom was also a total fox."

I wrinkle my nose. "No, she's not. Wasn't."

"Oh, c'mon, have you seen her bone structure? Plus, she was so skinny, and so, like, intense looking. Which is super in right now. And she was what, five foot ten?"

"Five eleven."

"Yeah, she was a goddamn high-fashion model. It's obvious why they wanted her to work there."

"You think so? I never thought of her as pretty." I conjure an image of her in my mind, but it's hard to tell if it's the real Mammy I remember or the scarier, pointer, elongated Mammy of my nightmares. "I guess if you consider all her features individually, if you describe her, she sounds pretty. And in pictures, she looks pretty. But in person she was . . . I don't know. I never felt that way."

"That's fair. I mean, I don't think you're supposed to think your mom is hot. And I never met her in person." Emma trusts my assessment generously. "I only ever saw pictures, like you said."

"You know what's weird?"

"What?"

"I don't remember her being so tall when I was little." I chuckle a little, to illustrate that I'm being ridiculous and I'm aware of it.

"You don't?"

"No, like before I was six or seven, I remember her being tall, but not so much taller than the other moms. Like I don't think she really stood out, you know? But as I got older, it felt like she kept getting taller and taller. Especially after Da left us."

"That's weird." Emma scrunches her lips to the side as she considers. "I feel like it usually goes the other way, right? We think our parents are bigger when we're smaller."

"Yeah, weird." I chuckle again, trying to dispel the unsettling mood I find myself carrying anytime I think about Mammy for too long. "My memory is pretty bad, though. I must be imagining it."

"Maybe," Emma allows, but she still looks unhappy with the conclusion. "Well, I have to get to bed soon. It's an early day with the twins, you know."

"Oh, yeah, of course." I smile brightly, pretending not to mind. "I've got stuff to work on here too. We'll talk again soon?"

"Yes! I promise."

"Good night."

"Night!"

Emma hangs up on her end and my screen goes mostly dark. I groan and stretch, catching the bird out of the corner of my eye as I do. It still sits on the window ledge, listening in on me.

"Feck Blondie, am I right?" I say to it.

It lets out a grating bark and takes off, leaving me alone.

"Well, feck you too," I mumble, and open a new tab on my web browser. I type into the search bar "cats for adoption near me" and try to guess which one Emma would like best.

You'd think my subconscious would give me one night off from Mammy, wouldn't you? But you'd be wrong. Mammy returns in my dreams, looming ever taller above me.

Day 6

I wonder if I am evolving into something more resilient, incapable of being killed (though still very capable of being hurt). I know evolution doesn't work like that, that it requires generations upon generations at a larger population scale to actually count as "evolution," but a girl can dream, right? Bending the rules of evolution would make a nice explanation for how I'm not dead yet despite the physical agony of yesterday, the absolute exhaustion from so many days of too little sleep in a row, and having eaten nothing but a bit of overpriced, scalded soup over the last thirty-six hours.

A more unpleasant explanation would be that I'm not dead yet because I'll be dead any minute now. I don't yearn for death, so I don't love this second option.

Channeling my natural optimism, I decide to conduct myself as if death is not imminent and pour myself another bowl of dry cereal, once again making a mental note to schlep to the grocery store for milk soon. My stomach is threatening to flip itself inside out, so instead of coffee, I make myself a gentle cup of tea. It won't make me feel as awake, but I'm prioritizing keeping my stomach acid safely ensconced inside my body over alertness today.

I glance toward the list of tasks on the fridge, the one I've made little headway on, what with the rotten food and day of pain and tooth in the bread (sorry, Carol), and realize I never really finished the kitchen. I still have to go through all the cabinets and decide what to keep and what to give away. Might as well work on that while I sip my milkless tea and crunch my milkless cereal.

My physical misery has shortened my temper, so I'm uncharacteristically quick as I decide what to chuck and what to keep in the kitchen. All the expired or suspicious pantry items go immediately into the bin (I'm looking at you, hardened brick of brown sugar), and for any duplicate items, like Mammy's heavy green enameled cast-iron frying pan versus my nonstick bargain-bin one, I just keep the nicer of the two.

Actually, Mammy's frying pan really is quite lovely, with a satisfying heft to it. I bounce my wrist a few times, admiring the fancy French quality, before returning it to the cabinet. This move isn't a total loss after all.

However, many of the items are suspect. Mammy had an odd penchant for single-use kitchen utensils, as if she had never actually eaten before, and so treated a paring knife and a specialty avocado slicer as having equal importance. The shredder claws, pizza scissors, hamburger patty mold, and containers shaped like tomatoes specifically for storing tomatoes (and tomatoes only) all go in a box to go to the charity shop, along with the duplicates. The mismatched and chipped dishes will be donated as well. All of this makes enough room in the cabinets to store the majority of the hand-painted shamrock porcelain from the hutch, which I've decided to keep. I want to see one of the tiny cups in Emma's tiny hands. So sue me.

When I open the extra-wide, shallow drawer I put the tooth in, the one with all the sharp utensils, it is with trepidation. I've been studiously avoiding thinking about the tooth, and I'm not looking forward to acknowledging it.

I'm glad I was cautious. I see a man's face inside and am able to slam the drawer shut with a shriek before he can escape. I stumble several steps backward until I'm leaning against the door to the fridge, holding my hand against my cantering heart. After several tense moments in which the drawer that is much too small to hold a man anyways does not move, I remove my hand from my chest. I slide open the drawer again and, of course, from atop the potato peeler and Microplane, Jesus gazes up at me, as merciful as ever.

For a moment, I am frightened, my brain running through scenarios of demon possessions or, even worse, this being a message from God that I am to be virginally impregnated with his second son. Jesus continues not to move. I stare down at him for a long while, until the situation starts to feel humorous. I pick up the picture, and it's just a picture, the same as always, and I begin to laugh in earnest at the stupidity of it all.

"Jesus," I chide, "you can't keep sneaking in like this. I told you to wait in the car. What would someone say if they found us here, like this, together? The scandal, Jesus! Think of your poor, sainted mother."

I giggle at my own joke and put Jesus in the charity shop box, a corner of his robe getting scratched up by the sharp point of a strawberry huller, and turn back to the drawer.

My merriment dies in my mouth. The plastic baggie, the one I put the tooth in, contains only a small grey pebble.

I snatch the bag and hold it close to my eyes. It's just a stone, oval in shape, slightly more bulbous on one side than the other, dark grey. Not even remotely tooth-colored. I tear through the plastic film, not bothering to undo the zip, and roll the pebble in my fingers, thinking maybe if I pay attention, I'll feel the roots I remember so clearly. I can feel the surface of the rock, faintly rough; I can feel the sweat on my palms; I can even feel the whirls of my own goddamn fingertips; yet I can't feel a single root, a single ridge, a single fissure.

It's a pebble.

But it isn't. Anger flares in me, irrational and irresponsible, and I stalk the kitchen in small circles, still fondling the stone in my hand. It isn't a fecking pebble. I saw it last night and it was a tooth, it was definitely a tooth. I know what a fecking tooth looks like. Last night I tried to talk myself out of it, tried to convince myself it was an animal tooth, but I know what a human tooth looks like. I can't be fooled so easily.

Except . . . I can, obviously. My stalking gradually slows until I come to a stop in the middle of the kitchen and look down at the pebble in my hand.

With my bad memory and my fanciful imagination, I can be fooled very easily. I have somehow fooled myself into believing I have internal, unhealable damage; I conjure up pain that crushes me under its pointed heel, pain caused by an ailment that clearly doesn't exist. Do I really believe someone broke into my house just to pour trash all over the floor, that someone other than me is moving a picture of Jesus around? Or am I so desperate for attention or excitement or agency I pretended a small rock that made its way into some poorly regulated flour was a tooth?

I sigh, and I'm not sure if it's in defeat or in self-disgust. I let the pebble tumble out of my hand and into the trash can, and resume going through the kitchen wares with the solemn subjugation of a monk. When the task is finished, I carry the boxes for donation out to my car and pack them into the trunk, making sure Jesus is there, too, where he belongs.

And there's the bird, that fecking bird again, sitting on the low oak branch it likes to spy on me from. I remember the next item on my list, to search for its nest and call animal control if I'm able to find it, and make a careful sweep around the house. When the first search is fruitless, I go around again, more slowly this time. The bird follows behind me as I continue my methodical journey. I watch it out of the corner of my eye in case it swoops into a particular nook or cranny.

The bird is crafty and gives nothing away. I am unsuccessful in the end.

Back in the kitchen, I examine the list on the fridge and relish crossing off the top few line items. I'm tired and want to take a break but know if I give my mind a rest, it'll just ruminate on the tooth (pebble), so a break is not allowed. The next task is to go through the stuff in my room or, more accurately, the guest bedroom that was once mine, and donate what I don't want to keep from there. I make my way down the hall.

Choosing the first item to go is simple. I take the abstract painting with its aggressive birdshapeshadow off the wall and stand it on its side in a giveaway box so it faces away from me. I feel a little thrill at my boldness. Mammy got it specially commissioned when she redid the room. I don't know why she'd request such a thing; it's horrible. But she loves that painting. Loved.

Suck it, Mammy.

The various knickknacks go the same way. Cloying scented candles, weird decorative bowls and orbs, and fake flowers have no place in my home. I keep the lamps, because I do enjoy lighting, but make a note to try to get new lampshades. Maybe the charity shop will have some acceptable ones and I could make a trade. I wonder how many lampshades you can get for an unsettling abstract painting. I'm prepared to throw in Jesus to sweeten the deal.

When I get to the closet, I pause for a moment ("I killed your mother and put her in the closet. And now, I'm coming for you.") but only a moment, because I know there're no bodies in the closet. This closet is much too small to fit a body. That would be ridiculous. It's Mammy's massive closet that's worth worrying about.

There are no bodies in any closet, I remind myself.

Despite Mammy having the master bedroom's closet all to herself since Da left us, a significant portion of her mountains of clothes have made their way into this one, some with the tags still attached. None of them would fit me, of course. Even though I'm tall for a woman, I'm significantly shorter than Mammy. I'm portlier, too, with a distended, swollen lower abdomen that changes size from week to week, as though I were gestating and losing a fetus in perpetuity. It's one of my less attractive features.

I make to dump all Mammy's clothes into giveaway boxes, but I stop myself when I remember she was considered quite fashionable and dropped loads of money buying whatever struck her fancy. It seemed as though money hardly even existed to her. But, for once, one of her bad habits stands to benefit me: Some of these clothes might be worth something at a consignment shop. I put anything new looking or with a brand name I recognize as fancy in separate boxes. In the end, only about half of the clothes are in the giveaway pile, but that's still plenty for a cat rescue. And now there's more than enough room for me to hang my few nice things.

It's a small room, and I'm already almost done. Once I stuff the guest sheets and comforter that used to be on the bed into another giveaway box, all that's left is to go through the dresser. I open the top drawer to reveal a layer of sweaters made of cashmere so delicate they ought to have snagged on Mammy's sharp collarbones. I glide my hands across them tenderly, loving how the softness of the wool is so complete I feel as if I'm touching nothing, and pull a camel-colored one out. Maybe I'll try it on. Mammy's much thinner than me, but if it fit her loosely, it might fit me snug. As I shake it out and hold it up to assess its dimensions, a torn piece of paper flutters out from between the folds and down to the floor.

I set the sweater down on the bed and pick up the paper, wincing as the motion to bend over aggravates the pelvic pain, and flip the scrap over. There's a message inscribed in black ink, written with an extra-fine-nibbed pen. I immediately recognize Mammy's elegant script. It reads:

You ungrateful little bitch.

Same as always, same as when she would hiss her words into my ear as I sat at the kitchen table or on the living room couch or in the chair in her room or on my bed, because no room, no place, no spot was safe from Mammy, I do not react.

I do not crumple the paper in my fist, or toss it to the floor, or turn away from it. I do not even cry; I hardly ever cry anymore when faced with Mammy's judgment. I used to cry a lot when I was small, after I became unlovable but didn't understand yet that I deserved it, before I learned crying only brings about more punishment, more consequences. No, I do not resist.

Quietly, graciously, I take the words into my heart.

I am unappreciative and entitled, self-absorbed and self-obsessed, unreasonably concerned with my own well-being and suffering, not concerned enough with others, and especially not concerned enough about Mammy. I should be searching for her, demanding the police investigate more, contacting news outlets, printing posters. Not living in her house, eating her food, selling and disposing of her things. It is the truth. Mammy is right.

She's always been right.

I fold up the sweater to place it back in the drawer, only to realize I've ruined the careful organization of the other sweaters. I take one out to refold, and a strip of paper falls from it as well. Same pen, same handwriting. I read:

I know what you're doing when you sneak around, you slut.

You can't fool me.

I inhale this truth, and exhale acceptance. Mammy knows every move I make. She always knows.

As I take every sweater out of the drawer, I gather the scraps of paper from each one so I might ponder them all together. When the sweaters are tidily tucked away, I do the same with the contents of the other three drawers (more sweaters—thick Aran cable knits—as well as slacks and a collection of silk shells), finding more scraps of paper. There is some real artistry, poetry even, in her words:

Do your little friends know how disgusting you are?

I love you, but I don't like you at all.

Stop lying. When you lie, you hurt me and you spit in Jesus's face.

I have no time for myself. You take over my life.

Your father wouldn't have left us if it wasn't for you.

You're selling your body with the way you dress.

Stop feeling sorry for yourself. Don't you know how blessed you are?

As I read them, I fan them out across the bedspread so I'll be able to see them all at the same time and bring them into my self-concept. It's no good to deny the truth, after all. Only by admitting our shortcomings can we hope to rise above them.

While I look over my collection, my gaze is drawn to the window. The bird stares at me through one cocked eye. If birds could have facial expressions, this one's would be smug.

I suppose it has never been a disappointment to its parents and can't relate to me.

I sit for a long while, accomplishing nothing other than stoking the cleansing fires of self-loathing, until I realize it is just about time for therapy with Carol. I gather all the scraps into a neat little pile on my nightstand, check myself in the mirror to make sure I'm looking as though I am definitely not a danger to myself or others, and power up my laptop for the session.

Carol is already on the call. Her face brightens when mine pops up on her screen. "Brigid! It's so great to see you. Happy Friday!"

I keep myself from pulling a face at her mispronunciation of my name. It's not her fault. There are multiple correct versions, and mine is the hardest to say. "Happy Friday," I repeat instead.

"How *are* you?" she asks in that earnest way she has, stressing the "are" and making her eyes wide.

"Honestly?" I scratch at my forearm. "I'm not doing so hot."

"Oh no, honey, what happened?"

"Um, a lot . . ." I stall for a moment, darting my eyes around the room, from the half-filled giveaway boxes to the carefully re-filled dresser to the horrible scraps of truth on the nightstand. I don't know where to begin. Therapy is about honesty, so I tell Carol that. "A lot has happened. I don't know where to begin."

"Okay." Carol nods, unfazed. "Last time, we made a list of things for you to work on so the big task of cleaning out your new house didn't seem too overwhelming. Did you do any of the things on that list?"

"Yes," I say, and through the dismal layers of self-hatred, I feel a small flicker of pride. Even when I'm worthless, I'm not entirely useless. "I got a few things crossed off the list. Like, I made the doctor's appointment, and they were able to fit me in for a tele-health appointment next week. On Friday."

"That's great!" Carol smiles indulgently. "Taking care of your health is hard to do, but so important. How are you feeling about the appointment?"

"I haven't thought about it too much. I'm not expecting much from it," I admit, "and I probably wouldn't have bothered schedul-ing it if you didn't ask me to. I don't think the doctor will be able to help, really."

"Well, thank you for scheduling it. I hope one day you do these things for yourself, but for now, doing them for me will be good enough. I'm really proud of you. You keep trying, even when it's difficult. You're a very strong person."

I find the compliments too overwhelming and have to break eye contact with the screen. My gaze falls on the paper slips and then skitters away as the rising self-revulsion turns my stomach. I want to believe all the nice things Carol says about me, I really do, but I can't. They aren't true. My throat clenches around nothing as the desperate wish I was what Carol says I am takes over. I feel my tear ducts kick-start. I almost never cry. I don't know why I'm starting to cry now.

Carol quietly waits with a soft expression, giving me space. For some reason, it makes me cry more, but not in a bad way. It feels like I'm being cradled in her hands; I don't have to carry the weight of my own spine for a moment. The crying itself feels good, as if there were a blockage, a rotting clump of hair and skin cells, in the pipes that bring my tears to the surface, and I've finally forced it out.

I should stop crying. I hear Mammy's voice in my head ("Your self-pity is disgusting, Brigid. Keep crying and I'll give you something to cry about."), and I'm a child again, afraid she'll leave me just like Da and I'll be all alone. But Carol won't leave. Of course, it's her job not to leave, but it's more than that. Even if I don't believe the nice things Carol says about me, I believe she believes them. She doesn't want to leave. For once, I don't have to stop myself crying.

When the tears finally slow, my nose is grotesquely plugged and my throat crackles with thirst. I look at Carol on the screen and ask to be excused for a moment, and she gestures in a way that communicates I should do what I need to with patient understanding. I blow my nose on some toilet paper in the bathroom, then return to my bed and the screen, taking a huge swig from my water bottle as I do.

"Sorry." I smile apologetically at Carol, still sniffling a little after my outburst.

"Please don't apologize," Carol answers. "I'm honored you trust me with your feelings. Was there something I said that triggered you somehow?"

"No, no, nothing like that," I rush to reassure her. "At least, you didn't say anything upsetting. I found some notes, Mammy must have hidden them before she left, and . . . I don't know, they said horrible things about me. It feels like she's still here, telling me all the ways I'm a failure, and it's making it hard to stay focused."

"Stay focused on what?"

"I don't know. Everything? The things I need to get done."

"Honey, you're going through a stressful time right now," Carol soothes, "but there's no race happening, no urgency. All the things you have to do will be waiting for you when you're ready for them. If you need to do them slowly, or take time to rest, both physically and mentally, that's okay."

I take a deep breath. "Okay."

"Would you mind telling me a little bit about what the notes said that made you so upset?"

"Of course I'll tell you." I scratch at my forearm and consider not telling her because I want her to keep liking me. Therapy is for honesty, though, so I'll be honest. "Uhm, a lot of it was just stuff she used to say to me all the time. It's nothing new, not really."

Carol waits in an encouraging way for specific examples.

I sigh and give in. I seem to have some sort of condition where I never developed a backbone. "Well, the first one just said I was an ungrateful bitch."

Carol winces in pain. I backpedal into a joke, saying, "It was elegant in its simplicity, really. You have to admire how concise of a writer she is. Was."

"I don't think we need to admire much about your mother."

"Yeah." I sigh again. Carol isn't letting me get away with jokes today. "Maybe not."

"What did the other notes say?"

I grab the stack from the nightstand next to me. "I have them all here. I can just read them to you."

I flip through them quickly, reciting the words in a monotone Gregorian chant, not pausing between them or looking up at the laptop screen. I'd rather not see Carol's reactions. If I see her realize the truth in the words, it will cause my heart to burst apart with such ferocity my ribs might actually crack.

When I finish the stack, I take great care in reorganizing and straightening them on the nightstand to extend the time before I have to acknowledge Carol. Alas, all good things must end, and I eventually do look at her again.

She waits until I do.

"Well," she says in a measured voice, "that was certainly . . . intense. She said things like that to you all the time?"

"Yeah." I shrug. I thought I had already told Carol as much, but maybe I hadn't made it clear exactly what the meat of what Mammy said was. That's another way Mammy's right about me being unlovable: I lie by omission a lot. I like when people like me, to the point of dishonesty.

"Brigid, I need you to understand something. Can you look at me?"

My lies have made me look away in shame. I snap my eyes up to the screen.

"Brigid, I know that you don't like to say what your mother did to you was child abuse. I know she was never physically abusive. But these sorts of things she said, what she wrote: These are clear examples of emotional abuse. She created an environment where you doubted yourself and thought less of yourself, where you were always scared of what she might do or what she might say. That's abuse."

I look away again. I can't help it. "It wasn't just that I was scared of Mammy," I mumble.

"I'm sorry, I couldn't hear you."

"It wasn't just that I was scared of Mammy." I raise my voice, almost to a shout. "It was more than that. She was this force, this powerful unstoppable figure controlling everything in my life. Any time she was angry or wanted something from me, I always shut down or gave in. I couldn't even imagine fighting her."

"Oh, honey, I'm so sorry," Carol soothes.

"I was terrified of her." My voice cracks again with tears, but I keep going. "I still am."

There's a sound from the open window behind me, a delighted rasp, higher pitched than I'm used to. I twist my head to look at the bird, laughing at me.

"Shut the feck up!" I pound my open palm against the wall next to the screen, expecting the bird to fly away in fear. It doesn't, of course. It's too stubborn. It mocks me with one last caw before taking off, dropping a few inches from the sill before its broad wings force the air to submit.

I turn my attention back to Carol. "Sorry, I know we were talking about something important. It's just I really hate that fecking bird."

Carol looks wistful, as if the bird flies off with a golden opportunity clutched in its talons, but then rearranges her face into a sympathetic smile. "You didn't have much luck finding the nest, then?"

"No. I did look for it, though, I promise I did."

"Don't worry, I believe you," she assures me. "I know you've been working off of the list, like you said."

"Yeah, the list has been helpful. Thank you again."

"Of course. Can you tell me what you got to?"

"Cleaning out all the crap in my room." I spin the laptop slowly around so she can see the bare walls and dresser top, empty apart from the Irish folklore book I've left out. "That's actually where I found Mammy's notes."

"In your room?"

"Yeah, in the dresser. They were folded up in her sweaters and trousers and everything."

Carol shakes her head slowly.

"What?"

She sighs. "I know you don't want to be pitied, and I don't pity you, but I have so much sympathy for you. Your mother took the time to hide all those notes in your drawers, where she knew you would find them. I find myself not liking her very much."

"That makes two of us," I jest. "We could start a club. Make jackets."

Carol just sighs again. My jokes aren't landing today.

"So, how far did you get in cleaning out your room? Are you feeling good about it?"

"I was almost done, but the notes derailed me. I ended up just folding everything back up and putting it away in the dresser instead of in the boxes." It's strange; I had felt so ashamed for considering getting rid of her clothes earlier. But now that I'm talking to Carol and the notes are more of a memory, I'm ashamed I haven't gotten rid of everything already.

"Would you like my help deciding what to keep and what to give away before we end our session? We only have a few minutes left."

"Oh shit, really?" I glance at the time. Sure enough, the hour is nearly up. "No, I think I'll be okay. There's something else important I need to talk about. The house was broken into."

"What?" Carol's voice leaps an octave.

"No, yeah, on Tuesday night, I think? The days are kinda bleeding together, they don't mean anything. Yeah, Tuesday."

"Were you hurt? Did they steal anything?"

"That's what was weird. Whoever it was didn't take anything, they just dragged the trash bags full of rotten food I had cleaned out of the fridge into the house and smeared it all over the floor. It smelled so bad, I can't even describe how bad, and took all day Wednesday to clean up."

"Oh honey, that's terrible. Did you call the police?"

"Yeah, they weren't . . . incredibly helpful. Emma thought I should get the locks changed. What do you think?"

Carol's eyebrows rise dramatically. "You haven't already?"

I scratch my forearm. Apparently, changing the locks was a more obvious solution than I had realized. "No? It's expensive, and I don't have a lot of savings left . . ."

"You need to change the locks," Carol declares. Carol never orders me around, so she must be serious. "Call a locksmith as soon as we get off the call. Okay?"

"Okay, I will. I'll do it right now. I think our time's up, and I don't want to keep you."

She glances at the clock and pulls a face of consternation. There's clearly more she'd like to talk about, but it's the end of her workday. "Okay, honey. I'll talk to you on Monday. Call the locksmith right now. Get them to come this weekend. Okay?"

"Okay," I agree again. "Bye."

"Goodbye!"

I told another lie, but this one is so small it hardly counts. Before I call the locksmith, I take all the trousers and cashmere and Aran cable knits and dump them unceremoniously into a box for the consignment store. In the end, I don't want to keep any of it.

It all works out, despite my lie. When I call the local locksmith, they promise to come tomorrow afternoon.

You would think the repetition of the nightmare would loosen its hold on me. In the daylight, that's how it works; I'm sure when I think about the dream tomorrow morning, I'll dismiss it as ridiculous. Maybe even a little campy. An over-the-top slasher movie: cheesy, but you still watch it every October for the nostalgia.

You don't remember how much it frightened you when the story was fresh, when it was new, when it felt like it was really happening.

This is happening.

She is not my mother.

She is coming for me.

Day 7

I have company over, so I am wearing an upgraded version of my chronic illness uniform: the leggings are plain black, and have no stains on them. Very chic. Sadly, the middle-aged locksmith, Al, does not seem to appreciate high fashion.

He's nice enough, though. We make friendly small-town small talk about how I'm settling in while he props the front door open and starts working. I offer to make him tea or coffee and it turns out Al is a tea guy, which I wouldn't have guessed. I make myself a cuppa as well, figuring I ought to skip the coffee even though I'm exhausted from so many fretful nightmare nights. I'd like to avoid another bowel episode. It might damage my blossoming friendship with Al.

While Al works and sips from his mug, I carry and push and kick the boxes full of Mammy's clothes and knickknacks from my bedroom to the kitchen. It twinges my pelvic pain a bit, but the satisfaction of having the bedroom feel like it could actually be mine is more than worth it. Between the contents of the bedroom and all of Mammy's weird single-use kitchen gadgets, I have a manageable mountain of boxes that looks like it'll just about fill my car. I decide today, pain allowing, I'll tackle scrubbing the bathroom clean. Tomorrow, I'll finally make my way to a consignment shop and the thrift store.

The idea makes me a bit giddy. It's the first unreversible step to making the house truly mine instead of Mammy's. Plus, I'll finally be rid of Jesus. I peek in the box I put him in yesterday to make sure he's still there. Miracle of miracles, he rests next to a plastic colander, peering up at me through the drainage holes.

His holy visage reminds me tomorrow is Sunday and the shops might be closed. I don't even know if there's a consignment shop around here. I pull out my phone for a bit of internet sleuthing, listening to Al mutter to himself as he works a few yards away in the entryway. My search begins.

The cat rescue/thrift shop combo is open from noon to five on Sundays. I'll try to go early; I'd like to have time to play with the cats, if they'll let me. I don't have luck finding a nearby consignment shop, but there's a high-end resale shop that will buy clothes from you outright that's not too far away and will be open all day. After a moment's deliberation, I decide that's a better option anyways; I might be stuck waiting months for an unguaranteed payment from a consignment shop, whereas this place will let me walk out with cash in hand day of. It'll probably be a tiny fraction of what the clothes are actually worth, but I have no interest in figuring out how to sell all this myself. Besides, high-end clothing resellers need to eat too. I'm just doing my part to keep the wheels of society turning.

In the corner of my vision, I see Al stand up from the open door with a groan. He places his mug on a shelf of the hutch next to a bud vase covered in shamrocks and calls out, "Alright, that oughta do it."

I take my time putting down my own mug and phone loudly, so it won't seem like I was watching him. I amble to the entryway.

The door mostly looks just like the same old loud-unless-you-know-the-trick-to-closing-it door, albeit with a shinier lock. Al hands me two loose house keys, which I immediately place on the hutch shelf next to his discarded tea mug.

"That was very quick," I tell him with a smile. I notice through the still-open door that the bird is on the porch again but endeavor to ignore it.

"Oh yeah, wasn't a complicated fix." He shrugs. "I'm glad I could help a nice young lady like you out on such short notice. I know it's tough, moving to a new town all by yourself—"

He's cut off when the bird takes off with a cacophony of wings and caws, and propels itself through the door. An inky razor feather slits into my right eyeball as it slaps its wings against my face and flies around me, making a sharp turn just past me to head for the hutch.

Blinding, literally blinding, pain overtakes my skull, centered on my right eye but spreading into my sinuses so my nose burns and drips while my tear duct spurts to help clear the irritation. I rub instinctively at my face and eyelid, curling into a question mark under the surprise of the agony, and hear the thunder of large wings in a small space. Al's voice rises, a yell of shock at first, turning into an angry order directed at the bird to "hey now, get out of here." The clump of Al's boots moves toward the hutch; there is a metallic *clink* and the scrabble of scaly bird feet against antique wood, followed by an increased, frantic beating-wing sound and fierce caws as Al continues to yell at the beast.

The sounds of the bird grow distant, caws shrinking away through the open door, which is then slammed shut, a screeching sound indicating Al does not know the trick to closing it quietly. The pain is less of an alarm now; my body has begun to embrace it as part of the new status quo. I begin to straighten up, keeping my hand over my injured eye, holding it shut.

Al lets out a low whistle, and through my one open eye, I see him rub at the back of his neck in befuddlement. "Well, I've never seen a bird do something quite like that before. I'm sorry, I guess I should've closed the door."

I try to smile reassuringly, but I'm certain it comes out more as a wince. "It's okay. It's not your fault. That bird is an arsehole."

My familiarity with the bird seems to befuddle Al even more than the bird's odd behavior, which I think is unfair. The bird is clearly an arsehole. I'm just stating facts.

"Do you need any help with your eye? Is there someone I should call for you or something?"

"No, no, I'll just put an ice pack on it. It'll be fine." I wave my free hand at him. "Let me pay you so you can get on your way."

He waits while I dig out my wallet and generously gives me a small discount for paying in cash. I wave to him as he leaves and shut the door behind him, grabbing my keys from the hook on the door to lock it. Of course, my key doesn't fit in the lock. It's a new lock. That was the entire point of this exercise. I would roll my eyes at myself, but my right eye still hurts and I'm still holding it closed.

I turn to the hutch to get the new keys Al gave me and find one sitting next to his empty mug. Just one.

I frown at it. Didn't he give me two? Am I imagining there were two keys? Of course I am. I imagined an entire human tooth in a loaf of bread. I'm capable of imagining a key.

Once the door is locked, I add the new key to my key ring. I keep the old key on there, too, since it'll still work on the side door. The side door has a chain on it in addition to the regular lock, so I didn't bother replacing it. I'm not made of money.

From the freezer, I grab a baggie of frozen peas and wrap them in a dish towel, holding the cold packet over my eye for a good ten minutes until the swelling is reduced to the point I can open my eye without it twitching itself back shut. Good enough.

After changing into my less-chic, more-stained leggings, I fetch the glass cleaner and bleach and rags and a bucket and pair of rubber gloves from under the kitchen sink. Time to scour the bathroom. Thrilling.

To be honest, I don't mind cleaning bathrooms as much as other people do. There's satisfaction in taking something shit covered and making it gleaming and comfortable. Besides, I'm used to it. Growing up, my chores included just about all the cleaning, and cleaning the bathroom was especially my chore. Mammy said it was because my disgusting shits made more of a mess than hers. She's not wrong, of course; I was having my bowel problems when I was as young as eleven or twelve, and they can get nasty. When you have a habit of leaving toilets embarrassing, the way I do, you also develop a habit of cleaning toilets so nobody finds out.

As I scrub the toilet bowl with the long-handled brush, I muse that there is one good thing about Da leaving so long ago. Nobody with a penis has peed in this toilet in almost two decades, so there are almost no pee splashes on the underside of the seat. Pee splashes are revolting. I know from when I worked in a coffee shop in college and had to clean the restrooms.

There would be no pee splashes in our house if I married Emma. I smile at the thought of decades spooling out ahead of us:

her soft, short torso tucked against mine as we watch period dramas before bed, a kitchen with cabinets full of her wonky bowls, a bathroom with no pee splashes anywhere. Of course, if we had a son, he might get urine all over the place. Well, that has a simple solution at least. Fantasy us will only have daughters.

I wipe down the seat and the outside of the toilet, then wipe down the counters and scour the inside of the sink. Once I've got the mirror shining properly, with the toothpaste scum and dried water droplet marks wiped away, I'm nearly there. Just the combo tub/shower and a bit of detail cleaning to go.

The tub and its walls are a pain, of course. They always are. Cleaning them requires a lot of stooping and reaching and leaning while the edge of the tub digs into my tender abdomen. Still, when the pain comes later (and it will come later, it always comes), I'll appreciate having a clean tub to curl up in while I let my tears mingle with pounding water pouring from the shower head. It will all be worth it.

The bathroom gleams, much cleaner than when I began, and I start cleaning the baseboards, beginning on the open side of the door. It's a small bathroom and the walls are mostly taken up by the cabinet under the sink and the tub, so I'm quickly to the baseboards that are on the back side of the door. The end of bathroom cleaning is in sight.

There's also a human finger in sight, poking out from the baseboard where the old-fashioned metal-spring door stopper should be. Still on my knees, I freeze stock-still. There is not a human finger instead of a door stopper. There can't be.

It really looks like there is.

I close my eyes. The right one is still sore from earlier. Could it be making me see things somehow? I let it rest, making sure the stinging is at a low point before opening them again.

I suck in a sharp breath. Still a human finger.

Tentatively, as if the finger might bend and beckon me to join it in its practical, wall-protecting purgatory, I reach out my rubber-gloved hand and nudge it. It wiggles slightly at my touch but remains firmly attached to the baseboard. It is cold, very cold, as if it was taken out of a freezer only a few hours ago. I look closer at it and, sure enough, it's sweating like defrosting meat. I remember the mystery meat defrosting in the fridge, and later dripping ominously from the ceiling.

The mystery meat was just a cheap cut of beef, I remind myself. I decided that. That's the most logical explanation. Like how the tooth was a pebble all along. I'm getting ahead of myself, that's all that's happening. I'm tired from the overwhelming week, dizzy from the bleach fumes, suffering from my mystery pain, and getting myself overexcited. I'll feel better if I take a bit of a rest, and tomorrow I'll see this was just a door stopper all along.

Still, if it is a human finger, the police would want it for evidence (evidence of what? I don't know. I don't think about it). I best put it in the freezer.

I turn on the fan and take the bucket of watered-down bleach out of the room, in case the fumes really are getting to me, and pour it down the kitchen sink and rinse it out. I decide the finger (door stopper) should probably be put in a plastic sandwich baggie to keep it clean, so I take off my rubber gloves to dig one out of the box and return to the bathroom.

My hopes that the finger was an illusion caused by bleach fumes are dashed when I return and it is still steadfastly stopping the doorknob from hitting the wall. Curiosity gets the better of me and I get on all fours to peer at it, getting so close it nearly touches my nose.

It's a large fleshy finger, probably a man's. It's basically my skin tone (very pale with a thick blanket of orange-gold freckles) and might have even had my red undertones before it was removed from its owner and the blood drained away. The bottom knuckles, closest to the wall, have sparse, wiry, ginger hairs sticking out from them.

That's what my da's hair was like: bright shock red and unruly. I miss him now, even though I barely remember him from before I made him leave. Dealing with a finger in the bathroom feels like something a da is meant to do.

He isn't here. It's up to me. Gritting my teeth and trying to not think too hard about what I'm doing, I wrap my hands around the frigid digit and gently pull, expecting it to pop off the wall. I groan loudly in frustration when it doesn't.

I yank harder, recklessly. I feel a little give, but the finger ultimately refuses to budge.

"Jesus, Mary, and Joseph," I complain, and wipe a hand across my face. "What are you? Screwed into the fecking baseboard?"

My hand freezes on my face. It very well might be screwed into the baseboard, I realize, especially if it actually is just a metal door stopper I'm imagining to be a human finger. Also, I realize if it isn't my imagination and it really is a dead human finger, I just smeared my hand all over my face after it recently grasped said dead human finger.

My stomach lurches and I stand up and spin, quickly turning on the bathroom tap to scrub my hands clean and wash my face. Once I'm clean, I fetch my rubber gloves from the kitchen and don them.

Gloved and ready to attack the finger (door stopper) again, I firmly grab it and begin to turn it to the right. It doesn't budge, and I grow despondent (will there be a finger rotting away on my bathroom baseboards forever?) until I remember the age-old adage of "righty tighty, lefty loosey." I turn the finger again, this time to the left, thinking hard about Lady Edith of *Downton Abbey* and her various foibles to keep from retching, and it mercifully begins to spin.

And spin. And spin. I rotate it several times, the fingernail facing the ceiling, then me, then the floor, then away from me over and over until it finally loosens to the point that I can pull it out. Sticking out from the end of the finger, out of the raw, gory meat flesh, is the associated metacarpal bone, but it has been delicately carved and doesn't resemble a hand bone any longer. It is carved, unmistakably and perfectly, into the shape of a screw. Of course it is. How else would you screw a human finger into a wall?

My instinct is to drop the finger on the floor, but I force my own hand to clasp around it vise-tight. If it's actually a finger, I can't risk damaging the evidence. If it isn't a finger, then there's no reason to drop it. I open the sandwich bag with my free hand and drop the finger inside, squeezing out as much air as I can while I zipper it shut. Once it's in the freezer, I decide that even though it's only the early afternoon, I've earned a break. It's been a stressful day.

Two weed edibles, three snacks, and one embarrassing voicemail message to Emma later ("Hey Emma, it's me. Brigid. You know that. I miss you! Call me back. Unless you're too busy with Blondie. What's her name? Shelly? Amy? Shit, I forgot . . . Sorry, I'm being a bad friend. I'll do better. I'm just really high. It's been a long day. Call me back, if you have time. But if you don't, don't call me back. Either way. Bye."), I have snuggled up in my bed, even though the sun hasn't yet set. I read a bit more of my Irish folktale book, reminding myself of the giant Manannán mac Lir, whose sorrow was so great he cried an ocean. I'd always loved him as a child; he was my favorite Irish mythological figure, though

Fionn mac Cumhaill gave him a run for his money.

When enough weed is in my system that the words slur across the pages and into the illustrations, to dance in circles along with Celtic knots, I give up on reading and return to *Downton Abbey*. I love the massive cast of characters, the ever-revolving wheel of faces. It makes me feel less alone in this empty house. Though I suppose I would feel differently if I were one of the servants cleaning the chamber pots and pee splashes.

One night, I'll have a restful sleep, one without Mammy, one without nightmares.

Tonight is not that night. She looms in the darkness, immaculate and inescapable.

Feck you, Mammy.

Day 8

When I awaken in the morning, I feel the thrill of triumph. An entire week. I made it an entire week in the house, and I'm doing fine. Better than fine. I've made some real progress, and today I'll bring the stuff I don't want to the resale shop and thrift store, and the house will be that much closer to truly being mine.

Still, though, unease slips into my mind like smoke from under a door (a door I'd rather keep shut, like the door to Mammy's room, or worse, her closet). Through the haze of sleep and whatever cannabis remains in my system, I don't remember the finger/door stopper right away.

Until I do. Ah, yes. That's the source of my worry. There's a finger in my freezer. I groan. Why do things like this only seem to happen to me?

I decide I can face the freezer after I'm dressed. I actually put on a pair of jeans, real ones with an actual button, since I'll be going to the upscale resale shop. I want to seem put together so they don't try to rip me off.

By the time I've begun to sip my coffee, however, the combination of anxiety about the frozen finger and the pressure from the waistband of the jeans has ratcheted my pelvic pain up to a tooth-grinding level and my bowel and uterus have entered some sort of knife fight with one another. I rush to the bathroom, not even bothering to shut the door behind me. I collapse onto the toilet for a nice, relaxing diarrhea explosion and am relieved to have made it, even as my poor butthole burns and my gut rings alarm bells of pain.

Alright then, body: point taken. I will face my problems head-on, and I will do so while wearing stretchy pants.

After a shot of generic Upset Stomach Reliever (which richy-rich name-brand types know as Pepto Bismol) and a change into my most stretchy, most worn-out leggings, I head to the freezer. I take a few deep belly breaths like the physical therapists said I should anytime I notice my body tensing up.

I am a strong, capable woman. I can handle any manner of body parts in my freezer.

I open the door suddenly, forcefully, before I can change my mind. Front and center, on the bottom shelf, lies the plastic baggie from the night before. It's a bit frosty, so I can't see the contents clearly at first. I lift it with the very tips of my pointer finger and thumb and peer through the murky plastic to see a regular spring door stopper.

"Ah, for feck's sake," I mutter, slamming the freezer door shut and trudging back to the still-stinking bathroom. I ought to buy some air freshener. I take a deep breath in the hallway before I enter and shut the door so I can reinstall the door stopper.

From the floor, a merciful, innocent face stares serenely up at me. I shriek in surprise and then again in rage. "Jesus!" I shout at the painting, shaming him for his blatant disobedience. "I put you in the fecking giveaway box!"

I snatch the painting, quite beat-up now between the broken and dinged-up frame and the scratched surface, and stalk back into the kitchen. I stuff him roughly into his rightful place in the kitchen giveaway box, scuffing up his face and not caring. "Now, you stay there," I order threateningly. This is the closest I have ever come to feeling like a mother.

In a sour mood, I return to the bathroom and sloppily screw the door stopper back into the baseboard where it should've always remained. My imagination is getting away from me. How would there be a finger in place of a door stopper? It doesn't even make any sense. I must be more stressed than I realize.

Stuffing fistfuls of Oaty-O's into my mouth at regular intervals, I use my pent-up frustration to ignore the constant pain and schlep all the boxes of junk to my car. The bird is, of course, watching me judgmentally from its perch on the oak tree for the duration. When I've creatively crammed every nook and cranny of my tiny car's tiny trunk and back seat, I refill my water bottle at the kitchen sink and toss it and a granola bar into the purple backpack I use as a purse. I walk down the driveway to my car, giving the bird the bird as I unlock the door and climb in. As I back out of the driveway and make my way to the resale shop, I see dark movement through my rearview mirror. The bird is flying close behind the car, following me.

It often followed me when I was younger, especially when I was a teenager, but not as boldly as this. It would pretend to be a more normal bird then, skulking on the edges of my vision, not drawing too much attention to itself. It was as if it wanted plausible deniability. I'm not following you, it said to me back then, why would I be following you? I'm just a regular bird. *Chirp chirp*.

Such illusions are gone now. It swoops in lazy circles when

I idle at stop signs. It keeps pace when I speed too fast down the quiet suburban streets. It follows me confidently, mockingly.

Jittery from pain, from the tension of being followed, from the stress of not being able to trust my own perception of what is real and what isn't, I enter the upscale resale shop. The older woman behind the counter is short and thin, her head barely coming up to my chin, but she is a delight to behold. Her outfit is sharp and perfectly tailored, a statement scarf popping out brashly against a tan blazer, and her makeup is boldly applied to her lined face. You rarely see such rich red lipstick on an older woman. For a moment, I forget to be upset, I so wholly admire the look of her.

She quickly scans my lazy leggings and shaggily grown-out pixie cut and seems mildly disappointed by the look of me, but slaps a customer-service smile on. I can almost believe she's happy to see me. I smile back in a way I hope is winning and deposit the box I carry onto the counter.

"Hi, I have some clothes to sell?" I uptalk at the end of the sentence, like it's a question.

"I'll be happy to take a look," she customer-serves, "but I'll warn you that we have very strict requirements regarding what we will and won't accept."

"Not a problem," I tell her, nodding. "I have a few more boxes, though. Is it alright if I get them?"

"Sure," she permits as she opens the box with visibly low expectations.

By the time I return with my two other boxes, her opinion of me and my wares has improved considerably.

"Where did you get these?" she asks as she carefully folds a dress I had carelessly tossed into the jumble.

"My mom lived in St. Charles before she, ah, passed away. I'm cleaning out her house. She was really into fashion."

"I'm sorry for your loss."

"Thanks," I reply awkwardly. "She worked at a boutique that's only a couple blocks away actually. Anneli Green. It's next door to the store with all the horror and monster stuff, on Main Street near the river."

The shopkeeper nods, rescuing another dress from my mistreatment. "I know Anneli Green. They don't carry things quite this . . . remarkable, though."

I shrug. "I couldn't tell you where she got it all, to be honest. We weren't close."

"Well, I can have an offer ready for you in about thirty minutes. Feel free to browse in the meantime."

I poke around aimlessly, not expecting to find anything I like. The way my abdomen is tender to the touch makes it difficult to be fashionable, and I'm usually too tired to dress up anyways. But despite all odds, I do eventually come across a wrap dress I love, knee-length silk, white with a pattern of dark green curling leaves. The fabric is sleek liquid slipping through my hands, and I think it would drip off my frame in an inviting way without pressing on my stomach. I imagine wearing it on a date with Emma, the dress inviting her to run a hand around my waist. I imagine the feel of her lips is even softer than the feel of the silk.

I look at the tag in the neckline. Diane von Furstenberg, size 8. I haven't heard of Diane, but I do usually wear a US 8. I check the price tag. Eighty dollars. Eighty dollars? For a used dress? I hastily stuff it back onto the rack and hold my hands behind my back.

Mercifully, the woman behind the counter calls my name. Mispronounces it, of course, even though I said it to her myself, correctly.

She seems put out by my empty hands. "You didn't find anything you liked?"

"There was one dress, white with green leaves on it? It's pretty. But I don't think I can quite afford it."

Her eyes sparkle a little, the way passionate people's do. "The Diane von Furstenberg dress? That one's lovely. You have good taste."

I blush a little at this kindness and look away. "I don't know about all that. It has a nice feel to it, though. The silk, I mean."

"It does," she agrees, and winks. "If you'd like to trade in some of the stuff you brought today for store credit instead of all cash, I'll knock twenty-five percent off the dress."

I bite my lip and look at the small mountain of Mammy's folded clothes in front of her. I have no idea what it would be worth. "How much can you offer me in cash?"

"Six hundred fifty."

My eyes bug out. "Dollars?"

"Yes." She laughs a little. "Though if you want the dress, it'll be five ninety."

I pretend to mull it over, even though I will obviously be taking the money.

She seems to know I'm putting up an act, but she generously makes another offer so there's the illusion I'm getting one over on her. "How about this?" She turns to the display of purses behind her and grabs one, a small green crossbody. "Six hundred even, you can have the dress, and I'll throw in this bag to go with it."

I'm not much of a purse person, but even I know that my purple backpack would look stupid with a silk dress. "That'd be perfect."

She fetches the gorgeous dress and nice enough purse, placing them into a brown bag that's been handstamped with the shop's logo. She then hands me six hundred dollars cash, straight from the register. I walk out buoyed by my new riches and the rare treat I've allowed myself. The trauma of the mysterious not-finger is forgotten. I don't even scowl at the bird still waiting for me by the car.

My phone rings and I'm delighted to find it's Emma calling. Maybe she sensed my acquisition of the sexy dress through the ether.

"Em, hi!" I chirp into the phone. "I was just thinking about you."

She laughs. "Good things, yeah?"

"Only good things, for always and forever."

"Good."

"What's up with you?" I ask, deciding not to bring up my embarrassing message from the night before if she doesn't.

"I actually need your help with something. Do you have a couple minutes?"

I grin from ear to ear. She needs help with something and she calls me. Suck it, Blondie. "Of course! I always have time for you."

"Okay, thanks. So, as you know, I've got pottery again tonight and Kelly's gonna be there and I think I'm gonna finally make my move and kiss her after class. So, I need to pick an outfit. Something sexy, something that says 'yes girl, you are so gay for me' but also that I can wear to pottery class without looking ridiculous and also not too flashy because I don't want Jess to know what's up, you know?"

The grin slides off my face. Of course she's calling about Blondie. Kelly. Whatever.

"Brigid? Are you still there?"

"Yeah, sorry, I got distracted for a second." I recover my chipper voice. "I don't know, you're better at fashion than I am. Maybe some tight jeans and a low-cut top, so like during class you're wearing the smock and Jess won't see anything, but then afterward you can show off your great rack?"

"And my combat boots! So she knows I mean business."

"Yeah," I reply, wishing she meant business with me. But I'm a good friend. My advice is sincere. "You should wear that red top, the one you wore for Halloween a few years ago when you did the slutty vampire thing. You look great in that."

"Yes! And the matching lipstick, yeah?"

I almost groan at the mental image. Emma's plush lips and plush breasts, color-coordinated in overt welcome. "Definitely. Definitely wear the lipstick."

"Awesome, awesome. Thank you so much, Brigid, I was going in circles staring at my closet. I gotta go in a few minutes, but how are you? I feel like we're not chatting as much recently."

"Yeah, I'm alright. You know, just . . ." My voice catches a little in my throat. I'm weary from the yo-yo of emotions. "Just working on the house. Missing you. Nothing too exciting."

"Awww, you're sweet. We'll talk soon, yeah? A real talk."

"A real talk," I repeat. "Bye."

She hangs up, and I consider how pathetic I am. Buying a secondhand dress and feeling like some hot girl for a moment. I wish I wasn't so alone.

The bird, staring at me derisively from a few yards away, doesn't count as a companion.

I make my way to the thrift shop, the one with the cat rescue inside. I drive slowly, not even trying to outpace the bird still flying directly behind my Honda. It's too fast for me to escape on these small-town streets. At some point, I ought to head over to the highway. Give it a real workout.

Despite my bad mood, the idea of the ominous bird flapping desperately, disappearing into the distance as I sink the pedal to the floor and my four-cylinder engine whines, makes me smile to myself. Stupid bird.

I pull up outside the thrift shop and stack the remaining boxes from my car onto the curb, checking to make sure the paintings of Jesus and the creepy birdshape are among them, then lock it up and carry the box containing Jesus through the door. I want to be rid of him.

Inside the shop, it's crowded with all manner of porcelain and picture frames, blankets and board games, tablecloths and trash and discarded treasures, all made equal in the benevolent eyes of the cat rescuers. The cat rescuer in charge today, an older man with an awe-inspiring handlebar mustache wearing a shirt seemingly sewn from an American flag, approaches me with the enthusiasm of a used car salesman.

"Hey there, neighbor! Welcome to Precious Paws!"

"Hi." I feel an incredulous smile break through my icy demeanor. It's difficult to withstand the infectious force of Midwestern friendliness.

"What is it I can do for you on this beautiful day? Are you here to meet one of our many fine feline friends?"

"Actually, I came to make a donation." I heft my box in his direction. "I have a few more boxes outside too."

"An offering! What luck!" He claps his hands twice as if summoning a butler but takes the box from me himself. I laugh and begin making trips from the curb to the shop with the rest of the boxes, focusing on my amusement instead of my increasing pelvic pain. After I put the last box down, while the cat rescuer is carrying them into a mysterious back room for sorting and pricing, I surreptitiously open my cheery purple backpack and dig out a bottle of ibuprofen. I pop four, just to be sure the pain won't get too severe for me to drive. (That happens sometimes, and I get trapped until the pain abates, which can take hours.)

I wander over to a large window looking into a room where some of the cats available for adoption live. For such a small room, there're an awful lot of cats in there. I think I see about fifteen, but every time I look at a new crevice, I realize what I thought was an empty fuzzy bed or dark shadow is actually another cat. I look away, worried if I continue looking, I will make more cats appear from the void between universes. This place clearly doesn't need any more cats.

"Anybody catch your eye?" The rescuer materializes behind me and I jump. "We have so very many friends who would so love to complete your heart! Just tell me what I need to do to get you to leave here with a cat today, and your wish is my command. We've got orange ones, grey ones, big ones, little ones, pretty ones, ugly ones, and the perfect one for you!"

Against my better judgment, I look back through the window. There are an awful lot of them, all without homes. I imagine Emma looking through the same glass with me, her tender heart breaking for each and every one.

I also feel my thigh getting scorched by how big of a hole the six hundred dollars is burning in my pocket.

"Hypothetically," I begin slowly, shooting the man a serious glance so his excitement doesn't become so overwhelming his heart gives out, "how much does it cost to adopt a cat and get everything they need? And how much would you expect vet bills to cost?"

"I am so happy, no, delighted, that you ask!" I have failed. He is too excited. "Our cats come with a variety of adoption fees, from one hundred and fifty dollars for brand-spankin'-new kittens to only twenty-five dollars for our wisest residents who have been around the sun their fair share of times! Their needs, especially in the case of our more mature friends, tend to be simple. A hundred dollars would be more than enough for food, dishes, a litter box, and a few toys to get you on the road of the most rewarding journey of your life. And, if that's not enough, all Precious Paws companions come neutered, dewormed, and with all necessary immunizations! Plus, with our new 'Helping Helpers' partnership with the Magnolia Veterinary Practice in town, if you adopt a friend with special needs or past a certain age, their future veterinary care will be offered at a heavily discounted rate."

"That doesn't sound too bad." I put my hand against the glass and stare thoughtfully at the roomful of lonesome fluff.

"It's not too bad at all! It's too wonderful!" His smile is blinding. He knows he's got me. "Who might you be interested in meeting?"

"I guess . . ." I pause. I can't believe I'm doing this. I am doing it, though. "Do you have any cats eligible for the discounted vet visits who like to hunt?"

The man nods emphatically. "We certainly have athletes who are getting on in years, but are still packed with vim and vigor! We do require anyone you take home to be a strictly indoor cat, though. Many of our friends came from rough lives on the streets, and it's our goal to make sure they don't return to such unfortunate situations."

"Oh, of course," I quickly agree. I just don't want the bird in my house again. "It's just that I live alone and I get bored. I'd like a playful cat." I stop again and consider my dream of living with Emma. She already has her two cats, of course. "Though there's a chance I'll get a roommate in the future, and she has two cats already. So, a playful cat eligible for the cheap vet visits, who gets along with other cats too."

The man thoughtfully strokes his handlebar mustache for a moment and throws me a considering glance. "What are you hoping for, in terms of appearance?"

I shrug. "I don't really care what they look like."

He claps his hands twice again, the sharp sound ringing through the cluttered store, then offers me his arm for a promenade. "If you would do me the honor of accompanying you, I would like to introduce you to the highly esteemed Mr. Odie."

I giggle and rest my hand atop his star-spangled arm. "Certainly, sir."

He walks me to a back room through a small hallway, passing the boxes I brought on the way. (I see Jesus staring out from the one on top and resist the urge to flip him off.) This back room is filled, impossibly, with even more cats. These ones seem significantly scruffier and lazier than the ones in the front room, though the scruffiest cat of all, a large black one with a white chest, is attacking a ball in a circular track with gusto.

"This is our senior cat room, for our gently used residents. But don't let his advanced age fool you! Odie is a rapscallion, his roguish nature barely disguised by his distinguished tuxedo coat, and is more than up for the adventure of a lifetime in your home." He gestures, of course, to the scruffy black-and-white tomcat.

I crouch on the floor, ignoring my protesting abdomen, and look closer at Odie. He's not a looker, that's for sure, though he might've been in his younger days. His coat is long and scraggly and his tail is scrawny, as if someone took a smaller cat's tail and stapled it to his backside. Most striking and most unfortunate, however, is the deep scar running across his nose, misshaping one of his nostrils so he snorts and grunts softly as he plays.

Poor little nose. Poor little guy.

I reach a hand out cautiously to him and he abandons the ball to sniff my fingers curiously. Then, bold as can be, he stuffs his fuzzy head directly into my palm. I laugh and, recognizing the request for what it is, begin scratching at his ears.

The man waits, uncharacteristically quiet, while I continue to pet and wiggle my fingers at Odie. Eventually, the warm feeling in my chest grows stronger than my good sense and I ask, "Do you mind if I change his name?"

The smile that emits from under the handlebar mustache could light up a football stadium. "Not at all, he's yours to christen and treasure. If you'll come with me, I'll have you fill out the paperwork! How lovely! A lovely day! I knew when I woke up this morning it would be lovely. I said to myself, it's a lovely day, and here it is, being lovely."

He smiles indulgently at me as we leave the room, and I spare one last glance at my new cat. Half an hour and a few binding signatures later, I place Odie in his cardboard carrier in the passenger seat of my car, pleased by the sound of him snorting away, and pleased the bird is nowhere to be seen.

As I begin to drive away, I see a woman approach the thrift shop through my rearview mirror. She is young and tall, ever so tall, elongated to the point that her high ponytail will kiss the top of the doorframe. Before she opens the door, though, she turns her head toward my car. Our eyes meet briefly in the reflection and I startle, slamming the brakes on impulse. The car shudders to a stop and Odie meows a complaint.

I shake my head. I don't know the woman; I've never seen her before. I must have been imagining the contempt on her face.

As soon as I get home, I set Odie up in my bedroom with the disposable litter box the enthusiastic cat rescuer gave me and, after making a few soothing sounds and promises to return soon, shut the door on him. The rescuer told me to keep him in only one room for the first week to make his new home less overwhelming. I, myself, am frequently overwhelmed, so this advice seems sound.

Even though I don't want to overwhelm him, I do want to spoil him. I make a run to a pet store and purchase everything the cat rescuer told me to and a few extra toys and treats besides, preferentially choosing brands I've seen in Emma's apartment because I know she only buys the best for her kitties. After a quick jaunt to the grocery store to purchase myself some significantly lower-quality treats, I rush back home to check on Odie.

As I set the oven to preheat and hastily put away the groceries, I think about what to name him. Renaming is definitely necessary; all I can think of is the dog from *Garfield* when I say Odie. It simply won't do for my fierce, boisterous gentleman. Besides, I'd like it to be something Irish. (He might be from Chicagoland, but he's an Irish cat now.) I think back to my folklore book; I could go for Manannán mac Lir, but that's a mouthful, and he's the sea god and cats don't like water. Fionn mac Cumhaill is better, and I could just call him Fionn for short, but it still doesn't quite feel right.

Then I remember Cú Chulainn, the famous warrior, and smile to myself. He was named because he filled the role of a guard dog; *cú* is Irish for "hound." Even though I don't speak Irish, the idea of a cat named Dog makes me laugh. And I'm hoping this cat will be my guard dog in a sense; I'm counting on him to keep the disgusting bird from coming inside again. Cú is a fitting name. Besides, it's fun to say.

Into the oven goes the celebratory frozen pizza I bought myself (with toppings and everything! Truly, a luxury item), and I sneak to my bedroom to check on Cú. I open the door with loving tenderness in case he lurks on the other side, planning an epic escape, but I shouldn't have worried. Cú has made himself at home on my unmade bed and glances up at me with his tongue out, paused mid-lick. I see he's already groomed some black fur onto my white sheets.

"Are you cozy? You look cozy."

He doesn't have much to say, but that's okay; it was a stupid question. He flicks his tongue back into his mouth.

"Do you mind if I join you?" I rhetorically ask as I sit on the bed a few feet away from him and hold out my hand for him to sniff. Like in the thrift shop, he plops his noggin into my palm for more scratches.

"I'm glad you're not too scared." I continue talking as I pet him, "I'll just get your new stuff all set up, and then we can have dinner, yeah?"

He purrs loudly, almost aggressively. I take it as acquiescence and fetch the pet store bags from the entryway to set up the bedroom, then fill up his new ceramic food dish with a mixture of his old food from the rescue, generously provided by the cheerful rescuer, and a bit of the new, expensive food I bought. I get him a bit of water and show him his new toys as well, just in time for the oven to beep at me for my dinner.

Sitting on my bed, with most of a mid-range frozen pizza on a plate at my side while Cú explores what might be hidden under the bed, I feel surprisingly cheerful. I hurt of course (I always hurt, and it was a busy day), but I don't feel as scattered as I have over the past week. I send a quick text to Emma (*I have something exciting to tell you! Call me!*), but she doesn't answer; probably too busy hooking up with Blondie.

I ignore my jealousy and fire up my laptop for *Downton*

Abbey, then pop a small edible into my mouth to help with the pain. By the time the first episode ends, my pizza is gone and the weed has taken effect and everything seems lovely. Midway through the second episode, Cú jumps up onto the bedspread next to me and curls up in the pit of my knees. I nearly sob from happiness. For the first time in I don't know how long (maybe ever?), I won't sleep alone tonight.

Of course, I forgot, as I often do, I am never alone. Even gone, even dead, the specter of Mammy haunts me, looming large in my subconscious, leaking out when I dream.

The dream starts the same way as it always does. I am in bed, feeling like I was just awakened and blearily seeing the form of Mammy bending over me. She appears even taller than before; if she stood to her full height, her hair would tangle in the ceiling fan. My imagination makes a giant of her.

There is one noticeable difference in the dream tonight: Cú is here, more alert than I am but still curled up in the crook of my knees. I think silent gratitude to my brain for allowing me to have him in my nightmare. Even if my ally is a small elderly bundle of fur, he's still an ally.

Mammy doesn't acknowledge him or even notice he's there, she's so intent on leering at me. When my eyes lock onto her shimmering aqua irises, her leer elongates into a predatory grin. "I am not your mother," she rasps, as she always does.

"*Mrow*," Cú croaks at her. His tail swishes decisively back and forth, and he shifts his weight into a preparatory crouch. His dark-vision pupils have locked onto a necklace dangling from around her throat.

And the nightmare fractures. Mammy deviates from the script. She shrinks six inches and leaps backward, holding her manicured hands out in front of her for protection. "What is that?" she shrieks, all menacing richness gone from her voice.

I sit up, optimistically confused. I didn't realize how much my subconscious treasured Cú already, but here he is, frightening the monster of my nightmares. Good imaginary cat. I'll have to give the real Cú an extra-special treat when I wake up.

Dream-Cú's eyes still track the necklace swinging on its chain. He chirps at it, pulling back his lips and emitting an *ek-ek-ek* from the back of his throat, displaying his tiny, pointed fangs.

"You got a *cat*," Mammy spits. She is obviously addressing me but can't drag her nervous eyes away from dream-Cú. "How could you do this to me? Bring such a vile creature into my home, after everything I've done for you?"

Normally, I wouldn't argue with her. I never argue with Mammy. How could I, when she strikes me through like a pinned butterfly? But this isn't Mammy. This is all a dream, and here in the dream, Cú is protecting me.

"I didn't do it *to* you, Mammy," I tell her, my voice barely shaking. "I did it *for* me."

Dream-Cú stalks his prey, stepping across the bedspread slowly, closer to Mammy.

She backs up quickly into the hallway, shrinking further as she does, until she's about my height. Before she slams the door shut, she lets out one last scathing decree. "You-you selfish— Selfish, ungrateful, horrible little bitch!"

Dream-Cú glares at the shut door and continues swishing his tail. Nightmare over, I lie back down and cuddle deeply into my comforter, feeling quite comforted. I sleep well.

Day 9

From the kitchen where I drink my tea, I happen to glance into the entryway. That's when I notice him. He's a little worse for wear but appears to be as merciful as ever: my old nemesis, Jesus of Nazareth.

Shock opens my hands automatically. The crash of the mug breaking on the tile floor (and hot tea splashing over my feet and calves) tears my eyes away from the miraculous picture.

"Feck!" I shout in surprise. Then, as I look down and see my favorite mug destroyed and the mess my thoughtlessness has made, I groan, "Feeeeeeeeck."

Gingerly I pluck up the broken pieces and chuck them in the trash. Bitterly I grab a handful of rags and sop up the spilled tea from the floor. Aggressively I spray all-purpose cleaner onto the tile and wipe that up as well. Angrily I rifle through the junk drawer until I locate a black permanent marker. It is exactly what I need.

I stomp over to Jesus, hanging there on the wall again even

though I specifically told him not to. He never listens, does he? Thinks he knows better than everyone else. I suppose that comes with the territory of being the son of God, but the joke's on him: I don't believe in God, so to me, he's just some guy. Sucks to suck, doesn't it, Jesus?

"How the feck did you get back here, Jesus? I took you to the thrift shop. I saw you there, in a box in the back. I *saw* you."

He refuses to divulge his secrets.

"Very well. I see you have fallen mute." I narrow my eyes at him and slip my voice into a bad facsimile of a German accent that is almost definitely offensive. "But we have ways . . . of making you talk!"

I uncap the permanent marker and attack, scribbling a spiky mustache onto his blessed upper lip. I jump back as if the painting might bite me, then watch the ink dry. Jesus pretends my assault has had no effect on him.

"You are brave," I whisper to him. "Very brave. But even you are not brave enough to withstand *this*!"

I leap forward again, on the offensive, and cover his eyes with two thick, unsightly *X*s as if he were the untitled Blink-182 album. To be honest, I would rather have Blink-182's album artwork hanging on my wall than Christ, and they're not even my favorite pop-punk group. I was always more of an AFI girl.

I step back and lean against the front door, still staring at the picture. I'm not sure exactly what I'm waiting for, and now that my initial anger is fading away, I'm becoming more fearful. What if the house really is haunted by a Catholic nun or something, and I've just provoked her further? But I don't know what I could've done to provoke a Catholic ghost in the first place; it's not like I'm sinning left and right. I haven't even lost my virginity, for crying out loud. I'm as pure as they come.

But a memory wiggles its way into my brain, unbidden. I was young, maybe only eleven. It was after I became unlovable, after Da left, but before I knew what *whore* meant or why it was considered bad. Mammy was calling me a whore, telling me the bikini I wore to the pool was too revealing, saying she was embarrassed to be my mother. How could I wear such a thing in front of other people? Didn't I know it would shame her? Didn't I know she wouldn't approve? I must've known and done it anyways to spite her. I was a spiteful, selfish, disobedient girl, and I would suffer for it. Honor thy mother, she hissed into my ear. It's one of the Ten Commandments. If you break one of them, you descend straight to hell.

I sigh, looking away from the painting. If there *is* a Catholic ghost, I know what I've done to upset it. I've been dishonoring my mammy at every turn since the moment I arrived in this house, and for years before. In every single choice I make where I place my needs above hers, I dishonor her.

There is no ghost, Catholic or otherwise, of course. And there's nobody else doing this either; I changed the locks specifically so no one else could get in. There is only my own guilt, festering deep in my small intestine, making my guts kink and roil. I wonder if I ever even brought the Jesus painting to the thrift shop. Maybe I just told myself I did while my subconscious guilt drove me to hang it back up on the wall. For all I know, I hung it back up while sleepwalking. I might be a sleepwalker; I can't be certain I'm not. I've lived alone for years now. There're a lot of things about myself I might not know.

I hear my childhood bedroom's door rattle a little in the frame, and the sound makes me nervous. Is there a Catholic ghost, after all? Does it hang out in my bedroom during the day? Before I go over to examine the source of the sound, I place the permanent marker on the hutch and cast one last wary glance at Jesus.

There isn't a ghost in my childhood bedroom either. The door is rattling because of Cú; his little black-and-white paws are flitting in and out from the bottom of the frame in a bid for either playtime or freedom. I wiggle my fingers under the door next to him and feel him pounce on them, but the cat rescuer trimmed his claws short, so he doesn't cut me. His paws are merely fierce marshmallows.

A smile creeps across my face, and I feel some of my fear melt away. Ghost or not, I'm less alone this morning than I was yesterday.

Knocking on the front door breaks me from my reverie. I groan as I stand, feeling a stab of pain in my lower abdomen, and lean against the wall for a moment in the hopes that the sensation passes. After twenty seconds or so, it begins to seep away, and I breathe a sigh of relief. The person knocks on the door again.

"Coming!" I call out. I have no idea if they can hear me. I also have no idea who it might be. I don't have any friends here in St. Charles.

I rush to the entryway, not wanting to keep the mystery person waiting, and pull open the door. I look up and up and up at the towering woman, eventually reaching her face, and am surprised to see Carol. I've never met her in person before, just via telehealth, but I had always imagined her to be average height. Still, her soft smile, gentle eyes, and cozy cardigan are unmistakable.

"Carol, hi! Come in." I gesture for her to enter without stopping to question why she's here, but the wondering begins as she takes off her shoes. We have a telehealth session in a few hours. She should be over an hour's drive away, in Kenosha, Wisconsin. She has my address of course, I gave it to her so she could mail me my bills, so I know how she found me. But why?

Once she arranges her shoes neatly on the doormat, I see her look up and clock my defacing of the painting of Jesus. I laugh nervously. "Oh yeah, that. I was just having a bit of a laugh, that's all."

A critical "hmm" is her only response. It puts me on edge. I'm not used to Carol being critical.

"Come inside." I urge her away from the entryway, into the kitchen, and pull out a chair at the small table. "Do you want something to drink? I could make some coffee or tea, or get you a glass of water?"

"Tea would be lovely."

"Sure." I begin to fill the kettle. "I only have one type, though. Barry's. It's an Irish breakfast tea. It's, like, a black tea; it's pretty strong. And caffeinated. Is that okay?"

"That's the only kind I drink. With milk and sugar, please." She flashes me a saccharine smile.

I put the kettle on the stovetop and scratch anxiously at my forearm. I'm on edge, having Carol in my home. Our relationship has always had a very strict therapist/therapee vibe to it; her being here is blurring the line more than I like.

I clear my throat and start to talk, wanting to fill the heavy silence. "I didn't know you like Barry's. I've actually never even met a not-Irish person who drinks it. Well, except for my friend Emma, but that's only because I introduced it to her."

Carol smiles benignly.

My discomfit grows. I'd feel better if she talked, if she reassured me in her usual Carol way. "Do South Koreans drink a lot of tea?"

"I'm not sure."

She barely fits in my kitchen chair, she's so tall. Her legs sprawl outward, far past the underside of my little table, and her shoulder blades float high above the back of her chair. How have I never noticed her height before? Even via teleconference, you'd think I would've paid attention to a trait so unordinary.

"Oh, sorry. I just figured you would. Since, you know, you're the kid of immigrants, like me."

Another benign smile. My skin crawls. Why is she here, and why is she acting so unlike herself?

The kettle begins to whistle, and I plop tea bags into two inferior mugs (may my favorite mug rest in pieces). I pour the boiling water and set a timer for five minutes.

"So," I begin, casual, too casual, "were you in the area and decided to stop by, or . . . ?"

"I wanted to check up on you. You've been stressed recently." Her plastic smile remains plastered to her face, devoid of warmth.

"Oh . . . well, thanks, I guess. That's a long drive, just to see me."

She tilts her head as if she just learned something new and is committing it to long-term memory. "Nothing is too much for my favorite client."

I scratch at my forearm, harder this time. "I thought therapists weren't supposed to have favorites."

"We're not." She grins at me. Too large, too wide, a leering grin splitting her face open. I can see both rows of her teeth. "But you're my favorite anyway. You can keep it a secret, can't you? Don't tell anyone."

I stare at her incredulously and she stares back, still wearing the rictus grin. She actually expects an answer. "Sure," I say, if only to end the staring contest.

"Great."

Another tense silence descends. The only sound is Cú, rattling my bedroom door again.

She jerks her head toward the sound, fear etching its way onto her forehead. "What's that?"

"Don't worry." I laugh at the unreasonable panic on her face, then swallow my mirth. It's not kind to laugh at someone who's scared. I've spent enough of my life scared to know that. "It's just my new cat. I was going to tell you about him during our session this afternoon. I adopted him yesterday! He's super cute. He's a black-and-white tuxedo cat with long fur. Really playful."

She still looks stricken. "It's locked up, isn't it?"

"Yeah." I sigh in disappointment. The smile on my face from talking about Cú melts away as quickly as it arrived. I thought Carol would be excited to meet him; I wanted to show him off. "He's in my bedroom. The guy at the shelter said to keep him confined to one room for a week or two so he can adjust to living here. So he doesn't get too stressed."

"And you're going to do that?"

"Yeah, uhm. Of course. I'll do what's best for him."

"Do you mean that?" She peers closely at my face.

I scratch my forearm some more. It'll start bleeding soon if I keep this up. "Yes."

"And do you trust me?" Her eyes bore into mine.

"I . . . yes, of course I do."

"Good." She nods perfunctorily. "Then you'll just have to take it back to the shelter. Immediately."

"What?" I sputter. Carol's never directly told me to do any-thing before, at least not anything this extreme. She prefers to slowly guide me to the well of understanding. I feel my natural obstinance kicking in like a bad habit. "No. Why do you say that? He's my cat. I'm keeping him."

"Ha." Carol laughs in a single sharp note. "You said you wanted what was best for it. You can't keep it."

"Yes, I can." I cross my arms, both to convey my anger and to keep myself from scratching anymore.

"Oh please." Carol snorts. "You can't take care of an animal. You can't even take care of yourself."

I feel the blood drain from my face. My arms fall to my sides.

"I mean, look at you." Carol continues her onslaught without stopping for breath. "No job. Living in your mother's house. Making up some imaginary illness. And for what? For attention? For pity? To have an excuse for what a failure you are?"

"I'm not . . ." I mumble.

"What was that?" Carol mocks, putting a hand to her ear to hear better. "You're not? Not what? Not capable? Not an adult?"

I stare at the floor, spine curled under the weight of my shame, unable to look at her.

"That's what I thought." She stands and walks to the door, slipping on her shoes. "Get rid of the cat."

She opens the old, creaky door silently and, as she leaves, shuts it behind her without a sound.

I remain still. For a minute, the only thing I hear is Cú, still rattling away, oblivious to my shortcomings. Eventually, the timer for the tea begins to beep.

I turn it off. I leave the tea undrunk and sitting on the counter, choosing instead to drag another giveaway box to my bedroom. I'll donate all the cat stuff I bought yesterday to the shelter when I take Cú back.

It shouldn't take long to pack Cú's stuff into a box, but somehow, I stretch the chore into a multi-hour affair. At first, it's because Cú is so hyper and playful; I tell myself it would be cruel to put him in his cardboard carrier box and into the car when he's so energetic. So, I spend a good forty-five minutes jiggling a stick with bits of ribbon on the end for him to enthusiastically murder. Then, I realize that even though he's been here less than twenty-four hours, he's gotten a fair amount of fur on my sheets. I'd like to get those cleaned up sooner rather than later, so I take the sheets to the washing machine in the basement and run them through with the growing pile of dirty rags. Once they are in there, I have to wait until they're ready for the dryer, and then wait for the dryer to finish so I can remake the bed, of course. I might as well pet Cú while I wait.

It only mildly baffles him when I keep pausing to pick him up, reverently examining each perfect bit of his perfect little body, burning every feature into my memory.

Soon enough, the time for therapy with Carol approaches and Cú is still living in my bedroom. I oscillate between options: If I join the call and she sees I still have him, she'll be angry with me, but if I don't join at all, she'll suspect something is up and be angry with me. Eventually, I settle on pretending as if I've already gotten rid of him and not explicitly saying I didn't unless she asks me. I hate lying, but if she just assumes I listened to her, it's less of a lie.

I sit on the bed with my laptop on my lap, smiling my regular bland smile while I wait for her to join. When her face pops up on the screen, though, the practiced smile falters and I tuck my face into my shoulder instinctively. It hurts to look at her now.

"Hi, Brigid! How are you doing this afternoon?" she cheerily chirps.

I visibly wince when she says my name wrong. It's harder than usual to be charitable today. I must harbor some bitterness against her for telling me the truth about my inability to take care of Cú.

That's unfair of me; I know it is. It's not her fault I'm worthless. I should be thankful for her telling me the truth.

I take too long to respond.

"Brigid . . ." she asks, "is something wrong?"

"No, no." I pull my head up and slap a peppy expression on. "I'm doing great."

She eyes me with tender suspicion. "Are you sure? You seem a little on edge."

"No. I'm great." I nod my head five, six, seven, too many times.

"Brigid, I know you're very independent, but this is therapy. This is a good time to talk about your feelings, even the hard ones."

"Hard ones?" I cackle, a noise like shattering glass I don't think my throat has ever produced before. "Hard feelings? Why would I have any hard feelings? No, I can't imagine why I'd have hard feelings. Not involving you, or therapy. Especially not today. Can you?"

"I'm . . ." Carol looks actively concerned now. "Brigid, I'm not sure what you mean."

She pronounces my name wrong, she makes me get rid of my cat, she reminds me how useless I am, and now she pretends like nothing ever happened. The liquid rage in my stomach starts to roil, bubbling up into my esophagus, burning my heart.

But then I remind myself again: I pay her to care about me, to want what's best for me. Carol is trying to help, and she knows what's best for a person's mental health. I need to accept her tough love.

It's only my own shortcomings that hurt me. I knew I wasn't responsible enough to care for another creature, and I adopted Cú anyway. When you make a mistake like that, you deserve to be hurt. There must be consequences. I swallow the rage again, and digest it into humility and acceptance.

Carol's eyebrows crease with worry as she watches this storm cross my face. Quickly, then, her eyes flit to something behind me, rest on it for a beat, and then return to me. Before I can ask what she sees, Cú comes flying up from the floor and smacks his front paws on the window next to my head.

I shriek in surprise and grab him around his midsection, loosely tossing him toward the foot of the bed, hoping Carol didn't recognize his shape as that of a cat in the brief moment he was on camera. I turn my head to see what was in the window that drew both Carol and Cú's attention.

It is the bird, of course, flying away. But it's not flying with its usual lazy, ominous dips; no, it's flying frantically. Like it's afraid. Like, for the briefest moment, it had a taste of mortality.

When I look at the screen, at Carol's face, her expression has changed to one of surprise and delight. "Brigid," she says, "was that a cat I just saw?"

I feel my intestines drop to the base of my pelvis as my anxiety ratchets up the volume of my chronic pain to a sharp staccato stab. "I'm sorry." I rush to get the words out. "I know you told me to get rid of him, and I will, I just haven't had time yet, it's only been a couple of hours—"

"Hey, hey, hey, slow down, slow down. You have nothing to apologize for. I think it's wonderful you got a cat! Is it a boy or a girl?"

The muscles in my face go lax with shock. "You think it's wonderful?"

"I think it's so wonderful," she gushes. "Oh honey, you know I never want to tell you what to do, but I was so worried you'd be lonely in your house. I'm pleased you decided to get a pet. I truly believe it will help improve your mental health. And you made the decision all on your own! You're prioritizing your needs and facing your fears of being 'not enough.' I'm so proud."

"But . . . earlier today, you said I needed to get rid of him. Just this morning. You said I couldn't take care of him!"

"I—this morning?" Carol's worried look returns. "Brigid, honey, I didn't talk to you this morning."

All of a sudden, the room feels frozen. Goose bumps materialize on my arms.

"You came to my house," I tell her, my voice soft, timid.

"I've never been to your house," she answers, firm and gentle all at once. "This morning, I walked my dog and had sessions with two other clients. Could this be a dream you had?"

"I-I don't think so." Tears of frustration (and maybe of fear; I'm really losing my mind; it's actually happening) start streaming down my face. "It felt very real. I was drinking my tea, and then I . . . There was this painting I got rid of, but it was back in the house, and so I scribbled on it with a marker, and then you knocked on the door and you were only here a few minutes but you told me I couldn't take care of a cat and I ought to take him back to the shelter."

"Okay." She nods, accepting the story at face value. "So, there's a painting you thought you threw away, but it was still there too? Has anything else strange been happening?"

"Uhm . . . yes. A lot actually," I admit, sobbing more now. I don't want to tell her how delusional I am, but I know I have to. The only way she can help me is if I tell her. "The bird is still following me, everywhere. Not just around the house, to stores and stuff too. And you remember when the person broke in and spread all the trash around? They like, hung this chunk of meat from the ceiling, too, it was really weird. And . . ."

"And?"

I hesitate, begging through my tears. "Please don't make me go to the hospital. I don't want to."

"Honey, I won't divulge anything to anyone unless you or someone else is in immediate danger, okay? You know that."

"I know, I know. Just please, don't."

"I won't, as long as you're safe."

"Okay, well, the other day, I thought I found a human finger in the bathroom while I was cleaning? And it really frightened me, it really did, but I thought maybe I was imagining it, so I just put it in the freezer, and in the morning, it wasn't a finger anymore. It was just one of those metal-spring door stoppers. You know, the things that keep the doorknob from hitting the wall? It was just one of those. It was never a finger."

"Okay, honey, it's okay," Carol comforts, as if she's heard a hundred people admit they found fingers that aren't fingers in their homes. Of course, for all I know, she has. "I'm sorry this is happening to you. All of that sounds very scary."

"It is!"

"I know it is," she soothes. "When did all this scary stuff start happening?"

"I don't know for sure." It's hard to think straight. I've always been scared. I haven't not been scared since I was six years old. "Mammy always said I had a bad memory and too much imagination. She would tell me to do things and I wouldn't remember, and she'd get so angry with me. Or I'd remember her saying something, something terrible, her yelling at me, or her doing something strange or twisted, but then she'd act like it never happened, and if I ever brought it up, she'd tell me it didn't happen that way."

"Was stuff like this happening in your apartment? In Wisconsin?"

I think back to the little apartment I miss so much. Now that she mentions it, it did feel safer there. Predictable. "No. I was sad to be moving away toward the end, but nothing weird happened. Nothing like this."

"Okay, well, so we know it has something to do with the move then." Carol smiles broadly, as if this is good news.

"I guess."

"Brigid, this might seem like an odd thing to ask, but do you know if your house has carbon monoxide detectors?"

I pause. The house hasn't been updated since my room was turned into a guest bedroom, and even then, it was only my room that was changed. Much of the house is outdated, frozen in the late '90s. "It might not. Mammy didn't do a lot of upgrades. I don't know for sure."

"Have you been having headaches? Or feeling dizzy, nauseous, anything like that?"

"Not any more than usual. Maybe a little more nauseous. More tired. I feel stressed out, you know?" I'm crying less now. Carol isn't treating me like I'm insane. She's acting like she has the situation under control. Like there's a reasonable explanation for everything.

"Sure, honey, that makes sense. Moving is stressful even in the best of times."

I nod and sniff. Cú saunters over from the foot of the bed where I tossed him to curl up in my knee pit once again. His warmth makes me feel better too.

"Right now, I'm thinking you might have a carbon monoxide leak in your house. It can cause you to see things, or to forget doing things you did, and can be really scary. I know money is tight for you, but I think you need to see if somebody could come out and check it out for you. Your local fire department might even do it for free. Do you think you can call them as soon as we get off the call?"

"Yeah," I eagerly agree, clinging to this hope. I'm not crazy. It's just a carbon monoxide leak. A carbon monoxide leak is bad, but surely it's not as bad as me being insane.

"Thank you. Another possible explanation is that you might be having some hallucinations, but I don't want you to panic if that's the case either, okay?"

I feel myself beginning to panic again. "No?"

"Hallucinations are very common." She opens her eyes wide to make sure her eye contact is landing well. "When my first dog died, for months afterwards I swore I could hear her toenails on the tile in the kitchen, the way it sounded when she wanted to go for a walk. They happen all the time, to lots of people, and there's lots of ways to help. I can refer you to a psychiatrist, a really nice doctor I've worked with before, and she can work with you to find a good medication regimen. So even if it isn't a carbon monoxide leak or something like that, there are still lots of solutions we can try, and it doesn't mean anything is bad or wrong with you. Okay?"

I take a steadying breath. "Okay."

"Okay." She smiles and waits for me to say something. When I stay silent, she changes the topic of conversation. "Would you like to tell me about your cat?"

"Oh!" I smile back. Now that I know she isn't going to tell me to get rid of him, I'm desperate to talk about him. And I'm thankful she's letting me distract myself from the possibility of hallucinations. "He's so wonderful! I got him from a shelter yesterday. He's older, the rescue said he was twelve, but he's still really playful. And handsome! He's black with some white—like a tuxedo? And he has a scar on his nose so he snorts a little."

"He sounds great! What's his name?"

"At the shelter, they called him Odie, but I named him Cú."

"Coo?"

"Yeah," I answer, even though it isn't quite right. The sound should be rounder in her mouth. "It's Irish for 'hound.' He's a cat named Dog."

She laughs brightly. "I didn't know you spoke another language."

"I don't." I shrug. "I know it from a book of Irish folktales my da used to read to me a lot. You know, before he left."

Carol's face grows more serious. "You don't talk about your dad a lot. How old were you when he left?"

"I was six." I wince a little at the memory. Having the Mammy nightmare as a little girl, and then in the morning, waking up to the real Mammy telling me he was never coming back, that he had someone else he liked better than us. He didn't even say goodbye to me, and I was his favorite person in the whole world. At least, that's what he'd whisper to me when he tucked me into bed at night. I guess he was lying. He liked his mistress more, in the end. "I don't really like to talk about it. I think it was my fault he made the final decision to leave."

"Why do you say that?"

"Well, because just a couple days before I had . . ." I hesitate again. I've never talked with Carol about how I ruined everything. I haven't talked about it with anyone before. I even skirt around thinking about it in my own mind. This is a difficult session today. "I had ruined everything a few days before."

"How so?"

"Well, there was this boy who was in my class at school, right? We were in kindergarten, I think, or maybe first grade. And he lived on my street and we were friends, and he was at my house, and we were playing in the backyard. And I don't know exactly how it happened, my memory is a little fuzzy because it was a long time ago but . . ." I swallow, nervous.

"Honey, no matter what it is, this is a judgment-free space, okay?"

"Okay. Yeah. Okay. Well, so we're playing in the backyard, and somehow—I don't know how, I don't know if it was my idea or not—we both took our clothes off. And I remember looking at him, at his—you know—and being excited, and reaching out and touching it, and he wasn't mad or scared, he was laughing, but I guess Mammy saw through the window because she came outside screaming . . . Just like, screaming."

I glance up at Carol to see how offended she is, see how disgusting she thinks I am. I'm ashamed to be recounting it, but she isn't reacting much. Her eyebrows just curve upward in that empathetic way they often do.

I continue, "So yeah, she's just yelling at me. And I'd never heard her yell at me before, she'd always been so nice, so patient before that, and I got so scared and tried to run away, but she grabbed my arm and kept yelling. And it hurt, like, she pulled my shoulder really hard, and it's not like it hurt that bad, but she'd never hurt me at all, ever, before that, and I was so scared. So, so scared. Then Da came out and told her to calm down, and she got in the car and drove away, and Da told us to get dressed. And I think we walked the boy back to his house? Because the next thing I remember is it being bedtime, and Mammy wasn't home yet and I asked Da where she was and he said she went to church to talk to God and would be back soon. And then in the morning, she was back, except . . . I don't know, it felt different somehow. She didn't love me anymore. She started saying mean things to me, yelling, being scary all the time. Because I was bad, you know? What I did was too bad. She stopped loving me."

I feel like I should be crying at this stage, but I'm not. Maybe I've cried too much today already. Reached my quota. I just hang my head. It weighs too much for my neck to support.

"Wow," Carol whispers.

"I know." I hang my head lower. My only comfort is Cú, still purring and snorting next to my legs. "It's bad. I'm like some sort of predator or something. But other than that time, I've never hurt anybody. I promise! I've made sure of it. I've never dated anyone. I've never even kissed anybody. I don't want to take advantage of anyone."

"Oh, honey, no. That's not what I meant at all," Carol rushes to explain. "What happened—that sort of sexual exploration—that's very normal for kids that age. It can shock parents, especially if they're religious or conservative, but it's actually really common. There's nothing wrong with you."

Cogs turn in my head, trying to fit this new information into my self-concept.

"It's normal," Carol repeats, her tone matter-of-fact. "There's nothing wrong with you."

"But I'm . . ." Some of the numbness leaches away, and I begin to cry again. So much for the quota theory. "But I'm a bad person! I know I am."

"Oh, honey, you're not a bad person."

"But . . . Da left just a few days after. I woke up one morning, and he was just gone. I know he had his mistress, that's what Mammy told everyone, but why would he leave, why then, if it wasn't because of me?"

"I don't know." Carol mourns with me. "I can't tell you that. But it wasn't your fault. None of this is your fault."

"I don't even know where he is." I cry harder, wiping my face with my T-shirt, getting it soaked and snotty. "I can't even find him and ask why."

"I'm sorry," Carol tells me. "This is so hard, I know."

I keep crying and Carol quietly supports me, letting me have all the space for my feelings I could possibly need. A long time passes.

Eventually, she says, "Brigid, I'm so sorry to do this, but I have another client in a few minutes. Are you going to be okay?"

I take a shuddering breath. "Yeah, no, yeah. I'll be okay."

"You'll call somebody about the carbon monoxide testing, right?"

"Yeah."

"And you'll take it easy tonight, right? Snuggle with Coo, do something relaxing?"

"Sure," I agree, and wipe some snot off my face with the back of my hand. "Can do."

"Good. Call me if you need to before Friday, okay?"

"Okay."

"Goodbye."

She signs off and, for a moment, I feel more alone than ever before. Then Cú lets out a particularly bold snort, so loud even he jumps a little, and I find myself laughing. Somewhere, somehow, underneath all the heaviness I always carry, I feel an incredible lightness.

I sleep soundly, like the dead, like a baby, like Cú all snuggled up in my knee pit.

Day 10

As it happens, Carol was right: The fire department is willing to come out and check the house for a carbon monoxide leak free of charge. Part of me wonders if I should get Cú out of the house until I know it's safe, but at the same time, I've been living here for over a week and am doing fine.

Mostly fine. I'm ignoring the hallucinations. They're just hallucinations. Not real.

I decide to renew my dedication to the to-do list and organize the office while I wait for the fire (and/or carbon monoxide) fighter to arrive. I rescue the giveaway box from my bedroom (Cú yawns exaggeratedly from the bed when I disturb his nap and it's so cute I nearly gasp; how could I have ever considered getting rid of him?) and get a few more, anticipating I'll be disposing of most of what's in this room.

I go through the bookcase first, putting everything other than a few collections of landscape photography and travel guides (all about Ireland, of course) into the boxes. I actually have one of the boxes stand in as a recycling bin instead, since some of the books are entirely worthless. (Why does Mammy even have a Windows '93 guidebook?) It's baffling how unchanged the house and its contents are from when I was little. Other than turning my bedroom into a guest room and Mammy's expansive wardrobe, of course.

It makes me wonder what the point of updating my room was at all. At the time, it just felt like she was doing it to make me uncomfortable. I haven't come up with any better reason since.

From that very room, the door begins to rattle again, thanks to Cú's desperation to explore the house. I smile to myself as I chuck a moldering romance novel into the recycling box. (*Ascent Through Hell* by Colm Finnegan: Will Sister Mary Robert be able to escape temptation—and the devil's clutches?) Maybe Cú can be released from my bedroom a few days early. He certainly doesn't seem nervous, and it'd be nice to have him hang out with me while I clean.

I move on from the bookcase to the desk drawers. I slide the first drawer open and find a jumble of pens and paper clips and scissors and other detritus, like I remember from when I was a kid. I leave it be, figuring junk drawers always come in handy.

The second drawer is more surprising. When I open that, instead of finding Post-it notes and a few rolls of tape like I expect, there is a large anatomical heart with slick beads of sweat dripping down its frozen surface.

I slam the drawer shut as if it were the door to my parents' bedroom and they were having sex. I don't need to see it. It doesn't need to affect me. I can just pretend it never happened and continue on with my life.

After eyeing the third drawer's handle with a healthy dose of skepticism, I slide it open. It contains a few reams of copy paper. I nod approvingly at the stack and shut the drawer again.

I load the old desktop computer and monitor and its various accessories into a few giveaway boxes and schlep them all to the entryway (because there's nothing of note in any of the drawers) and line them up against the wall beneath Jesus. He still hangs there benevolently with his mustache and screamo eyes, willing to shepherd the lost sheep back to his flock despite my many sins.

With the office basically cleaned out aside from needing a dusting (and having a human heart in a drawer that needs to be dealt with; except it's not a human heart, it's probably a roll of duct tape or something. Nice try, carbon monoxide leak, you can't fool me), I decide I've earned a break. My pelvic pain is rearing up anyways from all the bending and carrying, so I pop a few ibuprofens to get ahead of it. I put the kettle on the stovetop for tea, then scroll through Instagram while I wait.

After I've enjoyed my tea for a few minutes, there's a knock at the door. It can only be somebody from the fire department. I let her in, a middle-aged woman with a low ponytail and cargo pants covered in more pockets than I thought was possible, and offer her tea. She politely refuses and goes about her mystical scanning and measuring while I return to my tea and algorithmically curated image feed. A few pictures of Emma appear, and she looks great in all of them. I comment with multiple fire emojis on my favorite. I even post a rare picture to my woefully underpopulated page. It's not of me (it's one of Cú napping I took earlier this morning), but still. It counts.

"Well, I've got good news for ya," the firewoman says from behind me, breaking me out of my social media trance.

"Yes?" I wonder how a carbon monoxide leak could be good news.

"No carbon monoxide leak! House seems to be in good condition." The woman gives me a cocked smile and a thumbs-up.

"Are you . . . sure?" I ask, not wanting to be difficult but also not wanting to consider the implications of there being no leak. "I've been having some weird symptoms. I was sure it was carbon monoxide."

The woman shrugs a single shoulder and gestures to her device. "As sure as I can be."

"Ah, well." I try not to look overly disappointed about my house not being filled with a toxic gas. "Thank you for checking for me."

I see her to the door, stepping out onto the porch to say good-bye to her and sighing once she's out of earshot.

Feck. It's official. I am going crazy.

I guess that makes a certain degree of sense; I'm crazy enough to imagine agonizing, inescapable pain, so I'm probably also crazy enough to imagine a heart in a drawer. I'll have to ask Carol for the number of the psychiatrist she mentioned.

The bird is on its favorite branch on the oak tree, staring down its inky beak at me, relishing my distress. At least it's over there and not peering through my bedroom window at me. Cú makes sure of that.

I head back inside and decide to get back to work despite my misery. I need a distraction; if I think too long about how I'm seeing things, I'll have an anxiety attack on top of the hallucinations. And besides, it's not like wallowing will make the office any less dusty. I get some rags and all-purpose spray from under the kitchen sink and, after a moment's deliberation, also grab a plastic grocery bag from my bag of bags.

The heart is a hallucination. I know it is, because I'm not so insane I don't know I'm insane. I open the drawer and consider it again. It looks authentic: not blood red like you would expect to see in a fakey Halloween decoration, but a dull, dark pinkish brown with off-white globs of fat clinging to the tops of the chambers, letting off a sheen as it defrosts, a small puddle of juices collecting underneath, staining the bottom of the wooden drawer. I've never seen a frozen heart before. (Where would you happen across something like that?) The fact that my imagination is able to conjure up one so convincing is almost more impressive than disgusting. Almost.

Which is what gives me pause. It's similar to how I keep going to gynecologists about my pelvic pain even though I know it's all in my head, or how I cut off contact with Mammy even though I knew her treatment of me was my fault for being a bad person. There are these little voices, little niggling bits of myself, yearning to defend me. No, these minuscule pieces argue, no, my pain is real. No, they staunchly refute, I was never bad or evil, I was just a regular kid. No, they insist, I am not hallucinating. There is a human heart in the office, in the second drawer on the left-hand side of the desk. It is real. It is there.

It is this bit of me, this lying piece I think a psychologist would refer to as my ego, the morsel of me wrongly maintaining I can't be wrong, that is the bit that puts the plastic over my hand and picks up the heart from the drawer, covering it and tying off the bag like I'm picking up dog feces.

I hold the bag away from me by the handles as I carry it to the freezer in the kitchen, just in case it's a real heart after all, even though I know it isn't. But when I grabbed it, it squished slightly under the plastic film the way you'd expect a hunk of defrosting meat to give. It feels, looks, seems so real.

The drawer is still open when I return to the office, and I see the juices I imagined leaking from the heart are still pooled in the bottom of the drawer. I groan. If this is a hallucination, couldn't it at least be a clean one? I take a rag and soak up the liquid, but the light wood is stained. No matter how much I scrub at it with the all-purpose cleaning spray, it remains a sickening off-shade of pink.

I shut the drawer and decide to focus on literally anything else. I dust the rest of the office, wary whenever I have to shift a curtain or move a pillow, just in case I find a hunk of liver behind them.

When that's done, I move on to dusting the living room. The living room has less crap in it overall, but I'll still need to drag some giveaway boxes in here at some point to get rid of the gratuitous knickknacks. On the piano alone, I count two teddy bears, three framed photos, and a wooden carving of a small piano. The tiny wood piano feels particularly egregious and twee. I dust around them for now, just to check the chore off my list, and because the pain is gnawing at me through the ibuprofen. I don't think I can manage all the lifting and bending required to pack giveaway boxes right this second.

As I walk past Mammy's bedroom with the dusting rags in hand, I consider getting all the dusting done now. All I would have to do is pop into her room real quick and then it'd be done; the weight of cracking the seal on her sanctum would be off my mind. I reach out for the doorknob, even rest my hand on it, but then the memory of the chair, the "family meetings," and Mammy's cool stare are conjured.

I remind myself the pain is flaring and I don't want to push it, and I take my hand off the knob. Besides, as Carol always reminds me, there's no need to get everything done all at once. I can take my time.

Dinner tonight is a peanut butter and jelly sandwich with some raw baby carrots on the side because I'm starting to get sick of microwavable burritos and frozen potpies. Emma has a T-shirt with two slices of bread on it, one with peanut butter and one with jelly, and they have little smiles on their little faces, and they're holding hands. It says "Best Friends Forever" right under the little peanut butter and jelly bread people. It's a little funny because she can't eat gluten.

I miss her. Very much.

She never answered my text from the other night, when I wanted to tell her about Cú. Once my sandwich is eaten, I nudge her again. I don't want to be annoying, but surely two texts in three days isn't too much. We're supposed to be peanut-butter-and-jelly-best-friends-forever ourselves, after all. I text her a picture of Cú, the same one I posted on Instagram.

Ten minutes later, I'm sitting in bed jiggling the ribbon toy for Cú and my phone rings. I smile when Emma's name pops up on the screen. I knew a picture of a cat would get her to call me.

"Hi, Emma! Are you calling to speak with the man of the house?" I joke, keeping my spirits high by focusing on Cú and not the heart in the freezer. (What heart in the freezer? There's no heart in the freezer.)

"The man—? Oh, is the cat a boy?" she asks, sounding significantly less excited than I think she ought to. Instead of peppy, her voice is gummy and thick.

"Yes! He's a very distinguished gentleman. I named him Cú."

"Yeah, no, he's cute. I like his tuxedo fur." Emma sniffs.

Much to Cú's disappointment, I put down the cat toy to pay better attention to Emma. "Are you okay? You sound upset."

"No, yeah, I'm . . . I'll be fine. It's just that you were right."

"Well, that's new. I'm hardly ever right." I flip through the files in my brain, trying to determine when I most recently might've been right, and come up empty-handed. "Out of curiosity, what was I right about?"

"About Kelly! I should never have gone after her. I should've stuck to the rule about no bi-curious girls."

Guilt pierces me through. Poor Emma.

"Oh no, Emma, it's not your fault. You weren't wrong. I just said that before because I was jealous." I stop before I accidentally divulge my feelings for her. Even if Carol says I'm not some dangerous predator, I still can't tell Emma. I'm not any better than the bi-curious girls who hurt her again and again. Time to backtrack with the whitest of lies. "I was just scared you might like somebody more than your old pal Brigid, that's all. I would never blame you, and you shouldn't either. It's not your fault."

"It is my fault! I knew she probably wouldn't actually be interested. I knew I was getting my hopes up. Kelly's so . . . so basic! So obviously straight! I should've seen it coming from a mile away."

"Emma, there's no way you could've known. C'mon, it's impossible to tell when someone's straight or gay just by looking at them. Not for sure, anyways. You know that. I know you do. You whine about it all the time."

Emma sniffs again. I hear a peck on the glass behind me and turn to see the bird spying on me again. I frown at it because I do not have time for its bird-based shenanigans right now. Thankfully, Cú is a reliable guard cat. He flicks his tail, wiggles his butt, and pounces at the window. The bird flies off, panicked.

I turn my attention back to Emma and carry on with my clumsy comforting. "Besides, basic chicks are hot. With their makeup all perfect, and the messy buns, and the way they always smell like vanilla or pumpkin spice or whatever? Who could blame you?"

"It's just, god, it was so embarrassing, Brigid." Emma sighs but sounds a bit more like herself. "It was right after pottery class, so Jess was there."

"Uh-oh."

"Yeah, and I was dressed all hot, like we talked about? And I was feeling myself, and I went right up to Kelly and like tried to hold her hand while we walked out together. And she didn't take it, and that should've been the sign right there. And I know Jess saw it because she like, smirked at me—you remember, that bitchy smirk she does?"

"Oh, I remember." She smirked at me a couple times like that, always after planting a showy kiss on Emma's lip, and always just out of Emma's line of sight.

"Yeah, so, she does the little smirk, but I just sorta ignore it and think maybe Kelly just didn't notice me reaching for her hand, no big deal. But then we get outside, and I'm planning my big move, right? Like, I'm gonna say something about how incredibly beautiful she is and then I'll kiss her and it's gonna be super amazing and then she'll fall into my arms and come back to my place and we'll have such a wild night of passion we're both late to work in the morning. But instead, she gets all serious and is like 'can we talk?'"

"Oh, feck. Oh no."

"Right? That's like, the least sexy thing a person can say to another person."

"Yeah, and why do they even ask that?" I commiserate, thinking of Mammy asking me to have a "family meeting" with her in her bedroom. It always devolved into me sitting in the chair in the corner for hours, agonizing as she explored in excessive detail and at excessive volume the myriad ways I was disgusting and ungrateful. "It's not like you can say no."

"Yeah! Once they ask if you can talk, what are you supposed to say? 'No thanks'?"

I put on a preposterous falsetto. "Actually, now's not good for me, but I could pencil you in for next Thursday?"

Emma laughs, haltingly. She's a bit tearful again. "Exactly. You're like, trapped."

"Yeah," I say softly, trying to give her space to cry, the way Carol does for me.

"Anyway." She exhales deeply. I can see the tears track down her round cheeks, all the way to her pointed chin in my mind's eye. My heart breaks a bit more. "You can imagine what it was she wanted to talk about. The same old shit about how I was so great and she was so sorry, but she just wants to be friends after all, and how this was such an eye-opening experience, and she'll never forget me, and blah blah blah."

"Well, please allow me to say, Kelly sounds like a huge bitch. I'd like to start a petition to officially rename her 'Blonde Bitch' within the context of our friendship."

"No, I don't want that, it doesn't mean she's a bad person," Emma disagrees. "I get that not everybody is so . . . so sure of what they want, like me. And it's not like I'm some perfect person either. I feel bad about even coming up with the stupid 'don't date girls who haven't dated girls before' rule. Like, what a shitty rule to have. I'm just being cruel to bisexuals and women who were slow to realize they're gay with a rule like that, but I don't know how else to protect myself. Every time I get led on and then rejected by someone who doesn't know what they want, by someone who's just like, trying on being a lesbian for shits and giggles, it sucks. It's like, really fetishizing, you know? Like I don't actually exist, or like I don't matter. And the fetishizing is, like, twice as bad since I'm Black."

Emma laughs her sad, broken laugh again and continues, "I just wish she'd, like, I don't know, considered that masturbating to lesbian porn doesn't mean you're gay? And that she realized I was like, a real person, with real feelings."

"I don't know, Emma, I think you're doing that thing again."

"What thing?"

"The thing where you're too perfect and patient and wonderful. But conveniently, I am none of those things, and so I am perfectly capable of speaking the objective truth and saying Kelly is being a bitch."

The laugh again, but this time it sounds happier. I smile in triumph.

"You're one to talk," Emma playfully retorts. "Your mom was like, the poster child for an abusive parent, and you still think you deserved it."

"Well, that's different."

"Uh-huh. How?"

"Because I did deserve it," I answer in reflex, but then I pause. I think back to what Carol said about me being a normal kid. Do I believe her? I'd like to, but is that just coddling myself? I don't deserve to be coddled. I'm mentally ill, dangerous. I hallucinated a heart in a drawer, for crying out loud. I need to be strict with myself.

Emma's voice brings me back to the conversation at hand. "Brigid, your mom was a total bitch. You did not deserve it."

"Can't both be true? Can't my mom be a bitch and I deserved it?"

"If you deserved to be abused, then I definitely deserved to be dumped by my girlfriend before I even got to kiss her."

"Touché." I laugh. "Fine. We are both blameless victims. Delicate infant babes thrust into a cold, uncaring universe."

"Yeah, exactly."

"At least we've got each other." I smile again, selfishly this time. If Emma is single, she'll call me more often. That's always how it works.

"Together forever," Emma says, then sighs again. "Anyway, enough about me and my pathetic love life. Tell me about your cat! What did you say his name was?"

"Cú." My smile widens. "It's Irish for 'hound,' so he's like a cat named Dog."

I can hear Emma's eyes roll through the phone. "You would."

"I did. You've gotta meet him, though, Em. He's the best cat in the world. So brave, and so friendly. And he's got this scar on his nose so he sorta snorts when he breathes?"

"Awwww, poor baby!" Emma coos.

"I know! But the shelter said it wasn't anything to worry about, health-wise."

"That's good. Does he snuggle?"

"He's so good at snuggling, you have no idea. He curls up in the pits of my knees while I sleep and watch TV. And, it's amazing, I haven't had a single nightmare since I adopted him. It's only been a couple nights, but still."

"That's amazing! You just needed a friend."

"No, yeah, I'm so thrilled! And the shelter said he gets along with other cats, in case, you know," I stammer, feeling a spike in my adrenaline, "in case you ever wanted to move in with me. I've got the house all to myself, you know, and there's another bedroom and I'd charge you, like, nothing for rent. And there's lots of rich white people here; I'm sure you could find a good nannying job."

"Hmmm," Emma considers. "Probably not much in the way of a queer community, though?"

"Probably not . . ." I admit.

Emma snickers, but a bit lamely. "Well, maybe I oughta take a break from dating anyway. I'm like, way over pottery class girls at least."

I let the topic of her moving in with me drop and tut at her. "I warned you about pottery girls."

"I know, I know." She laughs and it's finally a real laugh, no sadness at all. Good. Blondie didn't do too much damage in the end.

I yawn into the phone. It isn't late but I'm exhausted. The pain is getting bad, too, even worse than usual. I'll have to take an edible for certain, or I won't be able to sleep through it.

"Hey Emma," I offer, "would you want to get off the phone and maybe do a video call and watch *Pride and Prejudice* or something together? I'm wiped."

Emma yawns, too, proving the adage about yawns being contagious true. "Nah, I think I might actually go to bed early if that's okay. I didn't sleep well the last couple nights, since I was all sad, but I'm feeling better now."

"That's totally fine. I'm glad you're feeling better. Night, Em."

"Night, Brigid! Oh, and send me more pictures of Cú. He's adorable."

"Okay, will do. Night."

"Night."

After I take an edible, I wiggle the fingers of my left hand under the blankets for Cú to pounce on. In my mind, I send another thanks to the enthusiastic cat rescuer for trimming his claws; he'd definitely be cutting me through the comforter if they were sharp. I snap a few pictures of him being ferocious, then send those along to Emma. Once he's satisfied with the amount of murder he's committed, he starts purring and we watch an episode of

Downton Abbey together. By the time it's over, the weed has hit my system and the pain is buried in a box somewhere in the back of my mind. I fall asleep smiling, thinking about Emma.

I wake up soaked. My face is wet from tears tracking sideways across the bridge of my nose and temple and settling in my hair. And I'm wet between my legs, on my thighs and pajama shorts and blankets and sheets, a hot and raw and meaty liquid. The pain is dulldulldull and then SHARP, a high wave of sharp stabs stealing my breath my thoughts my self, making me gaspandgaspandgasp and then back to dulldulldull again.

Cú isn't on the bed, probably because in my sleep I've retracted into a tight ball and have taken away his favorite spot behind my knees. I try to figure out what's going on while the pain is dull and I can think. It's dark and I'm disoriented; it must still be night and the weed must still be in my system. This flare must be a gnarly one if I'm feeling it this badly while I'm high. Probably not helping my thinking abilities either, being high, but being high is the only solution I have for the pain that's rising again again it's rising again oh *feckfeckfeck* like an organ is tearing itself apart like an organ is trying to escape like an organ is trying to claw its way out through my abdomen feckFECK*feck* I wish I was dead I wish I was dead I wish I was dead the dead don't hurt don't hurt don't hurt like this, and it begins to fade down to the dull pain again, and I feel in the dark for my nightstand, grab the edible container and hastily stuff another into my mouth.

I wish I was hallucinating the warm wetness all over the sheets and blankets of this bed, but I know I'm not. My hallucinations have been fairly novel so far, and I'm all too familiar with this sensation. It's been happening to me for too long for me to not recognize it. Still, I reach my right hand into my pajama shorts and underwear and draw it back to my face, close enough so even in the dim darkness I can see that my fingers are covered in sticky menstrual blood. The scent is insistent and cloying, already beginning to resemble the smell of rot.

"Feck," I grumble, annoyed I'm going to have to do laundry, annoyed my cycle doesn't follow a pattern, so I can't predict it, annoyed I'm basically guaranteed at least a day of agonizing pain now. Speaking of pain, it begins to rise again, nearly predictable in its unpredictability, and I harden my jaw against it. *FeckfeckfeckfeckfeckFECKfeckfeckfeckfeck* and it is receding. I fumble around on my nightstand again, this time taking four ibuprofen and a glug from my water bottle. I smear blood from my fingers on the bottle's plastic surface and the pills get a bit of menstrual blood on them as well, but I'm too high and too in pain to truly care. When you bleed the way I do, streams and rivers and waterfalls of iron, it inevitably ends up in your mouth some of the time.

I strip the sheets and blankets off the bed and leave them in a pile in the hallway, next to the basement door. Thank God, the blood didn't seep into the mattress. (Reminder: buy a mattress protector.) I head to the bathroom and strip out of my clothes and add those to the bloodied pile as well, then curl up naked on the tile floor, shivering from cold while another pain wave takes me. Once it abates, I clean up the small puddle of blood that's gathered on the tile and spread the bath mat out next to the shower. I lie on that instead for a good twenty minutes, until both the ibuprofen and extra weed have had time to kick in and even the highest pain spikes are tolerable.

Of course, when you're this high, accomplishing any task at all is difficult. I turn on the shower and just stare at the water for several minutes before getting in.

Even once I'm in the shower with hot, soothing water flowing over me, I struggle. It hurts to stand upright, so I lie, curled into the fetal position, on the bathtub floor while the shower beats down. Eventually, I shift so I'm lying on my back, leaning against the back of the tub, looking down at my naked, tender body. Blood still stains my thighs and clumps my pubic hair together. I'm continuing to bleed, so much that as the water travels along the path of my body toward the drain, it rushes away from between my legs dyed bright red. I do a little experiment and bear down with my pelvic floor muscles. As I hypothesized, the water runs redder, richer, as more blood pours out. I smile dully. It would be fascinating if it wasn't my blood, my strength, my life running down the drain.

Eventually, I find the nerve to wash the blood off my skin. I wash my hair, too, for good measure, but stay sitting on the floor of the tub. It's hard in this position, but not as hard as standing would be. Once I'm out, I put on clean underwear and pajamas along with one of those ultra-maxi nighttime pads that feel like wearing a diaper. After a moment's consideration, I put in a super-plus tampon too.

I notice my pitiful lie down on the bath mat resulted in it getting bloody. Into the blood pile with the other laundry it goes.

And now, as I stare at the pile, I am forced to acknowledge there is altogether too much blood in this laundry. It'll set if I leave it until morning and then I might never get the things properly clean. I can't afford to buy new blankets and sheets and whatnot. Defeated, I return to the bathroom to fill the tub up with cold water, dumping the bloody cloths in to soak. I'd add a few capfuls of laundry detergent, but it's all the way downstairs and I hurt too much to brave the steps. Whatever, this is good enough.

I return to my bedroom and remember I don't have extra sheets to put on the bed. I could sleep in Mammy's room, I suppose.

The chair in the corner of her room, the punishment chair, springs into my mind's eye.

No, I can't sleep in Mammy's room. I absolutely can't. I get the throw blanket off the sofa in the living room instead, and curl up on the bare mattress.

At least I don't have any nightmares.

Day 11

The good thing about waking up in the middle of the night in a huge pain flare is that you already took a bunch of edibles in the middle of the night, so you're still high and pain-suppressed when you wake up.

The bad thing about waking up in the middle of the night in a huge pain flare is that even though you're high from the edibles you took in the middle of the night, the pain is still there in the morning. And you know you've got an entire day of trying to put up with it ahead of you. It's practically guaranteed to be a shitty time.

My marijuana-muddled mind ponders what to do with the expanse of miserable hours before me while I sit on the toilet. I've already finished emptying my bladder, but I got distracted by my own illogical thoughts. Now, I'm just sitting here, while blood drips out of me into the water, dyeing it a cheery Christmas red. Disgusting.

I toss the stained overnight pad into the trash with the old tampon and clean my labia up as well as I can with toilet paper, then put in a fresh super tampon. After a moment's consideration, I put a panty liner in my underwear too. Tampons almost always leak, for me at least. I wash my bloody hands (putting in tampons is a gory event), scrubbing under my fingernails with determination, and then turn to the tubful of bloody sheets and clothes and whatnot.

There is no good way to get the soaking mass into the washing machine in the basement without making a mess. I did not think this through last night.

To be honest, I'm having trouble thinking it through this morning as well. (I'm still blazingly high, after all.) I start by unplugging the tub, and watch the red sediment on the bottom fall down the drain, rushed along by the pink-tinged water. I tentatively press on the soaking mass and more water leaks out and drains away, but it's obvious I won't actually get the fabric measurably drier with this approach. I head to the basement to examine my options.

The basement in this house is inarguably creepy. It's bare concrete, floors and walls alike, with a rickety wooden staircase with no railings descending steeply and straight down into the depths. Once you're down the stairs, you can see it is dimly lit by only a few bare bulbs. It smells faintly of damp soil and laundry detergent. Every available bit of wall is bordered by a massive array of boxes and totes and bags and some straight-up piles of stuff. Mammy was a bit of a hoarder. Not in the reality TV show way, but in the Midwestern way. From Christmas to baby showers, power outages to societal collapse, every possible eventuality is prepared for in this basement.

But these solutions are poorly organized and unlabeled. I halfheartedly poke around the junk for a few minutes, not finding anything good for transporting a large amount of wet, bloody fabric, and noticing the odd shape of the basement itself. The basement also serves as the foundation for the house, of course, and so you would expect the basement to be the same size and shape as the house above. I realize now, though, something I never noticed as a kid: The basement is smaller than the house, with a rectangular area toward the back of it sectioned off by solid concrete walls. I stare at the walls for a minute, fumbling with weed brain until I determine the sectioned-off area must be under Mammy's room.

Maybe it's just another room in the basement? But the walls are all bordered by the junk, and the detritus is even thicker around these two oddly jutting walls. If there was a door, I wouldn't be able to see it. I begin dragging away a pile of crap, determined to solve this mystery, but the effort causes the pain I've been studiously ignoring to spike. Feck. *Feckfeckfeckfeckfeck*. I lean against a stack of boxes labeled "~~Christmas Lights Halloween~~ Da's Stuff," pressing my fingers into my lower abdomen to create a sensation other than pain.

It eventually recedes. Feck. Let that be a lesson to me. Today is a rest day, not an investigate-the-mysteries-of-Mammy's-creepy-basement day.

I decide a shitty solution is better than leaving the bloody sheets to grow mildew. Besides, I want to put the sheets back on my bed. Sleeping on a bare mattress sucks. I grab the laundry basket off the top of the dryer and go collect the laundry from the bathtub. Yes, I know laundry baskets have holes in them. My clothes get wet, and I leave a trickle of bloody water from the bathroom all the way down the rickety steps to the washing machine. This is why I called it a shitty solution. I change my clothes and grab a rag to sop up the blood trail, only having to pause to take a break due to pain once. I toss the dirty clothes and rag into the washing machine, too, and set it to run, then hold my left hand up in the air and high-five myself with my right. I'm killing it today.

On high-pain, high-blood days, I usually have to take two or three naps, so I figure I might as well start now. I lurch upstairs and collapse onto my sheetless mattress with Cú for a reward nap. My pain is low enough for me to lie in my regular position on my side again, and he snorts and purrs happily at the return of my knee pit.

I wake up disoriented an hour or two later, with my mouth desert dry and my stomach hollow. I drain the water bottle on my nightstand, feeling the room temperature water splash into my stomach acid, then pet Cú for a few minutes while I assess my body. I still hurt, and I'm feeling unfortunately sober now. I chow down on another edible, knowing it'll hit fast and hard thanks to my empty stomach, and go switch the laundry from the washer to the dryer.

It does seem like my solution of soaking everything in the tub kept the bloodstains from setting. My sheets look like sheets instead of props from a slasher flick. I high-five myself again.

Upstairs in the kitchen, I fix myself a pain meal. It's not a complicated recipe: First, you take a spoon, then a jar of peanut butter and then you just go to town. Bonus points are awarded if you can ignore your pain for long enough to choke down a banana as well. While I eat my Michelin-star-worthy creation, I also refill my water bottle. As I sip from it, my eyes catch on Jesus through the opening leading to the entryway.

He's changed.

I lurch over to him, holding my aching pelvis with one hand and a half-eaten, overripe banana in the other. The crossed-out eyes and mustache are still present, but someone has added a message for me.

You worthless, ungrateful freak.

My first instinct, probably fueled by the good mood marijuana puts me in, is to say something sassy and vaguely flirtatious to Jesus. But the words die in my throat.

I recognize the handwriting. It is the handwriting from notes on summer mornings telling me I was responsible for making dinner and cleaning the bathroom, the same handwriting that lashed out at me from an innocent stack of sweaters.

Mammy.

I stumble backward, banana flailing, until my shoulder blades hit the front door. I steady myself against it. Mammy is still alive. She must be. I'm not hallucinating. Mammy is still alive and she's breaking into the house and she's moving around the picture of Jesus and emptying garbage all over the floor and tying hunks of meat to the ceiling and hiding human teeth in the bread and human fingers in the bathroom and human hearts in the office drawer with the stapler and scissors and reams of paper, and I can prove it. I put the heart in the freezer; it'll still be there.

Abandoning my banana on the hutch, I flit to the freezer, stopping just short of the door. I stare at the handle, willing the heart to be where I left it, wrapped in plastic and stiffly cold. It will be there. It will.

I open the door.

Oh, thank Christ. The plastic bag is still there, wrapped tightly around something that's definitely human-heart sized. As I reach for it, my mind clocks that I'm happy there's a human heart in my freezer. That's probably a sign I'm fecked up somehow, but I'd rather have a human heart in my freezer than be completely unraveling. I snatch the bag and open it, certain I'll see the meaty muscled organ inside.

Of course, there isn't a human heart in the bag. In the bag is a mere rubber band ball. In a desperate bid, I search the rest of the freezer, but it contains nothing but regular freezer things. It is completely devoid of nefarious, leaking body parts. Somewhere deep inside, I knew that's how it would be.

I shut the door and sink to the floor, lying back on the hard tile and staring up into the kitchen light above me, rubber band ball in hand. I try to consider the facts logically, try to calm myself down and remind myself it might be easier to deal with hallucinations than Mammy's Machiavellian ministrations.

But I don't like logical facts when I'm high. I don't want to be hallucinating. I don't want to be sneaking around, doing creepy things and then forgetting it was me who did them. The idea of having to deal with that, of having to go to a psychiatrist and admit how far I've fallen, makes me want to cry. I follow Carol's advice to practice feeling my emotions and let myself, for once. The tears roll out of the corners of my eyes and track down into my ear canals, muffling the sounds of my own sobs. It could be someone else crying, underwater, far away. I don't cry very often, after all. It could be someone other than me.

But it is me. And it seems that actually, I cry all the time. These are my tears, this is my life, and that's my handiwork on the Jesus painting. I should be impressed instead of distraught. Spooky nighttime Brigid is an excellent forger. I really thought it was Mammy's handwriting for a minute there.

I'm too dehydrated to get a real good cry going, so I eventually give up my wallowing and rescue my banana. I look at the mushy flesh and feel my stomach turn; I'm much too upset to eat. I frown at Jesus and smoosh the banana and peel across his face, working it into the canvas with my fingers for several focused minutes until I hear the dryer buzz from the recesses of the basement.

The peel won't stick to the painting, so I toss it in the trash.

The banana-based defacing of religious iconography suggests I'm higher than I thought I was. Good. Nobody ought to deal with this shit sober.

I save my laundry from the basement, remake my bed, and play with Cú awhile. At one point, the bird arrives at the window again, checking to see if we're still here, but Cú chases it off. The fierce hunter and I take another nap. When I wake up, I eat some crackers and more peanut butter, grabbing them from the kitchen and retreating to my bedroom to snack in my bed. I'm not going to engage with the world again until I don't hurt so much.

I fire up the laptop for a proper *Downton Abbey* marathon. I even watch the first movie. It's a good time. Branson, the hot Irish guy, is in the movie a lot.

Cú must enjoy period dramas as much as I do. He doesn't complain once.

Day 12

I'm feeling better in the morning. The pain is back to its more usual background drone. Blood is still pouring out of me as if I were the Torc Waterfall, but I can deal with that. A little (or, you know, a lot) of blood hasn't bothered me since I was eleven. That's what having a heavy flow will do to you.

Emotionally, I'm doing better too. The weed has cleared its way out of my system, and in the sober light of morning, as I gaze upon the rotting smooshed banana distorting Jesus's face, I'm able to admit I may have slightly overreacted. Everything happening in this house is my fault. Jesus does not deserve to be a victim of banana-based vandalism.

Most of it comes off with a damp paper towel, but between the broken frame, scratched paint, permanent marker, and banana stains, Jesus is looking less holy than he once did.

"Sorry, Jesus," I whisper. The apology is sincere, for once.

I make myself some tea and crunch my Oaty-O's while I peruse the to-do list Carol and I made. It feels like we wrote it up a lifetime ago, but it was just last week. It's been rough recently.

To be honest, I've been doing a poor job of following the list. For example, "adopt the best cat ever" isn't even on there. Neither is "buy a silk dress with money you ought to be saving" or "completely lose your goddamn mind," but there you have it. Life is what happens in between your plans.

Even if I'm hallucinating, I can still accomplish simple tasks. I owe Carol, and myself, that much. The next undone item on the list is going through stuff in the living room to give away. I can do that. I finish my tea and cereal, wash the dishes, and build a few giveaway boxes. I carry two and kick a third into the living room, and settle them all onto the floor. I'm glad I already dusted in here. This should be quick.

I start by gathering up all three crystal flower vases, which is a baffling number of crystal flower vases to own, especially considering I can't remember us ever having fresh flowers. Those go into the giveaway box. I doubt anyone will be buying me flowers anytime soon, I joke in my head, but then pause.

What if I was actually able to convince Emma to move in with me? Maybe I would buy her flowers. She might like that. It's probably bad to get my hopes up, but here they are, rising up, regardless of my wishes. I save the prettiest vase, the one cut to resemble a castle tower, from the giveaway box and put it back on its shelf.

The coffee table books can definitely be given away, though, as can most of the throw pillows. I don't understand the point of all these throw pillows. There are so many you can't even sit on the couch. The teddy bears atop the piano are next to get the axe, and are joined shortly thereafter by the tiny piano-shaped knickknack.

I run my hand across the top of the real piano thoughtfully. I don't know why it's still here. (Probably just Mammy's laziness surrounding updating the house; that, and pianos are a nightmare to move.) I always used to dream about taking lessons, but I knew better than to ask Mammy. Neither she nor I ever touched it; Da was the only one of us who was any good at music. He played at church sometimes. The piano has sat unused since he left us two decades ago, and I wonder if he misses it. Of course, he probably has a new piano wherever he is, one better than this beat-up spinet.

After I slide back the fallboard protecting the keyboard, I experimentally press one of the white keys. It lets out a twang, sad and out of tune, like a saloon piano in a cheaply made spaghetti western. I wonder if I could teach myself to play piano with free internet videos. I wonder how much it would cost to get it fixed up.

I try to sit on the bench and place my hands on the keys the way I remember Da doing when I was little, but the bench won't close all the way. Something big is inside, forcing the lid to remain open. I open it to investigate, expecting to see a too-tall stack of discolored sheet music, and instead find a brutalized face.

An entire head, actually, messily sawed off immediately below its wide Adam's apple, leaking minutely from the ragged stump. The man's expression is neutral in death, mouth barely open and skin barely moist, and yet the flesh appears rigid even by corpse standards. His eyes are open, and small wisps of frost cloud the dark blue irises and black pits to create an illustration of the permanence of death. His hairline is receding, but the mess of red curls that do remain shine lustrous and thick, complimenting the golden spatter of freckles across his cheeks and forehead.

I know him, of course. It is my father. Unaged, unchanged, from twenty years ago.

I drop the lid of the bench on instinct but, in an uncharacteristic display of athletic prowess, catch it before it lands on his face.

I've already squashed him by sitting on the bench; I don't want to damage him further. I push the lid open all of the way and sink to my knees, tilting my head as far as my neck will allow to the left, so I'm making eye contact with him. I used to look into those eyes as he read me folktales before bed. Even now, frozen and rimmed by thawing lashes, they are the exact shade of storm grey blue I remember.

With great tenderness, I stroke across the top of his cold hair, neatening the mussy curls. Whoever hacked his head off didn't bother to keep him looking his best, but I will grant him this kindness, even though he left us. I can't help it; I love him still. It is difficult for a child to stop loving their parent.

My hand goes still in his hair. I continue looking into his dead, shallow eyes, eyes set in a frozen face that hasn't seemed to age a day in twenty years. Twenty years. He left us twenty years ago. "Left."

My da never left me. He was taken from me.

I gasp fiercely, surprising myself with the chest-shuddering force of my anguish. I ought to be frightened, I ought to be terrified, I ought to be desperate and puzzling out who killed him and why and if I am next, but I am none of those things. I am in mourning.

My da was a kind man, a soft-hearted man with a low, muttering midlands brogue, patient when times were hard, grateful when times were good, steadfast and honorable, and I hardened my heart to him for years and years and years, believing what I knew in my core to be a lie, believing, somehow, I was so unlovable as to drive such a dependable father away, believing he could be driven away from a daughter he loved so truly.

Such a man would never leave me willingly. And here he is, in my living room, home with me, and I love him like a small child might. He is my hero, even gone.

With tender hands, I lift his head from the bench and cradle it in my arms. I try to close his eyes, the way you see in movies, but they don't stay shut. I try again again again again, and I don't know if the movies are a lie or if he's been dead too long or if he is too frozen, but I can't get them to just stay closed, and it makes me cry harder harder harder still. The cold of him seeps through my shirt and leggings as I cling his head to me, curling around it as I kneel on the floor by his old piano.

A thought springs unbidden into my mind (what if as his head defrosts, I get his blood on me, what will I do?), but I force it away. I hate myself for even thinking it. This is no time to worry about laundry and messes, or even police investigations. Besides, if it comes to that, I'm excellent at getting bloodstains out of clothes. Lots of practice.

At one point, as I sob, I hear a rattling outside the living room window. It is the bird, of course, the goddamn bird refusing to leave me in peace. It taps on the glass and rasps a gloat, then preens its feathers showily, bathing in my misery. I look away, focusing on myself, on Da. The bird deserves none of my attention, none of my efforts. Not now.

My body uncurls as my supply of tears runs dry. I continue my mournful ministrations, straightening his hair, holding his mouth shut, neatening his bushy eyebrows, drying the condensation off his skin with my shirt as he continues to thaw.

It takes several minutes of fumbling care for me to remember: I am hallucinating.

He can't really be here. This can't really be my da's head. How would that even work? Twenty years ago, my da died (or was killed, probably was killed, he was healthy and young, and here is his decapitated head, which feels like a murderer thing to do, except the

173

head can't be here, it can't it can't it can't) and then somebody put his head in the freezer, and somehow, I never noticed it for my entire childhood, right there with the frozen pizzas and ice cream? Or they stored it in a freezer somewhere else, and no one else ever happened across it? It's ludicrous.

It's more likely this head is itself a tub of ice cream. Yes, that's it. I blacked out, took a tub of ice cream from the freezer, put it in the piano bench, then came to and "discovered" it. Now, my diseased mind imagines it to be my da's head, since I was just talking about him with Carol the other day. Yes. That makes sense.

I take a deep, steadying breath. And then another. A third for good measure. There. I feel better. I better put this ice cream in the freezer before it melts entirely.

When I stand up, I do notice a damp, grotesque bloodstain on my previously cream-colored shirt. I steel my mind against the stain and against panic. It is just melted ice cream, and I am imagining the color. I'll wash it later.

There is another snag in my logic when I reach the freezer. The head (ice cream) doesn't fit nicely. There isn't an empty spot where it ought to have been, and I can't think there ever was; the freezer has a shelf running through the middle of it and the spaces both above and below the shelf are too narrow to fit the head (ice cream). I don't want to squish Da (the container), so I figure he (it) must've come from the chest freezer in the garage.

I've hardly ever used that freezer; I haven't even bothered to clean it out yet. That's way at the bottom of my list, even lower than organizing the basement. Even when I was a kid, I barely went out there. I assume it's full of all sorts of out-of-date crap; Mammy never once cleaned it out, and I've never seen it empty.

I believe Midwesterners are legally required to own either a beer fridge or a chest freezer (of course, if you are upper-class, you will own both) and keep those extra chilling units in either the basement or garage. My family, being middle-class, elected for a sole chest freezer and put it in the garage because carrying a massive 18.5 cubic foot capacity chest freezer into a basement would be pure madness. I have no idea why we, or other Midwesterners, feel the need to have these freezers. I assume it's a holdover from ye olden tymes when someone would shoot a moose and then massive chunks of moose meat would be distributed throughout the neighborhood. Or maybe it's for winter, so if you get snowed in you still have enough food and/or beer to last you through the storm. We have meat counters and snow plows now, but the chest freezers remain, incontrovertible evidence that we are not from either coast, thank you very much.

And yet, even though this freezer has a capacity of 18.5 goddamn cubic feet, even though we almost never used the fecking thing, it is nearly full to the brim when I open it. There's a jumble of freezer burnt tubs full of gummy ice cream that expired years ago, TV dinners and frozen potstickers, pizzas and ground beef patties and popsicles and one of those big bags of ice you buy for parties. None of it is organized at all; it's just tossed in there in a remarkable mess.

I don't know, maybe it's the stress of hallucinating that ice cream is my da's head in a piano bench (which, by the way, I'm still carrying under my arm like a soccer ball), or maybe it's how frustrated I am by the way Mammy left such a ridiculous hoarder mess for me to clean up, or maybe it's simply the fact both Da and Mammy left me, both of them found me so unlovable they had to drive into a river or get decapitated or, I don't know, maybe they're both in Vegas, Vegas-ing it up, but either way, they're not here, helping me, they're off doing whatever, and I'm tired and I hurt and I'm suffering, and they're supposed to help me and they're not helping, all they do is create more shit I have to deal with, shit to deal with like the mess in this fecking chest freezer, this fecking giant chest freezer big enough to fit a goddamn moose that's filled with expired trash, and now I have to clean it out and you know what? Fine. FINE. I'll clean it out. I'll clean it out now.

I toss Da's head (the ice cream) onto the garage floor, ignoring the way it lands, with his lower jaw pushed unnaturally to the left while his open eyes stare at me, because it's not real, it's not my da's head at all, and stalk to the kitchen to get the roll of black trash bags from under the sink. Back in the garage, I start throwing everything from the freezer into the trash bags indiscriminately. I don't care if some of it is technically still edible. I don't care that I can't afford to throw away good food. It all goes into the garbage bags, layer after layer of it, and Da's head (ice cream) lies on the concrete, a few yards away, staring on with Zen-like acceptance of its imminent fate.

Fueled by my rage, I keep digging, ignoring the stinging cold on my bare hands, ignoring the stabbing punctuations in my pelvis, ignoring the sadness in my heart. And then here, almost at the bottom, deeper in this freezer than I've ever reached, so deep I have to bend myself over the lip to grab the TV dinners destined for the dump, I come across raw, unwrapped, frozen meat.

When I first see it, I roll my eyes. I assume someone hunted this meat decades ago, when I was a baby or maybe even before, that it's a deer leg some friend of a friend gave Mammy and Da. They probably bought this freezer specifically for it and then never bothered to actually eat the venison. But when I reach through the layers of frost and popsicle boxes for the hoof, my fingers wrap around rough cloth instead.

I snatch my hand back. It felt like denim. Like that stiff denim men wore in the late '90s. Like the sort of jeans Da would've worn.

Breathe, I tell myself. Breathe. This is another hallucination. My imagination is running away with me. I'm going to clear away the rest of the frozen stuff and then I'll see it's just a deer leg wrapped in burlap for some reason, with a raw edge poking out. That's all it is.

I clear out the rest of the boxes, trying not to look at what rests on the bottom of the freezer, but eventually, I can no longer ignore how the fabric is obviously not burlap. It is definitely denim, a dark blue loose-cut pant leg, sliced open at the thigh to reveal a pale frozen leg with red curly hair and sunshine freckles. In the middle of all this skin is a massive chunk removed, all the way down to the femur bone, torn roughly out by a poor excuse for a butcher.

My mind conjures up the hunk of thawing meat I found in the fridge right after I arrived here. The meat I threw unceremoniously away. I feel my bowels kink as my anxiety spikes. Oh, god. Oh god oh god oh god. He's been here. He's been here this whole time. And I threw a piece of him into a dumpster.

Terrified now, terrified to be right, terrified to be wrong, I remove more and more frozen goods from atop the body. I reveal the sleeves of a practical dark green button-down, rolled up, showing off thick freckled forearms. A pair of New Balance sneakers, but one of them lies empty, next to a stump of a calf and a limp sock instead of being on a foot. (The little bones, the sliver of toenail—what was it that I found in the garbage disposal?) The left hand is wearing a wedding ring, a gold band with a claddagh stamped on it, a ring that matches Mammy's. The right hand is missing a pointer finger. (The finger in the bathroom, the door-stop finger, it couldn't be, but it could be, couldn't it?)

I find the neck. The neck is missing a head. With great trepidation, I turn my own neck to look at the head (ice cream? Head?) I threw on the concrete floor. It is still there. It is still a head. If it was a hallucination, wouldn't it have worn off by now? How long do hallucinations last? If I hallucinated that ice cream was a head, would it look like a head to me forever? Or would it eventually look like ice cream again?

Wait. I know the answer to this one. At least in theory. I found the tooth in the bread and then later it was a pebble. And the finger was later just a door stopper. The head will become ice cream again.

Except. The body. I look at what I've uncovered of the body in the freezer again. It is missing a pointer finger. How clever are my hallucinations? Are they clever enough to hallucinate a missing finger to better align with previous hallucinations? Is this really just a deer carcass in the freezer that I'm looking at?

I consider the head resting on the concrete again. I really don't want to do this. I really don't want to investigate further. But I owe it to Da, don't I? And to myself, to figure out how insane I really am?

Kneeling on the cold concrete, I lift the head once again. As it nestles like a baby in the crook of my left arm, I gingerly place two of the fingers of my right hand in its mouth. My bowel kinks painfully again, twisting my guts urgently, and I know I won't last long before I have to go to the toilet. God, I wish anxiety didn't trigger my diarrhea; I don't know if I'll have the courage to do this later. Rushing, fumbling, I feel around in Da's cold, dry, dead mouth, telling myself it's just an ice cream container. Of course, ice cream containers don't have teeth, and Da's head does. I feel along the row across the top, and there are no gaps. No gaps on the bottom left either. I begin to sigh in relief (see? Everything is fine) but then stop.

The bottom right. Toward the back. There's a gap. A tooth is missing.

I pull my fingers out and pinch the mouth open, angling the head so the light shines inside. Sure enough, there it is. Or isn't. A space where a molar should be, still looking raw and empty and unhealed, like the tooth was pried from the jaw after death. I slam the mouth shut and squeeze my eyes shut, too, resisting the urge to throw the head to the other side of the garage and feeling my gut roil. I'm going to have a diarrhea episode any moment now.

But there's one more thing I need to check. I return to the body in the freezer and toss the smattering of frozen goods obstructing its chest over my shoulder, not caring where they land on the garage floor. There, I see, with the detritus cleared away, my fears confirmed for a third time.

The practical green button-down has been ripped open to reveal Da's chest, and the chest has been hacked open, similar to the brutalization of the thigh. My eyes squeeze shut against the image, but I open them again because I have to see. I have to know.

The wound is large and rough, on the left side, and the ribs have been cracked and splintered to allow access. In the center of the wound rests a human heart with its connecting aorta and vena cava and other tubes severed. It could be easily scooped away. It could be easily placed in a drawer, then put in the kitchen freezer by me, then taken out of that freezer and returned here.

With my realization, my anxiety spikes higher, and my bowel lances me through with sharp, insistent pain. I can't wait any longer; I need the toilet. I snatch the head from the floor and return it to the freezer, lining it up shoddily with the neck due to my rush, and slam the lid shut.

I make it to the toilet, but it's a small comfort. (Though, of course, if I had shit myself, I would be even more upset, so perhaps it's a larger comfort than I am acknowledging.) I try to focus on my deep belly breathing to calm myself, but it barely helps.

There is the sound of the insistent rattling of my bedroom door. Cú. Despite my stress, my terror, I'm calmed by the thought of him, much more than I was by the breathing. He's afraid of nothing, as far as I can tell. The finest guard cat-dog a girl could ask for. Maybe that's the secret to dealing with this anxiety, these hallucinations, at least until I can get on a medication that works. Just spend time with Cú. Focus only on taking care of Cú.

I'll go to the bedroom and play with him as soon as I'm done in the bathroom. I won't go back to the freezer. Why would I? There's nothing in the freezer.

As I try to scrub all traces of the freezer's contents from both my hands and mind, there's a knock on the front door. I scowl at my reflection in the bathroom mirror. So much for playing with Cú and his perfect little snorty nose. While I dry my hands, whoever it is knocks again, louder this time. "I'm coming!" I shout in the general direction of the door. Sheesh.

I rush to the door, and they knock again. They're an impatient arsehole, whoever they are. I've already decided I hate them. I pull open the door; it squeals the way it always does if you don't open it just right, and I snap, "Hi, yes, what can I do for you?"

Emma's face looks back at me in shock but then melts into a smile. "Brigid," she says, "I was in the area and decided to stop by! How are you?"

I stare at her, holding the door open, dumbfounded. It would be just like Emma to impulsively decide to visit, to drive the two hours south when she was upset, especially if she knew she would meet a cute cat at the end of the trip. She's a good friend like that.

But this isn't Emma.

Emma is short and plump, a bit like a teapot, but in the best way. It would be easy to wrap myself around her; I always picture myself as the big spoon when I'm fantasizing. This Emma has the same round face and same pointed chin and same elaborate hair and correctly proportioned curves, but she towers over me. I instinctively recoil, disgusted on a visceral level by the uncanny valley of seeing a disorienting, inaccurate facsimile of someone I know so well. Looking at this Emma feels like looking at a statue made by someone who has only seen a picture of her, a picture that lacked any reference to inform the viewer of her height. The sculptor guessed, and made her an Amazon.

They guessed wrong from a picture. Or, maybe, from a video chat.

The bird.

The bird, constantly looking through my windows, spying on my calls, listening in on every conversation. Carol was tall, so much taller than I had ever imagined Carol to be, and the bird had seen Carol through a video call, too, hadn't it? And then it turned out to be not-Carol?

And here is Emma, too tall and not-Emma, and where is the bird? Is it somehow projecting this image of Emma into my mind? I peek my head around not-Emma's torso to try to determine if the bird is hovering nearby and using telepathy, but I don't see it. That doesn't mean it's not there. It's never far.

Not-Emma titters nervously. "Brigid? Are you okay?"

"Yeah, no, yeah," I answer, waving at her passively with the back of my hand while I scan the branches of the oak tree with my eyes. I'm not worried about being rude to her. She's just a hallucination, after all. "I'm just looking for . . . something."

"Should I help you look?"

"No, no." I pull my head back and consider not-Emma. Maybe this is a good time to test the limits of my hallucinations. Does she feel solid? "It's so good to see you!" I give her a hug, repressing a shudder at touching the repulsive representation, noting that she feels warm and sturdy, like a flesh-and-blood woman.

She hugs me back and steps inside, saying, "I've missed you so much!"

I politely step aside to make room for her to walk in, continuing to gather evidence. Not a vampire. She didn't need permission to come inside. As ridiculous as it seems, unseen telepathic super-bird is still a leading theory. (Of course, the "Brigid is having a mental breakdown" theory is the front-runner still, but Da's imagined corpse in the freezer could also be caused by a telepathic bird. I'm not ready to discount the bird being a twisted, immortal perversion of Jean Grey from the *X-Men*, is what I'm getting at.)

Can hallucinations hold objects? Can they eat and drink? "Can I get you something to drink? Or a snack?" I offer.

"Sure," she answers as she examines the defiled picture of Jesus. "You've been feeling creative, I see."

"Oh yeah, just a bit of fun," I tell my hallucination breezily. "What would you like? Coffee? Tea? Biscuits?"

"Tea and biscuits would be great."

Interesting. Real Emma can't digest gluten and is therefore anti-biscuit unless they're made with rice flour or whatever. Not-Emma doesn't know the real Emma very well at all. If this was purely a figment of my imagination, I would know to imagine Emma turning down the biscuits.

Or I like to think I would. I don't really know how any of this works, do I? All of this "evidence" I'm collecting could prove nothing at all. Does trying to prove a bird is making me crazy actually prove I am crazy?

Jesus, Mary, and Joseph, I'm so tired. Overwhelmed. I can't

keep any of this straight. I don't know what to believe. What can you believe when you can't believe yourself?

Cú rattles my bedroom door again and the sound snaps me out of my pondering. I go to make the tea. Not-Emma follows me into the kitchen and pulls out a chair at the little table for herself. An involuntary shudder runs up my spine. She can interact with objects. She can come inside uninvited. She feels solid to the touch. This distortion feels more real (I feel less safe) by the second.

I busy myself with putting the kettle on the stovetop and arranging biscuits on a plate to buy some time. I put exactly five biscuits down and decide I will eat exactly one. I'll be sure to know if she eats, and how much, without raising suspicion.

After placing the biscuits in front of her on the table and taking the seat across from her, I try to ignore how unnerved I am by looking up into Emma's face, when I usually look down at it. I keep my mouth shut for several minutes, waiting for her to make a move.

"That rattling sound," she says eventually, "is that the cat you told me about?"

"Yes."

There's another long, quiet minute. I maintain the silence and do not start talking, even though it's difficult for me to remain quiet when I feel so anxious. I refuse to give this hallucination any more ammunition than it already has.

She breaks first. "What was its name again?"

"Cú."

She sneers in disgust. It seems automatic, a visceral reaction. "Like Cú Chulainn?"

I narrow my eyes at her. There's no reason the real Emma would know Irish folklore, would know the name Cú Chulainn, would know how to pronounce it.

She seems to realize her mistake and backpedals, laughing too brightly. "Oh, don't give me that face. I was listening to a podcast about Irish stuff the other day."

"Sure."

The kettle boils and I get up to pour the hot water into the mugs over the tea bags. Not-Emma still hasn't eaten a biscuit, but that doesn't necessarily mean anything. She could merely be waiting for her tea.

"Aren't you going to ask me why I was listening to a podcast about Irish stuff?" she prompts me, her voice grenadine sweet.

"Why were you listening to a podcast about Irish stuff?" I play along but stay over by the stove, where the tea is steeping.

"Because"—she stands up (too tall, much too tall, my brain does not like Emma being this tall) and sidles over to me, wrapping her arms around me and stooping so her lips are in my ear—"I know being Irish is important to you. And you're important to me. So important. I want to know every little thing about you, Brigid."

I clench my jaw. The words, her voice, the warmth of her breath on my skin. I want it all. Badly. But this not-Emma is perverse, the smell of her is wrong, and hearing her want me makes my gut twist anew. Less dramatically than before, thank god. It's empty after the anxiety attack imagining Da's corpse gave me.

"That's nice," I manage to eke out.

Not-Emma pouts, drops her arms, and saunters back to her seat. I fish the tea bags out of the mugs with a spoon and ask her if she wants milk and sugar.

"Both." She smiles. I smile benignly back. Real Emma only takes milk.

I fix up the tea and bring the mugs over, taking my one

allotted biscuit and dunking it in my tea. Not-Emma takes one, too, dunks it, and takes a bite, gluten be damned.

"So, I actually was thinking," she says, "about your new cat. Cú."

I nod.

"Do you really think this is a good time for you to get a pet? With all the stress of the new place, and cleaning out your mom's things?"

I make a noncommittal noise, egging her on, and scratch at my forearm.

"Because I was thinking, it's not fair to Cú. To be taken care of by someone who can't, well, no offense, Brigid, but by someone who can't take care of themselves."

I wince. I know not-Emma isn't Emma, she's some hallucination or something, but whether she's caused by the bird or by my own sick mind, it still hurts to hear those words in her voice.

"Sorry." She shrugs, decidedly unsorry. "It's true, though. You've got these health problems, and they're not even real, Brigid. I think you need to figure out your own situation before you involve a defenseless animal."

Cú continues rattling the door and I think about wiggling the ribbon toy for him, snuggling with him in bed, listening to his snorts and purrs. My heart breaks a little, my eyes tear up minutely. What if I really can't take care of him? What if this is a protective hallucination, my mind's way of telling me so?

"I know it's hard, but I think I should just take the cat with me now. It can live in my apartment." Not-Emma reaches out and pats my hand. "It'd be for the best."

I recoil from her touch. She still disgusts me. My mind keeps flip-flopping from doubting myself to doubting her. If she's a hallucination, why does she want to take Cú now? Wouldn't a hallucination from my own mind tell me to return him to the shelter?

Taking him now feels like a way to guarantee that he's out of the house. I think of the bird, fleeing in terror from Cú even when a window separates them. The bird would want Cú out of the house.

"No, the shelter said he didn't get along well with other cats," I lie. "He can't go to your place."

Not-Emma's face falls in disappointment. "Are you sure? I could just keep it in another room."

"No, they were very specific about it."

Not-Emma becomes angry, flaring her nostrils and furrowing her brow. "I have plenty of space. Give it to me."

Fear squeezes my heart, hard, once, but I ignore it. I'm too afraid of other people's anger, and Cú needs me to be brave. "No."

Not-Emma stands, stretching to a greater height, her face thinning and elongating until it is no longer Emma's sweet round face but a fun house mirror impression, all points and edges. "Brigid," she intones in Emma's voice, but a half step too deep, "give me the cat."

I duck my head and seal my eyes shut, unable to look at her, my spine bending in submission. "I'll take him to the shelter tomorrow, okay?" I give in, my voice quaking. "Tomorrow. Just one more night."

"Fine." It is Emma's voice again, but I'm too scared to look up at her to see if she has returned to Emma's appearance. I hear her grab her bag and walk to the door. "There better not be a cat here after tomorrow, or you'll regret it."

I listen to her leave, shutting the door quietly behind her. I try to listen for a car driving away, but I hear nothing. Now that I think of it, I didn't notice a car in the driveway when she arrived, when I looked around her body to try to see the bird.

That makes sense, I tell myself. A hallucination doesn't need to drive. Something you're imagining can be anyone, be everywhere, all at once.

I send an email to Carol, asking for the psychiatrist's phone number so I can get on some antipsychotic medications. I need to stop seeing my da's corpse. I need to stop my brain from making my closest confidants attack me in my home. I need to stop blaming it on some stupid bird.

And I need to rest. I carry my tea and the rest of the biscuits to my bedroom, take an edible, play with Cú, and watch some more *Downton Abbey*. Most of all, I wait for tomorrow. Tomorrow will be easier. It has to be.

Day 13

The grating tone of an alarm coming from my cell phone startles me awake. Why is there an alarm? I never set alarms; the pain makes me sleep so fitfully Carol recommended I sleep in whenever I can. Anything to help my body calm down its inexplicable rages. I only set alarms if there's something I absolutely have to do in the morning.

I sit up to stop the noise and, through the blaring, hear Cú's irritated grumble at the disruption of his snuggle spot. "You and me both, buddy," I tell him as I fumble with the nightmare rectangle. Finally, I manage to hit the cancel button and am returned to blessed silence. Apart from Cú's little snorts, of course, but those are a different type of noise. A cozy noise. They improve upon silence.

Still sitting up, still tired, I start to scratch behind Cú's ears. He purrs and his snorts grow louder, and I smile groggily. Much to his disappointment, I stop petting him once my mind has cleared a bit. I open up the calendar app on my phone to determine what

I thought was so important.

Oh, yeah, no, I'm clueless. Today is my appointment with the new gynecologist, Dr. Hämmerle. I had totally forgotten about it. (There's been a lot going on.) I was able to get a telehealth appointment, right? I swear, if I have to drive forty-five minutes to some godforsaken office park, I will flip my lid.

I search through my emails and find the intake paperwork, which I fill out somewhat lazily. When I first started seeing doctors, when I believed I was sick and not delusional, I used to fill these forms out with gusto, as if they were homework and I were the teacher's pet. I would be so detailed, so precise, trying to use medical terminology to prove I knew what I was talking about, trying to prove I was worth taking seriously.

Eventually, I realized most doctors give these forms only the barest glance. They allot a measly fifteen minutes per appointment slot; they don't have the time to do silly things like read about their patients' medical histories. This used to hurt my feelings, before I had the epiphany that it was my own fault for putting the expectation that they legitimately care about me on them. After that, I instituted a new rule: I fill out medical intake forms as shoddily as doctors read them, and in doing so, save myself both time and heartbreak.

Anyways, I half-ass the forms and e-sign away an appalling, yet somehow standard, number of my rights, then email the office an attachment containing the surgical report from the endometriosis expert who performed my second laparoscopy and the high-definition photos she took of my slimy internal organs. I make sure to use the word *laparoscopy* in the email so they'll know I mean business.

Not that it matters. The result of this appointment will be the ultimate result of all the others: Dr. Hämmerle will find no real source for my pain, and everyone, including me, will agree I'm overly anxious and overly imaginative.

I have some time before the appointment, so I figure I best put on real clothes and get some food in me. I studiously avoid thinking about what's in the chest freezer in the garage (there's nothing in the chest freezer in the garage, I know that, why would there be anything worth mentioning in the chest freezer in the garage?) by drawing out my tiny everyday decisions into complex, meaningful quandaries.

Should I have eggs instead of cereal today? Do I deserve to fill my stomach with the expensive and potentially cruelly gathered eggs of birds that have been brutally abused, eggs that are meant to house chicks and certainly are not meant for my entitled lips? Should I wear my new silk dress to increase my confidence, or will that convey that I'm trying too hard to be diagnosed with something, and therefore make Dr. Hämmerle dismiss me as a melodramatic hypochondriac? Or, will wearing nice clothes convince her I absolutely cannot be sick, because all truly sick people are unable to put on nice clothes? And beyond that: Do I deserve to wear silk, or does doing so prove I'm vain and shallow and don't care enough about the plight of silkworms, similar to how I don't care enough about the plight of chickens?

I really work myself up into a lather with these questions, and the time passes more quickly than it would otherwise. It's amazing what you can accomplish when you really harness your anxiety and self-doubt. I manage to settle on yes to eggs and no to the dress, though the eggs take longer to cook than expected, and I leave the dirty frying pan languishing on the front-right burner of the stove instead of cleaning up. After eating, I return to my bed and my laptop wearing my standard chronic illness outfit, albeit with a T-shirt lacking any logos or slogans.

Wearing the same carefully vague smile I do when I wait for Carol, I wait for Dr. Hämmerle. And wait. And wait some more.

I scratch my forearm roughly. I don't like doctor's appointments.

Out of the corner of my eye, I see the bird land on the windowsill behind me. It settles in, clearly expecting to eavesdrop on this conversation, too, but Cú spots it. He hides behind my legs for a moment, stalking it, and then explodes onto the window, slapping his paws against the glass. The bird flies away in terror, and Cú makes an excited trill of chirping sounds, eyes alert and tail swishing.

Good cat. I pet him until he calms down and returns to the foot of the bed for a nap.

The screen finally gives me a loading indicator and Dr. Hämmerle appears, thick-rimmed glasses fogging up slightly since she wears a medical mask over the bottom of her face. Her eyes crinkle at the corners as she smiles at me through the camera, and she laughs a little.

"Hello, I'm Dr. Hämmerle. It's nice to meet you. This is a telehealth visit, which means I can take this off." She removes her mask to reveal thin lips bordered by distinct smile lines. "That's better! I'm so sorry I'm late. I wanted to spend some time reading those medical history forms. Thank you for filling those out, by the way. I like understanding my patients' backgrounds as much as possible, so I appreciate it. Now, should I pronounce your name Brigid, kind of like Bridget, or is it Brigid?"

My jaw drops open slightly in surprise. This isn't how doctor's visits usually start. And her second pronunciation is right.

"Uh . . . the second one, Brigid," I answer, repeating her correct pronunciation. "Yes, the second one is right."

"Oh great!" She laughs again, warm and pleased. "I'll be honest, I actually looked up the pronunciation before I joined the call and found a couple, so I figured I better ask."

I quirk a half smile despite myself. "I looked up how to pronounce your name too. Before I scheduled my appointment."

"Well, aren't you thoughtful?" She tilts her head like a puppy. For a middle-aged woman, she's energetic. For a doctor, she's friendly. It shouldn't matter to me whether or not a doctor is friendly, but I find myself feeling lighter and safer. And she hasn't even done any doctoring yet.

"Now, Brigid." She pauses after she says my name correctly to wink at me. "I already read the forms, like I said, but I was wondering if you could tell me, in your own words, exactly what's been going on with you?"

"Uhm . . . it might take a little while. I have a complicated medical history."

She nods in understanding and folds her hands on her lap, the spitting image of an attentive listener. "Of course. Please take as much time as you need and tell me absolutely everything about your symptoms, head to toes."

And I do. I'm hesitant at first, scared of wasting her time or angering her. I try to skip through the first surgery by only saying it didn't work, but she slows me down with specific questions: Was it excision or ablation? Do I know what specialties the first doctor had? Did I have any symptom relief at all?

Emboldened by her attention, I start to give more details. How much it hurts, how I often struggle to stand, to breathe, to think. How hopeful I was for the second surgery, and how destroyed I felt when the endometriosis expert found nothing. How I've tried almost everything, from physical therapy to herbal supplements to mindfulness, and nothing seems to help. The pain consumes me.

Through it all, Dr. Hämmerle listens, nods, and says nothing other than asking clarifying questions. By the end of it, I've nearly forgotten I'm talking to a gynecologist; it's like I'm speaking with a therapist, or maybe even a friend.

I admit some things I've never admitted to a doctor before: Da leaving when I was little, Mammy's unpredictability, my struggles with my anxiety. I know it'll just give her more ammunition to tell me all of my symptoms are in my head, but since all of my symptoms are actually in my head, I figure it's best if she knows everything. She doesn't seem like she'll use my secrets to hurt me.

At the end of my monologue (which surely lasts longer than the regular fifteen minutes an appointment ought to take), I summarize my story for her.

"I know there's nothing physically wrong with me. They would've seen it during the second surgery if there was," I say. "But it really does hurt, you know? It's so painful. I just don't know . . . I don't understand why I'm feeling this much pain. I don't understand why my brain would invent it."

I try to keep my voice even, but it cracks a few times. A couple of tears eke out of my eyes.

Dr. Hämmerle's face is open and soft, her own eyes wide and soulful behind her unstylish glasses.

"It sounds like you've been through the wringer," she says. "I'd like to thank you for sharing all of that with me. I know people who have invisible health conditions can have a hard time getting good care, and it can be hard to trust a new provider."

"Yeah, no, yeah, you're-you're welcome." I'm thrown off by her authenticity, but at the same time feel incredible relief course through me. She believes me. She's listening.

"I do have a few more questions, if that's alright with you?"

"No, yeah, of course. Go ahead."

"Great. I'm wondering why it is you're convinced your pain is psychosomatic, or, like you said, your brain is 'inventing' it." She puts the quotes in with her fingertips.

"Uhm because . . . well, because that's what the second laparoscopy showed. What the endometriosis expert doctor seemed to think."

Dr. Hämmerle nods but doesn't agree. "I don't know if we have enough information to rule out a reproductive health condition, though. Your symptoms are definitely in line with something like endometriosis, but it's possible you could have some other condition too."

"I've had my hormone levels and everything checked, a couple of times. And ultrasounds and everything, you know."

"Of course, that all makes sense." She twists her mouth to the side in an expression of thoughtful consternation. "I wish I had access to that second surgeon's surgery report."

"I e-mailed the surgical report to your office this morning, the same time I filled out the forms. I sent the pictures from the surgery too," I say. "Did I send them to the wrong email address?"

Dr. Hämmerle sits up, straight and attentive. "You sent them? Do you mind waiting for a moment? I want to talk to my office manager, see if she's got them."

"Yeah, no, of course. Please."

"Great. Just one minute."

Dr. Hämmerle exits the view of the screen and I hear a door open and shut from her side of the call. I try not to let my hopes rise up. I know there's no way to fix my pain. There's nothing I can do other than suffer. It's been proven time and time again.

"Found them!" The doctor returns to the screen with a stack of papers in her hand, held triumphantly above her head like a trophy. "Sorry about that. We need a better system in the office, clearly. Is it okay if I read this real quick?"

"Sure." I scratch at my forearm and watch her eyes scan across the pages of the surgical report. I know what she's reading: a dry, factual detailing of how everything in my body is medically perfect.

"I see what you're saying," she says when she eventually looks up. "This doesn't really give us much to go off of, does it?"

"No, it doesn't. That's why I'm saying it's all in my head. There's nothing physically wrong with me."

As I repeat myself, she flips the report to the back of her stack of papers and starts to examine the pictures, one by one. She has her thoughtful consternation face on again, growing more pronounced with each image until she reaches the picture of my pink, shiny uterus. Even through the screen, I see her eyes spark at that one.

"What is it?" I ask.

"Your uterus. Do you have a copy of this picture you could look at with me?" She holds the picture up near her webcam so I can tell which one she's talking about.

"Yeah." I open the image on my laptop and set it to split screen, so I can see Dr. Hämmerle and the photo of my least favorite internal organ at the same time.

It sure looks like a regular uterus to me.

"Okay, so do you see how the uterus looks kinda chunky? How it's bigger in the back than it is in the front?"

I look at the image. It is definitely lopsided, but I hadn't thought anything of that before. "Yeah, it does."

"And also, can you see how on the back side, it's got sort of an irregular, wavy shape? The front is smooth, but the back isn't?"

Sure enough, it does. "Yes."

Dr. Hämmerle beams like a beauty queen who was just awarded Miss Superlative at the state fair. "So, that's textbook adenomyosis. Now, there are a couple of different ways we can treat it—"

"Wait," I interrupt, then wince. I never interrupt. "Sorry, I don't mean to be rude."

"No, please." She waves her hand permissively but still oozes triumph. "Ask any questions you have."

"It's textbook what?"

"Adenomyosis. You haven't heard of it?"

I flip through the files of my brain and come across a memory. The endometriosis expert mentioned it as a possibility during my first pelvic exam with her, when she noticed me recoiling in pain when she pressed on my uterus. But she never brought it up again after that. I saw the word a few times on the internet too. I think it's somehow related to endometriosis. I tell Dr. Hämmerle as much.

"Gotcha, sorry, I got carried away. So adenomyosis is similar to endometriosis, but for whatever reason, it doesn't get as much attention. That might be because it can't be definitively diagnosed without a hysterectomy—that's surgically removing the uterus—but honestly, if you know what to look for, these days, MRIs and sometimes even ultrasounds are getting good enough to catch it, at least some of the time. And, of course, if you know what to look for and it's severe enough, you can see it from the outside of the uterus, too, like here in these pictures."

"Okay." I scratch harder on my forearm. "And it's . . . what, exactly?"

"You know how endometriosis is when the endometrial tissue—that's the lining of the uterus—grows outside of the uterus, onto other organs and structures in a person's pelvis?"

"Yeah."

"Adenomyosis is effectively the same thing, but the tissue grows into the walls of the uterus instead. It causes very similar symptoms to endometriosis: increased pain, heavy bleeding, long cycles, bloating, sometimes bowel issues, all of that, but since all the damage is happening inside the walls of the uterus, when you do a laparoscopy, all of the other organs look perfectly healthy. It's also relatively common to have both endometriosis and adenomyosis. I'm thinking that may be the case with you, since the first surgeon found adhesions during your first laparoscopy."

"But shouldn't . . . shouldn't the endometriosis expert have known about this?" My mind spins dramatically, trying to fit this information into my worldview. It can't be true. I remind myself I need to keep my hopes down. "Shouldn't she have noticed during surgery?"

The doctor shrugs noncommittally, probably unwilling to speak poorly about another medical professional, but I see her eyes tighten sympathetically. Yes, her look says. Yes, the surgeon should've noticed.

I place my hands tenderly on my lower abdomen, still aching, as always. I picture bloody tissue growing into the walls of my uterus, ripping deeper and deeper into the flesh, scarring me more and more.

No wonder it keeps getting worse. No wonder it feels as though one of my internal organs is being slowly ripped apart. One of them is.

Dr. Hämmerle clears her throat. "So, there are a few different treatment options. We could try to be conservative and try you on a birth control pill or an IUD or something similar. That can help some women, though I'll be honest, it does take a little while for your body to adjust and, even then, doesn't seem to be very successful for pain control for most of my patients. Another more conservative approach would be—"

"What would be an unconservative approach?" I interrupt again. That's twice in one conversation, a new record for me. I feel bad, but not bad enough to stop.

"Well, the traditional treatment for adenomyosis is a hysterectomy—again, that's removing your uterus. We can safely leave your ovaries in place, though, so you wouldn't go through menopause. Though if we leave your ovaries, there's a chance if you have any microscopic endometriosis tissue left, it might grow back in time. If that happens, though, we could always try another laparoscopy. But, of course, with a hysterectomy, you would be giving up the option to ever be pregnant, and it isn't a miracle cure. There are potential side effects and complications. That's why I usually recommend a more conservative approach at first, until we know it's our best option. But ultimately, the choice is yours, since it's you we're talking about."

Never being pregnant. I squeeze my eyes shut. No children, at least not from my body.

I've never thought too deeply about whether or not I would have children; it's always been somewhere on the hazy "someday" horizon. And yet, the idea of having the option taken from me lances me through with sadness. It feels like giving up on a dream I didn't even know I had.

But, a voice whispers in the back of my mind, would I even want children? Think about it: Hurt people hurt people, don't they? What if I just pass all the terror Mammy instilled in me down to my child? What if I'm just like her?

Besides, could I even handle a child? My gut knows the answer to this one: no. You can't have a child if you spend multiple days a week bedridden from pain, if you have to get high every night to be able to white-knuckle through your misery. Even if I never scared them the way Mammy scared me, my broken body would keep me from being the type of mother I would want to be.

Dr. Hämmerle, to her credit, politely waits while I think through all of this. When I open my eyes, she tilts her head to make it clear she's listening.

"Would it work?" I ask her.

"The hysterectomy?"

"Yes. You said birth control isn't as helpful for stopping the pain. I assume the other more conservative options aren't either. But would the hysterectomy work?"

"I can't make any promises regarding the outcomes of a potential surgery, and again, a hysterectomy isn't a miracle cure for adenomyosis. It comes with its own risks and potential side effects," Dr. Hämmerle says as her eyebrows turn up empathetically. "But, yes, I think it would work. I believe that if you were to have your uterus removed, the vast majority of your symptoms would resolve."

I don't answer right away. My mind keeps spinning its tires.

"There's no need to make any choices right now, Brigid, so what if you think on it for a few weeks, and in the meantime, I'll send you some information about various birth controls or other medications you could try? And we'll schedule an appointment for you to come into the office as well, if that's alright? We'll do an ultrasound to make sure we don't see anything unexpected, and you and I can meet in person and discuss any questions you might have."

I hem and haw internally, but ultimately agree. "Okay," I answer. "Okay."

"Good." Dr. Hämmerle smiles. "Whatever you choose, I think it's great we have a better idea of what's going on. Now you don't need to think you're imagining anything! I'll have someone from scheduling give you a call to set up the ultrasound appointment, okay?"

"Okay, yes. Thank you."

"You have a great day! Bye!"

"Goodbye."

The screen goes dark and prompts me to rate the quality of my call. I give them five stars, exit out of the window, and make the photo of my uterus full-screen. Now that Dr. Hämmerle has pointed out its flaws, I can't unsee them. It looks chunky. I have a chunky uterus.

Adenomyosis.

I say the word out loud a few times, tasting it on my tongue and waking up Cú, for whom absolutely nothing has changed.

The doctor's parting words echo in my ears. I don't need to think I was imagining anything, because I wasn't. My pain is real. I have a diagnosis.

I ought to be upset, right? I ought to be devastated, feeling like my ability to have children has been stolen from me, feeling like my life is now forever immutably altered. And maybe I will be upset about it, later, maybe when I'm thirty-five and all my friends have children and I'm alone.

But right now, I'm not upset at all. I'm thrilled. Tickled. Delighted. I have a diagnosis. A diagnosis! Something tangible, something real, a fancy-sounding medical word I can say to people and they'll look it up online and read the little summary paragraph about how my uterus is tearing itself to shreds and they'll make a sympathetic face and tell me how sad, how terrible, how unlucky, and best of all, they'll believe me. I'll believe me. Because it's real.

I cover my face with my hands as if I'm about to cry, but start laughing instead.

It's real.

I pull my hands off my face and gasp.

What else is real? What else have I been tricked into believing?

I know I'm not some sort of sexual predator, that Mammy's insistence I was some lecherous slut was wrong. I know my invisible illness is tangible, that proof of it exists.

That's what I need. Proof.

I get out of my bed quickly, ignoring the protesting of my tender pelvic organs; there are more important things than pain right now. In the office, I open the drawer that previously contained a human heart and now contains a rubber band ball. I look closely at the inside of the drawer, at the light oak wood, and sure enough, there is a stain. Faint, as if someone after me tried to clean it again, but pink and indelible and undeniable and there.

Not believing my luck, I giggle delightedly at the bloodstain like a child who ran through a sprinkler. The mirth dies in my throat when I remember the other proof I'll have to check for.

After taking a deep, steadying breath, I make my way to the garage, passing the bathroom where I found the finger, the kitchen where I found the tooth and meat, and the entryway where Jesus continues his cruel vigil. I will not let the horrors of this house deter me.

The garage smells ripe and rotten, filled with the spoiling meat and TV dinners and popsicles I threw out of the chest freezer last night. It's stiflingly warm in the summer Chicago heat, but I hardly notice. I reach the chest freezer and stare at the lid for a beat before I locate my courage somewhere in my diaphragm. In a swift motion, I throw back the lid.

And there it is. He is. Da. Da's corpse. It looks like he's been shifted slightly—the heart now lies beside him instead of in his chest cavity, his head is lopsided, so his left ear touches the stump of his neck—but if anything, that only proves me more right.

Proves this as more real. Whoever is tormenting me must've tried to move the body and couldn't. Sure, they might be able to fool me by hiding a tooth or a finger, trick me into believing they're everyday objects. But in letting me find Da's corpse, they finally bit off more than they could chew.

A bitter and vengeful pulse swells in me. I've been tormented, been fooled, been tricked into disbelieving myself, and all in my own home, where I'm supposed to feel safe, where I'm supposed to be loved. I slam the lid of the freezer shut and stalk back into the house, where I'm greeted again by Jesus in the entryway. Jesus, with his horrible quote on his chest, the accusation written in Mammy's hand. I glare at him and remember all the times I've glared at him before: Mammy asking me where her sweet little girl had gone, Mammy telling me I was lazy and ungrateful, Mammy saying I was a liar and a thief, Mammy shouting I was a whore and a bitch, near the same goddamn painting, so close to the front door that could grant me my freedom. I never just walked through that door. I wanted her to love me, I wanted to be enough, so I would stay and I would listen and I would believe her.

No more. No more will I swallow what I've been fed; no more will I believe what others tell me about myself. I know what I see. I know what I feel. I know who I am.

I am named for a deity, the goddess of poets and a woman of wisdom, renowned for powers of healing and protection. I am brave. I am resilient. Whoever is fecking with me ought to know: It ends today.

Stalking back and forth through the entryway and kitchen, I grasp at the straws of a loose-weave revenge plot. How do I catch them at it, whoever they are? How do I stop them? I could call the police, of course, but no: They're clever enough to trick me, they'll trick the police too.

Besides, I want to bring them down myself. They killed my da; or at the very least, they desecrated his body. I want their blood on my hands.

On my eighth or ninth path through the kitchen, with eyes skipping from my tea mug in the sink to the stovetop with the dirty cast-iron frying pan on the right-front burner to the fridge with the chipper checklist, I see it through the window: the bird. Sitting on its fecking branch on the fecking oak tree. It has something to do with all of this. I know it.

It's as good a place to start as any.

I'll take down the crow.

I've got everything set up in the kitchen for my preposterous plan: cardboard cat carrier, blanket, plastic Tupperware with holes punched in the lid. I've remembered to unlock the side door and made sure Cú is awake. It's not too bad of a plan, not really. It's elegant in its simplicity.

That's what I tell myself, at least. It helps boost my courage if I pretend to believe it.

I need all the courage I can get. I even decided to rescind one of my morning decisions and changed into my new silk dress. It looks amazing and, aside from my pain, I feel amazing in it. I hope I don't get avian blood all over it. Even if I do, I know how to get out bloodstains.

Before I seal my fate and challenge the probably telepathic and potentially cosmically powerful bird, there's something else I need to do. I'm done letting other people's judgments of me determine my actions. Including Emma.

I call her.

. . . And it goes to voicemail. Of course it goes to voicemail. I roll my eyes. Anticlimactic.

When it beeps, I leave my message.

"Emma, hi. It's me. Brigid. You know that already, we live in the future and caller ID exists. Anyways. I have something important to tell you. Ask you? Tell you. I'm about to do something really dangerous and I have like, a lot of adrenaline, so it seems like a good time, now while I'm, like, brave or whatever. But maybe I shouldn't say it over voicemail? But now I've told you there's something important, so if I don't tell you, you're gonna get all scared and nervous, and I don't want to do that to you, that's not cool, so here goes nothing."

I take an exaggerated inhale. An exaggerated exhale. I scratch at my forearm.

"Yeah, no, here I go. So, the thing is, I'm in love with you. And like, I know sometimes we say we love each other because platonic love is legitimate and valuable and deserves recognition and I do also love you as a friend, but I'm, like, in love with you. In a gay way. A sexy way. I want to have sex with you."

I face-palm with my free hand. I thought I was going to sound all cool and suave, but instead, I'm fumbling. Hard. But it's too late to back out.

"This probably is a surprise to you because you think I'm straight, and to be honest I never told you otherwise because I don't really know what I am. And I know you don't want to date girls who haven't dated girls before, and I totally respect that and respect you if you don't want to date me, but maybe I could be an exception because I haven't dated anyone, I haven't even kissed anyone, so it's not like I prefer guys, or at least, if I do, I have no way of knowing. Also, I do think I like men at least a little because Branson can get it, but I like you more. I like you more than

Branson, the Irish chauffeur in *Downton Abbey*, and I don't know how to convince you that I mean it when I say I love you more than by saying that . . .

"And yeah, that's basically what I had to say. I'm going to be honest, I don't know how to end this message in a way that doesn't make me sound like a total dork. I hope you like dorks. I hope you like me. If you don't, though, I promise to always value our friendship and not be weird about it . . .

"Okay. That's all. Bye."

I hang up the phone, slam it down on the table, and raise my arms to the ceiling to bask in my triumph. It was such a lame admission of love, but I did it. I cut my stupid heart open and bled into her voicemail message box and no matter the result, I took up space. I did it.

Time for phase two of the plan.

I go to my bedroom door, which Cú rattles in his habitual bid for freedom. I open it and scoop him up, hugging him tight as I carry him to the kitchen.

"Alright bud, I didn't want to have to involve you, but I think you're my best bet. Your reflexes are better than mine and you've got some serious bloodlust. Are you feeling brave?"

He fixes his lamp-like eyes on the kitchen window, and I feel his feather-duster tail swish excitedly in my arms. He's ready.

I place him on the floor, and he explores the room a bit, then crouches behind a section of cabinets that allow him to keep looking out the window. I wonder if his eyesight is sharp enough to see the bird in its tree, even from in here. It seems like he can. I open the screenless window and hope he won't jump out of it before it's time.

It takes a couple tries, but eventually, I find a five-minute-long video on the internet of a cat making sad noises. I shudder when an errant thought makes me wonder what sort of bastard made the video and for what audience, but then I realize here I am, the audience, right now, and have a brief moment of guilt-laden paralysis. But no: This is a good reason. I have the moral high ground over any perverts who get off to the sound of upset cats.

I package the caterwauling phone with a heavy pot and a blanket into the cat carrier, so it'll look weighty and convincing. Then I carry it out to my car, making a production of apologizing to it the whole way.

"I'm so sorry, Cú," I say. I try to pretend I actually am returning Cú to the shelter and I actually believe in not-Emma. Just imagining Cú in the box is enough to make my eyes prick with tears and my voice turn thick. "I love you so much, Cú, but this is for the best. It'll be better in the long run, I promise."

Once the screaming carrier is snuggled into the passenger seat, I get into the driver's side and begin to pull out of the driveway. I peek surreptitiously at the bird in the oak tree, confirming it's the correct bird, with its ink-stain head and burnt-ash body, and making sure it's watching me leave.

I start to drive away and it doesn't follow me; it just looks between my car and the open kitchen window, weighing its options. Good.

When I'm halfway around the block, I pull over and park, then scramble to turn off the upset cat sounds playing from my phone. It's a migraine-inducing cacophony, and I have to be stealthy now. I set my phone to silent and slip it into my dress's pocket.

As I'm sneaking through the garden of the house behind mine, I remember my dress has a lovely pattern of green leaves on it. I hope it helps camouflage me. Maybe it does, because I reach my side door, crouch-walking in a way that probably makes me seem more suspicious, without anyone stopping me.

Gently, slowly, carefully, I turn the side door's shitty, squeaky handle, hoping to create as little noise as possible. I wish all those things Mammy said about me when I was a teenager were true. Maybe I'd have more practice with sneaking into the house quietly if I had ever snuck out.

Once inside, I stand stock-still, listening. The only noises are normal house sounds: a whirring refrigerator, the bathroom fan, Cú's little snorts, trees rustling outside. I sneak forward to a spot where I'm not visible from the kitchen window but can see most of the tile floor. I can also see Cú, still crouched like a proper little predator behind the kitchen cabinets, feather duster tail swishing in fervent anticipation.

We wait there, the pair of us, hiding for several long minutes. The lull in action makes me pay attention to the aching of my poor, scarred uterus. I rest a hand across my lower abdomen, feeling sorry for it. Feeling sorry for me. All this time there was an answer. It's enough to make me weep.

Maybe this is foolish. Maybe the bird is a bird, and I am hallucinating. It's possible to have two different illnesses at the same time, after all. Maybe I ought to just shut the window, scoop up Cú, and make my way to bed for some painkillers and *Downton Abbey* until it's time for therapy with Carol this afternoon. I can figure out what sort of treatment I want to pursue for the adenomyosis with her help. That's what a normal person would do. That's what I ought to do.

I start to move from my hiding place, but before my self-doubt can ruin anything, the bird decides the coast is clear and soars through the window. It lands on the lip of the stainless-steel sink and I jerk back behind the corner, hoping it didn't see me. I peek around to watch Cú's rear end. His pose has morphed ever so slightly; his body is lower to the ground and his back feet shift as if calibrating delicate equipment. He's locking onto a target.

The bird must still be in the kitchen, must not have noticed Cú and me. I don't dare to breathe. It seems like Cú might be holding his breath, too, because I can't hear his usual snorts.

There's a soft flutter of wings. I can make out the shadow on the floor growing as the bird approaches it to land. In a single explosive movement comprised entirely of grace and elegance and muscle and sinew and destruction, Cú leaps.

It happens so fast my eyes can hardly process it. I see three distinct pictures: Cú's feet leaving the floor, the bird's panicked flapping coming a moment too late, and Cú landing with the bird's neck and shoulder blades firmly pinned in his jaws. He bunches into a tense bread loaf on the floor while his fangs push through the bird's downy feathers, puncturing the flesh beneath.

The bird lets out frantic chirps of agony, drawn-out high-pitched noises scraping around the inside of my skull and filling my heart with pity. I don't know how Cú, with his sensitive ears, can stand the sound. The bird's right wing sticks out from Cú's mouth at a horrible angle, twitching wildly in concert with its feet, but Cú keeps his dreadful hold on the creature.

It will be hard to think of Cú as a harmless house cat after seeing this gleeful carnage. Regardless, I find it hard to regret my choice. This is not just any bird; it's been stalking me, tormenting me. Besides, birds get killed by cats every day. And I'm not even going to let Cú kill it.

I rush into the kitchen, snatching the blanket off the back of a chair. I'm going to toss it over the pair, then work the bird out of Cú's mouth and trap it in the hole-poked Tupperware container. After that, I'm not sure. See if the hallucinations stop? Take it to a wildlife rehabber? Buy a cage for it? I don't know. I'll cross that bridge when I come to it.

When I throw the blanket over the two, Cú lets out an irritated meow. He must've opened his mouth to do so, because under the blanket I see the flapping increase and separate from the blanket-draped form of my cat, making it seem like the bird is growing in size.

I step forward to grab the bird through the blanket and am given pause. The flapping shape does definitely seem larger than before. Maybe I underestimated the size of the bird from the get-go, but this bird seems too large to even fit in Cú's little mouth, and until a moment ago, Cú had it firmly in his jaws.

The flapping is moving in a different pattern, too, now appearing less like the beating of wings through the cloth and more like a tortured roiling. The blanket seems to bubble and jerk upward, growing higher and higher. Once it's reached the height of my hip, I've accepted this is not a bird trapped under the blanket.

This is something else entirely.

Terror claws at my throat and chest as I stumble away, hitting my back on the sharp edge of the table, then shifting to the side so I can back up farther. Once I hit the wall, I splay my fingers against it as if I might be able to press my body through the drywall and away from this unearthly perversion. And yet, as much as I want to escape, I seem incapable of tearing my eyes from it.

When the shape reaches the height of my shoulder, the blanket begins to fall away. The first thing I see fills my heart with desperation: a stretched, bony, feathered foot swinging back, then making contact with Cú, who is still trying to escape from the blanket. He yowls and struggles harder against the cloth, but only traps himself inside it more thoroughly as he pulls the fabric away from the monster.

I reach out instinctively to save my cat but am stopped cold when my brain finally processes the rest of the beast's form.

The larger it gets, the quicker it takes shape. Rapidly it grows taller and taller, skin going from scorch-mark black on its head and ashen grey on its body to an unmarred porcelain cream, feathers growing narrower until they are simply regular body hair, fine on the limbs but thick and dark on the naked pubic mound of the twisting, morphing woman. Her body is elongated and thin as she towers above me, but strong; she is corded in lean muscle, hard as steel, taut as piano wire.

As the blanket drips off her head, she unfurls to her full height, nearly scraping the ceiling with the top of her bare scalp. She considers me with pale eyes, so light they could be nearly considered colorless, but I do not maintain eye contact with her. I'm distracted by her other faces.

The face in the front, looking at me, is thickly drawn and proud, and is the only one that appears awake. The one on the back-left third of her skull is sharp and angular, thin-lipped with thin eyebrows, resembling a child's haphazard scribbles. Its eyes are closed, muscles slack in repose. The back-right third of her skull features the last face, plush and rich, with round cheeks and chin and bee-sting lips, also asleep.

Each face has its own pair of eyes, own mouth, own nose, but they share three ears between them, so each has one ear facing the wrong direction. It is this small detail that breaks my brain, filling me with uncanny valley revulsion at the perversion of humanity on display.

What even is this bird? What have I gotten myself into? Are the other faces alive, or are they illusions designed to unsettle me more deeply?

Before I can decide exactly how fecked I am, she lunges for me. On instinct, I jerk away, but she is quick and her limbs are long. She snags me around the waist. Her hands are so large that as her sharp-boned fingers dig into my back, her thumbs bruise my stomach, ratcheting up the pain that is my constant companion.

I twist in her grasp. My eyes dart around between the kitchen counter and appliances behind me, desperate for something, anything, to help. A shield, a weapon . . . a heavy cast-iron frying pan still sitting on the stovetop.

I snag the handle and clutch it like a tennis racket. The clear eyes of the main face go wide with shock (or is it irritation?) for the briefest moment as I turn, putting the weight of my torso into the torque of my swing. As the frying pan makes contact with the three-faced skull, I hear the stomach-turning, wet-sucking crack of a neck breaking. The monster's head turns too fast, too sharp. The plush face is now in front.

My muscles relax and I drop the frying pan, surely denting the wood floor. I've done it. She's dead. Her loosening hold on me and her upright stance must only be persisting through some sort of magical, quick-acting rigor mortis.

And then the soft face, with round cheeks and half-circle brows, opens its eyes. They are the same hardly visible blue of the face before. Her round lips part.

"Run," she whispers.

My brain jolts into action. I push off the monster's now-weak grip and tear into the living room, breaking for the side door, my phone tumbling out of my pocket and shattering on the floor. I skid to a stop just short of freedom. Cú is still trapped.

I hear another neck-breaking snap, followed by yowling, Cú's yowling, increasing in volume. Fearing the worst, I look through the doorway to the kitchen. The woman (women? Creature? Demon?) has reset her head to its original face and has lifted the tangled blanket Cú trapped himself in, holding the squirming, spitting bundle out as far away from her body as she can manage. Her face is twisted in revulsion and fear, eyes squinted and turned away as though she can't bear the thought of touching the cat.

I'm relieved he's alive, that I can still hear his outraged hollers, but she leaves the kitchen, quick and smooth, steps like a skipping stone. She carries Cú, his screaming moving through the house with her. A door opens and shuts, and Cú's sounds become muffled.

I turn on a dime and rush back to the kitchen, trying to determine where they've gone. I can't abandon Cú. Not when he's done so much for me.

When I don't see them in the yard through the kitchen window, I rush to the garage door. I throw it open and immediately am knocked back by the stench of the moldering and melted frozen food scattered throughout, but the space is otherwise empty. I slam the heavy door shut and make for the hallway, stopping only briefly to retrieve the frying pan from the floor.

The doors to the bathroom, basement, office, and my bedroom all hang open. That leaves only one place they could be.

Mammy's room.

I shudder to a stop with my hand on her doorknob. I don't want to go into Mammy's room. This is where the worst of it all would happen; where she would force me to sit in the corner while she stalked around me, detailing the ways I was a miserable pox on her life and a drain on society.

From my spot in that stiff wooden chair, I would stare at the door, wishing and hoping to slip out unnoticed. But she noticed everything I did. She relished my suffering. They would last hours, these screaming lectures, and if I said anything, if I tried to argue or defend myself, it would simply start her internal timer anew. My bladder would be full to bursting by the end, even as my throat and eyes were swollen and desert dry from tears and dehydration. My head would pound from the stress of being trapped, of knowing how worthless I was. At the end of these "family meetings" as she called them, these torture sessions, I would slink into the bathroom to relieve myself, then turn on the faucet to cover the sound of me banging my head against the wall. Crashing my forehead into the tile made the headaches worse but felt better than being myself.

No, I don't want to go into Mammy's room. But Cú protected me. It's my turn to protect him. I open the door.

I expect to find the creature and Cú inside, but the room is as empty as all the others. The windows remain shut tight. It smells stale, dusty, unlived-in, but looks the same as I remember from my childhood. Same king-sized bed with the dark blue bedspread. Same designer purses displayed on shelves on the far wall. Same horrible wooden chair in the corner. Same closet set into the wall to my right.

Of course. The closet. I remember my nightmare, the one that plays on a loop in this house. Or did, at least, before Cú.

"I am not your mother. I killed your mother and put her in the closet. And now, I'm coming for you."

Avoiding looking at the chair in the corner as much as possible, I turn to the closet door and wrench it open, bracing myself for the worst: an altar to Satan, a mummified corpse, a mural painted in blood. Instead, I am met with disappointment. It is just a regular closet, filled with a long row of long dresses.

I let out an angry grunt, like a bull being taunted by a matador. I have let my imagination get away from me, again. I've been busy concocting some fantastical story, some mystical myth mining meaning from a nightmare, to explain my life rather than accepting the truth. Like I always do. I can't be weak anymore; Cú is depending on me. I hang my head in shame as I resolve to check the basement.

My gaze hits the floor, and I pause. There's something there: a thick metallic ring. Usually in this spot there's a big bin full of Mammy's shoes, but it's been pushed to the side.

I'm not crazy. I'm not imagining a thing. There is something in the closet after all. I yank on the ring, ignoring the way the movement hurts my abdomen, and a section of the floor lifts up.

A trapdoor, with a ladder leading down into a concrete bunker. I remember the odd shape of the basement, how part of it seemed sectioned off and inaccessible. Of course. This house was built during the early days of the Cold War. It seems obvious now, but I hadn't even considered there being a trapdoor to a bunker in Mammy's room.

How many secrets can a house I lived in for all of my childhood hold? Quite a few, it seems.

It's dark inside. I scratch my forearm nervously and consider walking away, but a woman's voice with a distinctly Irish lilt calls up from below.

"Brigid, I know that's you. I know you're up there. Come down here."

Still, I hesitate. It's clearly a trap. And a realization pops into my mind. An Irish lilt to her voice? A shape-shifting scald-crow?

Was I right again? Is this the Morrígan, made flesh?

The voice turns stern, impatient. "Brigid. I still have the cat. Or have you decided you don't care for it?" I hear a bang and Cú yowls deeply, mournfully, in miserable fear. "Uh-oh! Better come down here quick. Who knows what I might do to it next."

I jerk from the force of the rage filling me. All the anger I should've been using to protect myself all these years, all the spite and hatred stuffed away into the crevices of my joints, flares to the surface, mobilizing me against this threat to my cat. Three faces, eight arms, ninety-seven anuses: I don't care what the monster's got. Cú needs me to be brave. I need me to be brave. I descend the ladder.

It's a difficult climb, between balancing the frying pan in one hand and ignoring the constant and increasing pain. My confidence wavers again by the time my feet touch the concrete floor, but I screw up my courage and turn to scan the room.

It is dim and I can't quite make out the form of a pile of detritus sitting in the far corner. The only light is coming from the trapdoor above me, though a bare light bulb with a pull chain is ominously attached to the ceiling in the middle of the room. It must not have been replaced in years; it's one of those old-school incandescent light bulbs, the type I would've used to bake cakes in my Easy-Bake Oven. Maybe it's dead. Maybe that's why the creature hasn't turned it on.

Or maybe she wants to frighten me.

The creature stands beneath the bulb, the blanket that had trapped Cú puddled at her feet, still oppressively tall but hunched over somewhat in this bare concrete box. She is clothed now, wearing a long, body-hugging grey sheath dress I recognize as one of Mammy's favorites from when I was in high school. On Mammy, it reached the floor, but on the monster, it's barely knee-length. The dress is so tight, and she's so thin, I can count her ribs through the cloth. The proud square face has returned to its spot in front; the angular and round ones rest in their respective places on her scalp.

I wait for the creature to attack me with her elegant fingernail claws. She fixes her face with a mocking smile instead. But somewhere in the edges of the curve of her mouth, I also read wariness. There is a hint of terror, her eyes flicking from my face to something behind me on the floor.

Twisting my head to see what she fears, I find Cú. A relieved exhale escapes me when I see he's unhurt, though he stands with his back arched, tail bottle-brushed, and fangs bared.

I take a shaky step toward him, willing my bravery not to falter, making soothing sounds as I reach out my free hand. Cú's eyes glance from me to the creature and back, but he doesn't recoil. I take this as a willingness to be saved and scoop him into my arms, but it's difficult to hold him and the frying pan all at once. He affixes himself firmly to my chest, digging his claws through the thin silk of my nice dress. He nearly cuts into my shoulders, but his claws are still somewhat dull from being trimmed at the rescue and he can't break the skin.

As I rise and turn back to face the creature, she recoils with a half step backward, and her mocking smile falters into anxious revulsion. Her fear of Cú is fascinating. I suppose it makes a certain measure of sense; she was being crushed in his mouth as a bird only a handful of minutes ago.

My eyes dart to her right arm and chest to see if the wounds Cú inflicted on her bird form persisted when she shape-shifted. Sure enough, her right arm is held at a stiff angle as though it pains her, and a deep red stain is beginning to spread across the front of her dress.

I feel my confidence increase an iota. She can be hurt, and she's scared of Cú. Even if my hunch is correct, if she is a god, she isn't an invulnerable one. I hold more cards than I thought I did.

Of course, I don't know what other cosmic powers she possesses, aside from shape-shifting and surviving broken necks. And I don't know how badly she's hurt; she might still be able to turn back into a bird and fly away. In the end, I may not be holding any cards at all.

I can't risk Cú's life any more than I already have. His safety is my responsibility; I would never be able to live with myself if she hurt him.

As if she can sense my self-doubt, she slaps the sneer of mockery back on. "Brigid, how lovely of you to join us. It's not much of a party without a guest of honor, is it?"

"Listen," I demand. My voice only shakes a little. "You don't want Cú, right? It's me you're after? And you're scared of him. You don't want him here, ruining your plan. Let me put him upstairs."

"Oh no you don't, you tricky little bitch," she hisses. "You can't use the cat to escape, not this time."

"If I hold him up, he'll be able to jump out himself. I'll keep my feet off the ladder. I'll stay down here with you until you let me leave."

"And what if you don't? What do I get if you break your word?" she asks.

"What?" I'm thrown by the line of questioning, phrased as if there's some cosmic punishment that could be doled out. "I don't know. I just promise, I guess?"

She taps her chin with a long fingernail, considering, then her eyes alight. "I know. If you touch that ladder without my permission, you must commit suicide within the following twenty-four hours, or the cat's life is forfeit."

"What?" I'm still baffled. Are we bartering?

"Do we have a deal? You can release the cat, and in exchange, you mustn't touch the ladder or you have committed yourself to death by your own hand."

"Uh, sure." Maybe it's a foolish thing to agree to, but my desire to keep Cú safe outweighs my desire to figure out exactly what's going on. Besides, I don't see how the whole kill-yourself-or-your-cat-dies situation is enforceable, unless there's some cosmic judicial system for god-monsters I'm not aware of. "We have a deal."

As I say the words, the dead light bulb glows faintly for a moment, and a shiver of electricity, like an oncoming storm, trickles across my skin. Feck. Maybe the cosmic judicial system is a thing after all.

Still, what's done is done, and at least Cú will be safe. I gingerly put the frying pan down next to my feet, keeping a firm grip on Cú as I unhook his claws from my ruined dress. Then I lift his tense body into the air. Mercifully, he seems to understand what I'm trying to do and jumps the short distance from my arms to the floor of Mammy's closet. I hear his paws patter above us as he runs out of the room.

My shoulders relax, and I exhale a breath of relief knowing he's safe. As I bend to retrieve my frying pan, sharp fingers materialize around my neck, lifting me into the air and slamming me against the back wall, hard. As pain explodes like paint splattering through the inside of my braincase, the handle of the pan slips through my fingers and clatters to the concrete floor.

I dangle from the throat, at the end of her uninjured left arm. My feet hang below me, searching for the purchase of the floor. I try to focus on inhaling through my narrowed windpipe, gaining only the meagerest sips of air for my efforts.

"I could just kill you." The fingers tighten, the nails nipping into soft flesh, and my shallow swallows of oxygen are gone. "I could crush your larynx, your windpipe, and watch you suffocate. I really could."

My eyes widen in fear, and I try to pry her hand away from my throat, even a little bit, just the tiniest bit, just enough for one more breath. I scrabble against her marble flesh, not able to grant her any suffering with my stubby, useless fingernails.

She laughs with delight, tossing her head back. Her skin seems to glow for a moment, luminous, and she is terrible in her beauty.

"But that would be over so soon," she purrs, then adds in a singsong voice, "and you've given me so much, so very much, but you've *still got more*." She taps my nose with her right index finger three times, as she sings the last three words.

I notice through my tunneling vision that as she moves her right arm to taunt me, her shoulder wound bleeds more freely and her eyes tense in the outer corners.

She drags me, slowly, across the concrete wall, taking care to ensure my scalp is being scraped across the rough surface. Occasionally, she loosens her grip, just enough for me to gasp a single lungful of air, after which she strangles me again.

"Do you see where we're headed? Do you remember our deal?" She gestures with her triad head toward the ladder. "I haven't given you permission to touch it, have I?"

I kick, hard, pushing against the wall to try to break free, my vision turning ever darker as I waste precious oxygen fighting her steel grasp.

"Won't that be delicious? You spending all day unable to sleep, stewing in your own sweat, trying to decide: Will you risk it? If you don't kill yourself, will your wretched little pet truly die? And if you do kill yourself, how frightening it will be! Choosing the knife, or the gun, or the rope. You won't have much time. Which do you think you'll choose?"

She drags me a little closer, relishing my panic. The ladder is within striking distance now, and I crane my body away from it as much as I am able to.

"Personally, I think you'll use the coward's method and go for pills. You've never had much conviction. But I do hear that that can actually be the more painful way to go. Funny, isn't it, how these sorts of things play out?"

With the last of my air, I summon all the willpower within me. All the hours of standing tall through Mammy's cruel barrages, all the nights spent writhing in pain knowing the only way out was to live through it, all the years of carrying on even when everything in me yearned to give up, all of them practice for this one moment.

I push my legs off from the wall as hard and quick as I can, and aim my missile feet at the open wounds in the creature's right shoulder.

They make contact, and I feel the tip of my left ballet flat sink into the gristle of her. Blood flows over my shoes, onto my ankles, and as she screams in agony, she loses her grip on my throat. I drop to the floor, feeling the pain of landing on concrete reverberate up through my bare knees and into my screaming uterus. I lock the sensation away and flop onto my stomach in a wild dive for the frying pan.

She sees my lunge and makes a desperate lunge of her own, sloppy from her own inexperienced pain. She falls short by several centimeters and struggles to rise through the agony as her shoulder weeps onto the hard grey slab of floor.

I scramble to my feet. For once in my life, I do not hesitate. The frying pan comes down hard, onto her right shoulder again, and something in her snaps. I move on to her left, pummeling, smashing, raining all the fiery pits of hell down onto her as I grasp the cast-iron club in both hands. Her beautiful, fine-boned frame crumbles under my onslaught.

"You! Fecking! Bird! Monster! God! Bitch!" I wail, accompanying each word with a new wound. "Following! Me! Attacking! My! Cat! Feck! You! Bitch! You! Bitch! Feck! You! Feck!"

I slow down, gasping for air, feeling my own pain begin to

overtake me. She lies on the floor, her inhuman form now bent and broken into a horrifying alien mess. Still, though, her chest moves as she breathes. The blood pumps out of her in time with what I can only assume is a heartbeat. I slump slightly against the wall but retain a strong grip on the frying pan, pointing it at her as though it were a saber.

"Why are you following me?" I demand.

"Following you?" She raises her head to look at me with the forward, conscious face and curls a lip. "I think I'm doing a bit more than that, don't you?"

"Stalking me, then. Tormenting."

"I think I would prefer the term *terrorizing*," she muses, shifting her weight gingerly. I wave the frying pan a minute amount, and she settles to a wary stillness, both arms hanging limply from her broken shoulders.

"Sure, *terrorizing*. Whatever you want," I say, impatient. "Why?"

She beams like I'm a waiter carrying the meal she's been waiting for out from the kitchen. Or perhaps, like I am the meal itself.

"See, Brigid, that's something I've always loved about you." She puts on an appallingly accurate facsimile of my own Midwestern voice. "'Whatever you want.' 'Yes, ma'am.' 'I'm sorry for this thing that obviously can't be my fault, but I'm so sorry anyways.'" She returns to her own Irish lilt and the grin grows wider. "It's delicious, the way you grovel. And with hardly any provocation!"

My stomach turns. I'm not that pathetic, am I?

"Though I suppose I deserve some credit there. I'm the one who taught you to be that way," she comments smugly, glancing up at me with a flash in her eyes.

Memories tumble through my mind: Mammy telling me I

was misremembering, I was melodramatic, I deserved everything she threw my way. She's right; she did teach me to wallow, to beg, to lessen myself until I hardly could be said to exist. But even when I cut off contact with her, the feeling persisted, following me everywhere, especially into doctor's offices where experts quickly concluded I was healthy even as I quaked with pain. Mammy was the first to teach me self-loathing, but her torch has been carried by those too powerful to spare me a second glance ever since.

The monster's hands snap up to her head, grasping both sides of her face and quickly torquing it. The wet snap of a breaking neck rings out and the creature's head turns. I brandish the frying pan to beat her again, but pause: The round face, the one that told me to run, is in front.

"Brigid, listen to me," she implores, still in an Irish accent but with a more musical note than her sister. "Get out of here. Find some way out without touching the ladder. Run away. As far as you can. Go somewhere unpredictable, somewhere she won't think to search for you. She couldn't find you before. That's why she disappeared and left the house empty. To draw you back. Don't come back this time. Hide. Go."

The massive hands return to the head. Another gruesome crack, another turn, and for the first time, the angular face is awake. "No, stay!" she screeches. Her voice is sharp, like her cheekbones. "Stay with us. Don't you want answers? We want to tell you! We'll tell you if you stay. And I'll add you to my collection. It's a pretty collection, but not big enough, no, not big enough at all. There are more places to hide in this house, I know I can find more. In the walls, perhaps. Or, yes, yes, in the piano, yes! I'll hollow it out, take out all the metal and wire and pegs, and put you in the piano, and there you'll stay for as long as I keep you."

A third crack rings out, and again, I am confronted by the

face I have come to think of as the leader. "Don't you recognize me, Brigid?" She puts on a wounded countenance.

I try to take a step back, disgusted and confused, but only back farther into the wall. She crawls toward me in a weak, miserable motion. I twitch the frying pan and she stops, not fully closing the gap, but making it clear she has no intention of letting me flee.

"So ungrateful. Such an entitled little bitch," she tuts, wagging a finger at me. "You don't even know your own mother."

And she morphs, shrinking down to a human height, her limbs and fingernails shortening in concert until the dress is floor-length. The resting faces recede into her skin, and dark hair sprouts from her scalp, pouring over her ears and down her back. Her eyes darken to an aqua blue. Her face narrows and bends into a gorgeous visage: the bloodied, beautiful, unmistakable face of my mammy.

She laughs, grating and barking, like the crow she was. She transforms again, softening her bones until she is unmistakably Carol. "Do you recognize your therapist?"

Quickly now, she morphs to a darker skin tone, fuller lips, plusher curves: Emma, but too tall. "What about your most-trusted friend?"

"And if those forms don't suit, I can always return to my favorite. The scald-crow." She smiles at me, syrupy sweet, with Emma's lips, as if I needed to be reminded of the bird. And then, again, she becomes my mammy, mocking me. My mind reels. She can be any woman, real or imagined, and could, therefore, be anywhere, anytime.

I lurch backward again on instinct and only meet the wall. I keep my hold on the frying pan, held high aloft, muscles locked through fear.

Mammy is dead, I remind myself. Mammy is gone. She can't

hurt me anymore. But I don't know that. I never knew that, did I? Not for certain. The terror of her, the omnipresent threat of her reappearing in my life, always hovered at the periphery of my mind, an anxiety I could never quite shake.

"Of course, that's not the whole story, is it?" She deepens and projects her voice so the sound bounces off the concrete walls, overflowing from the room into my brain. "I am not your mother. I killed your mother and put her in the closet. And now, I'm coming for you."

It is the nightmare. My nightmare. I am literally living my nightmare.

I don't move this time. I can't quite seem to find my legs. My breathing quickens and hitches, my lungs twitch hyperactively in my chest. The frying pan quivers at the end of my arm.

I can't stop shaking.

Mammy reaches out a hand lovingly to stroke my face but stops short when I'm able to steady the pan. Hand still outstretched, she says in a gentle, mocking tone, "Oh, sweet Brigid. Sweet, stupid, gullible Brigid. All this time you thought it was a dream, when it was always me. Me, telling you exactly what I had done."

Her head turns quickly to her shoulder, and there's another gut-wrenching snap. Mammy's face falls slack for a moment, eyes wide and lifeless, and then it animates again, this time with an impish glee.

"Actually, if we are being very specific, and I prefer we are. You understand, don't you? I'm sure you do. I just want credit where credit is due, because it was me, which is to say it was Nemain, me, me, Nemain, me, who took your mammy and killed her and put her in the closet, and when Badb finally says it's time, it'll be me, me, me, to add you to my collection too. Nice to have the full set—it's been much too long since I had a complete set. But I will soon! Mam and Da and baby Brigid, all stiff and still in their quiet little house."

"You . . ." My voice quivers and cracks as I talk. I swallow in an attempt to make it hold steady. "You killed Mammy? And Da?"

"Yes, yes, yes! And what pretty work it was. You already saw your da, of course, which I think was clever storage. And your mammy's here, didn't you notice? Why don't you say hello?" She gesticulates excitedly toward the pile of detritus in the far corner, draped in shadow.

I take a few shaky steps toward the pile, holding the pan in the creature's direction at all times as a protective medallion. Once I'm past her, she shoves me sharply, her fingernails scraping against the soft silk of my dress. I stumble forward, catching myself before I fall face-first into the jumble of human bones before me.

The skull stares up at me from inside the pelvis. The body had been carelessly tossed in a crumpled heap to rot instead of being properly laid out.

"Mammy?" I whisper. How long has she been down here? How long has she been dead? I've been having the nightmares for decades, since I was six, since around the time Da left.

And in a flash, I know the truth: This monster has been raising me, abusing me, all this time.

And Mammy loved me.

The not-Mammy monster's neck turns and snaps again, the opposite direction this time, and Mammy's face hangs blank again for a moment before returning to its regal composure.

"Ugh, how gauche. My sister Nemain can get a bit overexcited from time to time. But yes, we killed your parents, and you will be next since you've outlived your usefulness. It's a shame because you really were an incredible source, but now that you've begun to piece it together, we'll have to start again from scratch."

"A source?" I turn to face her again, trying to arrange my tumbling thoughts. I haven't pieced much of anything together, no matter what the monster wearing Mammy's face thinks. "A source of what?"

"Goodness, you are stupid," she mutters, then raises her voice and chin to brag. "I am Badb, the battle crow, who sows terror and confusion into the hearts of those who would oppose me. With me are my sisters, Nemain, who personifies the frenzied havoc of war, and Macha, goddess of fertility and female sexuality, who grants kingship and protects the lands. We are the three Morrígna. You would know us as the Morrígan, Irish goddess of war and fate, though that is a gross oversimplification that you can thank your own holy men and scholars for."

My memory serves me flashes of illustrations from my collection of Irish folktales. The carnage of a battlefield. The bloody cloth for those fated to die. The scald-crow.

The Morrígan.

"Though I don't mind overly much what the monks did to us." She gestures at her broken body with a nonchalant hand. "We were complicated figures: celebrating assertive female sexuality and the creation of life, glorifying chaos and a warrior's death, reminding all of the cost of sovereignty. Sometimes we stood as separate sisters, often we worked and were worshipped as one. Much too nuanced for those staid Catholics to comprehend. Reducing our individuality made sense to them, and making certain we seemed evil by bringing me, the battle crow, front and center, helped them prove the wickedness of paganism."

"But—" I begin to argue, waiting to say she (they?) can't be real, that I must be imagining her. But I remember my epiphany from before: I am imagining nothing. I will believe myself.

Still, though, the story doesn't add up. "But you're supposed to celebrate female sexuality, you just said that. Why did you . . . ?"

"Make you think you were a pervert?" The twisted grin returns, then falls into an inauthentic simper. "Yes, Macha didn't like that either. But I needed you scared and to despise yourself, and that was an easy way to do it. And your mother's beloved church helped too. The guilt Catholicism sows in its followers is such a useful cudgel to beat a child with."

The creature wearing Mammy's face grows angry at the mention of a church she herself brought up and begins to rant in earnest, more to herself than to me.

"But one thing you devout worms never seem to grasp is gods are different from people and things. We exist only in the designs and dreams of mortals. By proving the wickedness of paganism, by painting us as an evil monolith hell-bent on inspiring fear and destruction, it became the truth of us. No more were we the complex, intricate sisters who served glorious purpose and protected balance in both peacetime and war. In fact, with every day, with every further reading of the tales reducing the three of us to one, reducing our multitudes to single points, there is less of a *we* at all."

The hair recedes back into her skull, her torso and limbs and neck and fingernails stretch themselves out again until she is once again the three-faced megalithic creature.

"And so, I am the Morrígan, goddess of terror, and it is terror and worship I seek." Her voice booms and echoes through the tight space, rattling the bones of my dead, decayed Mammy. Her arms grow longer, palms pressed into the floor, barely connected to her torso but still able to leverage her up and up until she hangs her head over mine and traps me without actually moving any closer. She opens her mouth to leer from above, and she has shifted her form again so her teeth are sharp spikes, rows upon rows of them in conveyor belt jaws, so long I don't believe her mouth could properly close around them, so sharp they would slice open her lips if she tried.

It is terror she wants. I will not give it to her. She cannot hurt me; she is weak in the face of her own suffering, and I am resilient from the persistence of mine. I close my eyes against the image of her twisted face, to the bones of my real Mammy, and focus on the feeling of the cold iron in my hands, the thrum of my heart, and the inescapable pain reminding me I have battles yet to win.

I do not fear her. She has no power over me. I have everything I need.

I open my eyes and raise them to hers, staring deep into the yawning voids within. I do not waver.

She sighs in exasperation as she shrinks, returning her arms and teeth to their normal lengths, and collapsing onto the floor in a melodramatic puddle. "See? This is what I'm talking about. You're worthless now."

"Why did you even choose me in the first place?" I ask. I need her to tell me more, keep her talking about herself. I have to figure out a way out of this bunker, and more information can only help me.

"Oh, *you*." She considers me with love in her eyes, not as a mother regards a child, but as a miser sees gold. "You were such a lucky find. Coming across your mother going to church, listening in on her little chat with the priest. You know he told her your little experiment was normal? That you only needed to be told not to do it again, and you were a perfectly good child? She was so relieved and was coming straight home. But I couldn't allow that. What an opportunity!"

"So, you killed her and took her place," I interrupt, sour in my gut.

As confirmation, the Morrígan beams. "It was perfect: What could inspire more terror and worship than an abusive mother? And doubly so if you can convince the child the cruelty is their fault. And she was Irish and beautiful to boot, so we enjoyed being her. The only snag was your father; he became suspicious of us, wondering what caused such a dramatic change in his gentle, limp-wristed wife. He started threatening a forced stay in a mental hospital. Of course, he was dealt with easily enough." She sighs fondly, reminiscing. "It was, in a word, idyllic. I'll miss it when you're dead."

"You can't kill me," I tell her. "Cú hurt you, and I got enough lucky swings in while you were distracted by your pain to break your body the rest of the way. You're stronger than me, sure, but I know a thing or two about fighting through pain. All I have to do is find a way out and lock you down here. Maybe I'll make gloves out of my dress and climb the ladder."

She frowns mildly, at the very corners of her lips. "Yes, you could try it. But will that count as touching it? It very well might. And what if you slip, or—whoopsie—I pull you down and your hand grazes a rung? Are you willing you risk your little pet's life?"

I hesitate.

She smiles, cold and certain. "Even if you do succeed, I am a goddess. I do not require food, or water, or rest. I merely have to wait until I heal. I will fashion a knife from your mother's bones and slowly scrape away at the door or wall or ceiling until they crumble. And you have my word, I will find you, and I will make the terrors you have suffered so far seem like fond memories of times long gone."

To illustrate her point, she rests her head on the floor and smiles softly, the image of patience and repose. My inescapable pain asserts itself in my mind, telling me it won't be ignored. My bladder has begun to complain too. How long can I hold out?

Not as long as a god.

I need to think of something. If she's telling the truth, if gods are made real and morphed by the tales we tell of them, then maybe the solution lies in a story. I think of my Irish fairy-tale book and every story my da ever told, flipping through legends of banshees and faeries and warriors and kings.

Cú Chulainn took the place of the hound he killed, in service to its master. Fionn trained with the warrior Fianna and ate of the salmon of knowledge. Brendan the monk traveled the ocean on the back of a whale he bravely befriended. But there are no great hounds, brilliant salmon, or kind whales here.

And, finally, it comes to me: In many Irish folktales, mythological figures love to make deals. Usually, these deals are used to curse the humans who make them, but sometimes a particularly clever human can make a deal to save themselves. Sure enough, wasn't it a foolish deal I made to not touch the ladder, trapping me down here in the first place? From her own mouth, the Morrígan laid it out: If it's in the stories told again and again, it becomes the truth.

It's a deal I need. So, what can I offer that the Morrígan, goddess of terror, would want?

As I think, the Morrígan grows listless, shifting her body into different faces and shapes in an effort to entertain herself and distract from her pain, always remaining giant to maintain her dominance over me, sighing theatrically as each new form fails to delight her. She may have the powers of a god, but she lacks patience.

The answer is so obvious it smacks me across the back of the skull like my frying pan on the Morrígan's thin frame. She wants to be an abusive mother, to have a human child she can raise to doubt itself and fear her, to tremble under her awesome power. But she lacks patience. It could be years before she lucks into another perfect victim, ripe for the picking.

But I can give her a baby. I have all the necessary equipment.

"What if we make a deal?" I propose.

Her eyebrows raise with interest, and she pushes herself up from the bloodied floor to sit upright, wincing as she does so. "What sort of deal?"

"In exchange for you allowing me to touch the ladder and then you leaving me alone, for you never seeing me again, you never even coming within a hundred miles of me for as long as I live, I will give you the first child I bear."

She sucks air in through her teeth appreciatively. "You'd give me your first child?"

"The first child I bear, yes," I agree. "The first fruit of my womb."

An elongated fingernail scratches at her chin as she considers.

"You can't use condoms or the deal will be broken," she states.

"Okay."

She continues thinking. "And no birth control pills either," she demands. "And no IUDs, or patches, or birth control shots, or implants, or rings."

"Fine." I shrug.

She eyes me for a moment, then breaks out a grin, making her teeth pointed and gruesome again. "You will have no contact with the first child you bear. When they are born, within the very hour they separate from your womb, they must be delivered over to me. Any attempt to keep them from me will result in your immediate demise."

I maintain fierce eye contact. "Agreed. But if you come

even an inch closer than one hundred miles from me, or try to communicate in any way with me or anyone I know, before or after the first child I carry is born, you will die, immortal god or not."

"Agreed." She cackles and offers a bony, massive hand for me to shake. I keep the frying pan in my right hand, holding it aloft as a threat, as I grasp her hand firmly with my left. Again, the light bulb above us flickers, brighter this time. I feel the crackling run across each inch of my skin, starting from the center of our palms.

"A pleasure doing business with you," she says. "You're just as selfish as I always said."

"Well, I ought to be." I smile tightly. "I learned from the best."

And with that, she transforms into the scald-crow, shrinking smaller and smaller, growing darker in color, arms thickening and sprouting feathers, legs shrinking into clawed matchsticks, until the bird I've hated for two decades hops out of the now-empty, bloodied sheath dress on the floor.

She raises her wings to take flight but can't even bring them entirely aloft before she collapses from the pain and blood loss. I scoff at her weakness; sure, there's blood smeared across the room, but not more than I lose on a bad night, and I still find it in me to wash my sheets, don't I?

She, still as the bird, looks up at me with a pleading expression.

"Really?" I ask, raising an eyebrow.

She shrugs her broken bird shoulders.

I sigh and scoop her up with the frying pan, balancing her as I climb up the ladder and into the bedroom. Cú is waiting at the top, meowing in excitement when he sees the bloody snack I possess. She squawks in a panic, and I hold the frying pan high out of Cú's reach.

"Not now, buddy," I tell him. "I'll give you some treats in a minute."

I carry the pan out the front door, to the end of the driveway, and dump her into the gutter. Laboriously she stands on her two matchstick legs and begins walking down the street. I watch her with narrowed eyes; she only makes it twenty or so feet before hanging her bird head. She turns and transforms into the horrifying, nude, three-faced monster again.

"You can't do that," I scold her. "The neighbors are going to see."

"I need your car," she says.

I gasp at the cheek of her. "What makes you think I would ever give you my car?"

"Well, I can't fly, so the scald-crow thing isn't as useful as it usually is, and you want me a hundred miles from you. I'm not sure what else to tell you." She crosses her wounded, limp arms, hissing at the pain of the motion. "The sooner you give me your car, the sooner I can get a hundred miles away and our deal can begin."

"Sucks to suck," I say. "I can't afford a new car. I guess you're walking."

She groans. "How about another deal?"

"What do you have in mind?"

"You give me your little junk heap of a vehicle, and in exchange, I will give you access to twenty thousand dollars' worth of wealth."

"Twenty thousand United States dollars?" I clarify, not wanting any tricky fairy-tale Zimbabwean-dollar nonsense.

"Yes, yes, United States dollars, real, actual value, which if you do not receive within two fortnights, my very existence is forfeit, blah blah blah." She waves a hand in a few small circles.

"Fine. Deal." A small crackle flits across my skin and in the air between us. "Where's the money?"

"Where are the keys?" she retorts.

"Nice try," I say, not even caring anymore if the neighbors see a giant naked mythological creature in the street. "Money first."

"Look, it's the purses, and the shoes, and the clothes in my closet. That's all the good stuff. I have a Birkin in there that's worth ten grand, at least. Do not, I repeat, not, take them to the consignment shop again. Sell them online. My things are worth so much more than you got." She sighs with great melodrama. "I can't believe I have to start all over again."

I roll my eyes. "Fine, I'll get the keys. But the car's parked on the next street over and the neighbors are going to start taking pictures if you stay like that any longer."

She hangs her head, then lifts it slightly to pout at me. "Could I have some clothes?"

"Jesus Christ," I mutter in response as I stomp back into the house.

When I come back out, she's a bird again. I put my shittiest pair of yoga pants and crappiest T-shirt next to a bush with the car keys. She gives me a withering stare, and I answer, "What? You should've made a deal for Ralph Lauren and bathroom access if it was so important to you."

She hops a bloody trail to the bushes. I go inside, slamming the door behind me.

Once inside, I finally get to use the bathroom. Afterward, I dig up a bottle of ibuprofen, popping four of them. I've earned it, I think, and treating pain I know is real feels good somehow. Like

I'm taking care of myself. In the kitchen, I find Cú lying on the tile, licking himself in a sunbeam, conflict forgotten. I shut the open window to keep him out of danger.

I catch a glimpse of Jesus, still hanging in the entryway, and walk over to snatch him off the wall. I don't say anything, just huck him in the trash.

I put the kettle on the stove to make a cuppa and stare into the burner as I wait for the water to boil, thinking of Mammy and Da. Real Mammy and real Da.

It has been so long since I have known them, the memories are flashes rather than entire scenes. Da practicing at the piano. Mammy pulling scones from the oven. The three of us walking up the sidewalk to church, with them holding my hands and swinging me in the middle.

The kettle boils, and I pour the water into a mug with the tea bag.

They were my real parents. Once they were gone, the absence of their love left the gaping hole in my chest where my self-compassion should be. They were the ones whose job it was to fill that hole, to give me the unconditional love I needed to learn how to love myself.

But they did love me, in the end. Da didn't choose to abandon me, and Mammy didn't decide I was unworthy of love. They were stolen from me.

The tea finishes steeping, and I add my milk and sugar. I take a healing sip.

I was never unlovable.

I lift my mug to my lips again and my eyes catch on the clock on the stove. Only five minutes until it's time for therapy with Carol. With all the excitement of the day, I had nearly forgotten. I head to my bedroom and crack open the laptop, not bothering to check myself in the mirror first.

When Carol logs on, her default smile turns to a look of concern. "Brigid!" she exclaims, pronouncing my name incorrectly, as usual. I wince. "What happened? You have scratches all over your neck! And bruises! And you look exhausted."

I look down and notice that, yes, the Morrígan's claws did manage to scratch up my neck and shoulders quite a bit, and much of my once-stunning dress is tattered. But I have more pressing matters to discuss with Carol.

"I'm fine," I say. "Nothing to worry about. There is something I need to tell you, though. Something important."

"Sure." She rearranges her face to her "active listening" pose. Like I said before, she's a good therapist.

"You've been pronouncing my name wrong. I don't say it Bridge-*id*. It's *Breej*."

"Breesh?" she tries.

"Breej," I repeat.

"Breejh," she copies. Close enough.

"Yeah, that's it. Thank you."

I smile at her. I feel better.

Day Whatever

I wake up disoriented and feeling strangely light. There's a woman I don't recognize wearing all blue. I blink at her a few times, trying to remember if I've seen her before, if she could be a threat, but my brain has gone all fuzzy.

I'm exhausted. I fall back asleep.

I wake up again. My mouth is cotton-ball dry. I experimentally feel around my gums with my tongue. It seems like I still have all my teeth. I look around myself. I'm lying down, covered in blankets, wearing a hospital gown. This is a hospital room.

And Emma is here!

She's so pretty. I smile, so big.

"You're sooooooo pretty," I tell her. My speech slurs.

She stands up from her chair and rushes to my bed, her perfectly groomed eyebrows quirked in concern. "Brigid!" she says.

"You're awake."

"I think so?" I uptalk. I can't be certain. Everything is a bit ill-defined.

"Yeah, no, you are." She laughs. "Can I get you anything?"

"A kiss!" I demand.

She laughs again and the sound is a wellspring. I pucker my lips out, but she sweetly pecks my forehead.

"No!" I groan.

"What?" She pulls back in alarm. "Are you hurt? Should I call the nurse?"

"No." I narrow my eyes at her in accusation. "That was a nanny kiss."

She looks at me, a little baffled.

"I want a *girlfriend* kiss," I stage whisper, "because I'm your *girlfriend*."

She rolls her eyes but acquiesces, leaning forward again to kiss me on the mouth. Her lips are soft and a little greasy from her lipstick. Fire-truck red today. It looks good on her.

"I like your lipstick," I mumble contentedly.

"You always like my lipstick," she teases.

"The cats!" The trio pops into my head. I'm not home to take care of them like I usually am. I try to straighten up in my bed, but my muscles aren't listening to me as well as they ought to. "Somebody needs to feed them!"

Emma places a calming hand on my shoulder and laughs a little. "I drove home and gave them their wet food while you were under."

"They're okay?"

"All three of them were on the big cat tree in the living room together when I left," she confirms.

I relax into the bed, and Emma becomes all business. A

proper caretaker. "How are you feeling?"

I scan my body hesitantly, searching for pain. It's there but far away, with a different quality than I'm used to. "Good," I answer. "Sorta weird? But in a good way. Like, light. Like there was something heavy I was carrying, and now it's gone."

"Well, you did just have your uterus taken out, so I think that makes sense."

Of course. I remember now.

Dr. Hämmerle made it clear this decision wasn't to be taken lightly: It's a major surgery with a long recovery time, and complications can range from minor things, like bloody discharge, to permanent damage to the urinary tract or bowel. My risk of having other pelvic organs prolapse will now always be higher. And I might even still have pain; my ovaries were left in place, so if there are any microscopic bits of endometriosis left, they could grow and cause havoc, no uterus required. It's possible I've traded my ability to have children for very little improvement, and, ultimately, we won't know what will happen until it happens. It was scary to decide. To be honest, I'm still scared.

But at least I'm doing something.

I reach out for Emma. She takes my hand in hers. "You think I made the right choice?" I ask.

"I think you made the right choice for you," she tells me, and kisses the back of my hand. "I think you'll be okay."

"Yeah," I agree.

She's right.

I'm okay.

AUTHOR'S NOTE

Brigid is not real, but her suffering is reality for thousands upon thousands of people. Adenomyosis and endometriosis are common causes of pelvic pain, heavy bleeding, infertility, and other associated symptoms for women and other people with uteruses. Yet, according to Yale Medicine, for endometriosis there is an average delay of four to eleven years between symptom onset and diagnosis. Adenomyosis, which is considered more difficult to diagnose because a definitive diagnosis of it requires examining the tissue of the uterus after hysterectomy, often has a much longer delay. This delay is present even for a clinical diagnosis, like Brigid receives.

Despite the presence of a goddess straight from Irish legend, I think the most unrealistic part of this book is the ease with which Brigid receives a hysterectomy. Even the most progressive doctors often refuse to allow young people to make this choice for themselves, even when other treatment options (such as birth control or medications which cause chemical menopause) fail or produce unbearable side effects. I believe these clinicians have their hearts in good places; the potential for unforeseen complications from hysterectomy should not be ignored and permanent loss of fertility should be seriously considered. However, when adult patients are considered unfit to determine which treatments are right for them, they are being infantilized, and I believe it is cruel to force someone to bear decades of intense pain because they might change their mind about wanting kids someday.

Now, I am a complex case, as the diagnosis and treatment of my own adenomyosis and endometriosis are complicated by other chronic, invisible illnesses I have. However, from symptom onset, it took me eighteen years, two emergency room visits, two surgeries, and fourteen gynecologists to get a diagnosis. I struggle with disabling symptoms of adenomyosis and endometriosis to this day.

In the very darkest depths of my agony, I have felt pain so intense I was certain death was imminent. And yet, the pain which has hurt me most profoundly and with the greatest lasting impact was the pain of being systematically disbelieved, accused of melodrama, and dismissed. When the people who are supposed to care for you the most, whose jobs are to care for you, determine you are unworthy of care, you find yourself drowning in despair and self-doubt. I often had the sense that I was reaching a hand into a great abyss, searching for someone to grab hold of, searching for someone who might comfort me.

I dream of a world where the pain of women and people assigned female at birth, and indeed the suffering of all people with invisible illnesses and disabilities, is believed and prioritized. This cannot happen if we do not believe ourselves. As impossible as it may seem, we must be our own advocates. We must demand more attention, more care, more funding for research, more treatment options, and more respect.

For a long time, I have been reaching a hand out into the darkness. If you have been reaching too, may this book serve as the joining of our palms.

ACKNOWLEDGEMENTS

Writing a book seems like it ought to be a lonely process, but thanks to my best friend and our frequent multi-hour phone calls, it never has been for me. Analise, thank you for seeing my vision, for helping me determine important plot points and aspects of character development, and for being my best and most reliable source of emotional support.

To my editor Amanda at Creature Publishing: I'm delighted you were the one who was moved by Brigid's story and saw its value. Thank you for bringing it into the world with such respect, care, and attention to detail. Krysta, your incredible copy-edits have saved me the embarrassment of people knowing about my addiction to commas. Thank you, sincerely.

Beth, thank you for your expertise and perspective on Irish literature and folklore, especially in regards to the Morrígan. I'm sorry I made her the bad guy; I know she doesn't deserve any more bad press.

Suzette and Colin, your enthusiastic beta reading convinced

me I wasn't wasting my time on this book. And speaking of enthusiasm, I owe an extra sincere thank you to Darren, who I consider my very first fan.

Finally, to my dog Westley and my cat Molly, thank you both for being the fuzziest, funniest, and snuggliest writing buddies anyone could ask for.

GRACE DALY (she/her) is a disabled author who lives near Chicago with her pets. She spends most of her free time with her dog, who is a very good boy. Her fantasy novella, *The Star of Kilnaely*, is forthcoming in 2026. *The Scald-Crow* is her first novel.

CREATURE PUBLISHING was founded on a passion for feminist discourse and horror's potential for social commentary and catharsis. Our definition of feminist horror, broad and inclusive, expands the scope of what horror can be and who can make it.